THE FERAL BUTTERFLY

SHEILA RAY MONTGOMERY

ISBN 979-8-9931041-0-2 (paperback)
ISBN 979-8-9931041-1-9 (hardcover)

Publishing company: SJBA, LLC
10/30/2025

Printed in the United States of America

Some things are always true.

Wild is always wild, even if you tame it. Cruelty is always cruel, even if you say it's kindness. Violence is always violent, even if it's justified. Pain is always pain, even if they tell you it shouldn't hurt.

The truth doesn't always set you free; sometimes, it ties you down.

Chapter 1

*N*othing *in this world is better than a clean house, coffee, and time with my dog,* she thought. *Living alone has its benefits.*

She smiled, the kind of smile that started on one side of the face and ended across the room.

The dog peered up from the floor, stretched, yawned, and joined her in the next room, curling up several times before finally settling on top of both of the woman's feet.

Somehow, her smile brightened even more.

"Well," she said to the dog. "You've finally taught me the greatest lesson of all: how to enjoy the moment in the middle of tragedy."

She crossed her legs and picked up her coffee, barely disturbing the dog. Breathing deeply, almost as if the air itself had depth and weight, she murmured, "This is gonna be a long day."

The phone rang. "Hello, oh, hi. How's your morning?" Her smile was completely gone. She covered the receiver. Looking down at her dog, she whispered, "She's gonna go on about what a good person she is; she doesn't like me. Why did I even answer?"

The dog offered sympathy, just the way dogs do. Back into the conversation, it was obvious by her twirling hand motions that whoever was on the other end was, in fact, going on and on.

Walking with her phone in hand, offering a 'yes' or a 'really' every so often, she entered her bedroom and opened her closet. She pulled out a pair of pants, changed her mind, and put them back. Then she pulled out a dress, again putting it back.

Over and over, she chose and returned items, tears breaching the corners of both eyes.

Clearing her throat, she said, "I have to go."

She hung up the phone, set it to silent and laid it on the bedside table.

The room was simple. A queen bed sat on one wall, with an old patchwork quilt on top. Old and worn, it always held its spot on top of the bed. The quilt had been a present from her mother and matched nothing in the room. On the other wall was a dog crate, and finally, a dresser.

No mirrors, nothing extra. She wandered into the adjoining bathroom. Looking up at the mirror, she said to herself, "I don't know why I have to, but I know I do." She drew in a very controlled breath. "Don't you dare fall apart. You can do this."

She stared at her reflection, taking in the gray curly hair tumbling around her shoulders.

Deep wrinkles from years of smoking ran beside her mouth, and crows' feet spread from her eyes. Tall, strong, and just a bit heavy, she was built like the song from the eighties and she knew it. She grinned, humming, '*She's a brick house …*'

Looking up, she said, "Dear God, you know I need help, and I'm done praying; it's time for doing. Just walk with me, help me hold my place and throw no stones."

She turned on the water, dropped her robe, and stepped singing into the shower.

Finishing, she toweled off, rubbed on the lotion from the counter, and took in the sight of herself again in the mirror. The dog had wandered in to lick the lotion off her legs.

Patting him on the head, she said, "We got this."

The doorbell rang.

"Crap, I forgot."

Jumping into the nearest outfit she could find and hopping into her socks, she made it to the front door. The doorbell rang again, almost insisting it be opened at once. She peeked through the eye hole. Her friend was standing there, holding two very large cups of coffee, tapping impatiently on one of the cups with her forefinger.

She opened the door. Her friend smiled and stepped past her, coming straight into the house. Setting the cups down on the small side table just inside the door, Sam hugged her.

"Sam, you forgot I was coming, didn't you?" It wasn't accusatory, but she added, "We've been friends longer than I can remember, and you always forget whenever you get overwhelmed. But this time, I thought I'd have to climb the back fence to get to you."

Eyeing her dearest friend, she let a tear fall.

She nodded, just once. "It's a lot, really. And it's not how I wanted this to end."

Her friend smiled, putting her hand on Sam's shoulder. "Let's have some coffee."

Sam followed her friend out to the back porch. Flowers and edibles lined it, beautiful greenery too. While it remained somehow very simple, the large space was open and inviting.

The two settled into the high bar stools at a square metal table. On its top were three freshly baked biscuits with butter and orange marmalade generously applied.

Comfortable, they both sipped coffee, lighting cigarettes. The air was cool, even for March.

Sam reached across and picked up her coffee.

Her friend was lean and tall, with sun-touched skin and short blonde hair that never covered her ears. "Biscuits," Ashley said, obviously pleased at their presence. "And that orange marmalade you're so obsessed with."

"Always my favorite," Sam replied, matching Ashley's smile with one of her own.

Ashley picked up a matchbox from the tabletop.

Pushing open one side, a simple smiley face appeared, written in black ink.

The matchbox was worn and weathered.

Ashley slid it the other way, pushing the matchbox open on the other side. A sad face appeared. Sam smiled and grabbed the matchbox from her friend.

Ashley said, "That little box always makes you smile, but you never tell me where you got it."

Sam pushed the box open to one end, then the opposite side. "Smiley face, sad face, smiley face!" Sam giggled loudly. "Oh, Ashley, that's such a long story from so long ago. If you have to know, it's a game of sorts."

Sam jumped at her friend, pushing open the matchbox, smiling, saying, "Smiley face," before pausing, then saying, "Sad face." Sam repeated the behavior over and over with great animation.

Ashley and Sam began to giggle, clutching their sides, trying to catch their breath.

They settled into the high-backed chairs.

Silence settled in like a blanket, as it sometimes would around good friends.

"Ashley, we've been through a lot over the years, but this one may be more than I can do."

Ashley responded, "Then why go? It's not as if they're gonna be kind to you."

"I don't know, I have to go. It's like taking your place at a table. I just have to be there."

Silence permeated the space, thick with emotion.

Breathing out gray smoke, Ashley finally said, "You know I'd go with you."

"I know you would, but this is a solitary journey, always has been. I'm just glad in a real way that it's ending."

"Sam, is it really? You'll have to leave it there for it to end."

Ashley tapped the table with two fingers.

Sam breathed in deeply, sighed, then said, "Well, I don't know for sure what's gonna happen. I do know I have to go, I just have to. And who cares if they like me or not? I'm good with me, and that's all that really matters."

"You don't have to do anything, and you know it. You're loved and cared for by so many people."

"Yeah. But they're not my family."

"So what? Besides, your family loves you. In their own way, but they still do."

"Hm, you think so? Because not one of them has called me this past week, just the joint text about times and dates. Not one has called to see how I am."

"Have you called to see how they are?"

"Yes. Several times. No Answer."

"Sam, I'm so sorry."

"Yeah, Me too." Sam let several tears fall and cleared her throat.

Silence again. This time, it was the type of silence no one would break. They sat there just being in the same space, comfortable with each other, watching the rain as it started to slowly mist down and fall around the covered porch.

They finished their coffee, also eating fresh biscuits with orange marmalade. They talked about old friends. They spoke about dogs, flowers, and planting season. When they rose, Ashley said, "Well, did you pick out your clothes yet? It's almost time to go."

Sam smiled; her friend knew her so well. "Yeah. I think so."

She walked Ashley to the door. "See ya soon."

Ashley replied, "Leave your phone on silent so I can text. And try not to lose it."

Sam hugged her.

"Okay." She closed the door.

Walking down the hall again to the bedroom, she picked up the last outfit she'd touched. Black slacks and a light gray shirt, long sleeves.

As she dressed, the dog stretched out across the bed, never taking his eyes off her.

Looking at him, she said, "I'm gonna be fine. You know I am."

The dog meandered with her to the back doorway, stopped, his brown eyes meeting hers.

"Really," she said. "I'm really gonna be fine. You have to trust me."

The dog cocked his head this way and that for a minute, before sighing, walking out onto the porch through the dog door. He settled on a dog bed, positioned perfectly to not get rained on.

Sam chuckled. "I love dogs for a reason."

She stepped back inside, grabbed her purse, keys and walked toward the front door. As she stepped out again, she yelled, "Oh, crap. Forgot my shoes."

She headed back inside, changed her socks and slid her feet into soft black loafers.

As she walked again to the front door, she glanced right, pausing, taking in the picture in all brown undertones. It had a wooden bridge path circling across into a forest full of beautiful trees.

She sighed again. "A path that goes nowhere, or everywhere. Oh, wait."

She wandered out the back door, picking up the matchbox off the square table.

Sliding it side to side, she said, "I may need you, my little friend." Putting the matchbox in her pocket, Sam jiggled her keys, stepped out the front door, locked it—and finally headed out.

Chapter 2

"Ouch." Sam's mom pulled and snatched at her hair.

"Really, you should brush this curly hair," Mom said in her snappy way.

Sam wiggled and squirmed.

Finally, her momma sighed, giving up, and she said, "Get out of here or I can't cook."

Sam ran as fast as she could, all the way out the back door. The concrete slab was not very large, and neither was the three-bedroomed ranch house in which they lived, but Sam loved it all.

The countryside stretched off to the left side of the house, and the neighbor's field ran all the way across the back. Sam slowed just a little, then ran out to the fence and stopped.

An electric fence ran along the border of the yard, grates sitting along the other side of the fence on the ground.

"Mooooo. Mooooo!" Sam called out.

She knew she shouldn't mess with the bull, but honestly, she could never help herself.

"MOOOOO!" Sam tried to put all her breath into it, always feeling as if she was conjuring up a great beast like the ones in the stories her mother read to her. "MOOOOO!"

He came stampeding across the huge field, blowing out of both nostrils, stopping right in front of the grate placed on his side of the fence. He took her breath away, so large and strong.

Sam yelled back at the huffing bull, "I wish we could be friends, but you're always so mean!"

The bull stood there with two horns just cut, all 1,000 pounds of him. He glared right at Sam. In his eyes, she saw something akin to curiosity and not complete violence, but just then, he stomped the ground with his massive cloven hoof. Sam jumped back, glanced around to see if anyone had seen her, then straightened. She tried to pretend nothing had startled her.

"Don't hoof at me; I'm just as big and tough as you!" Except, of course, she wasn't. But she continued, "Anyway, my birthday's tomorrow. Momma's baking me cupcakes. In fact, she's doing it right now. I will be eight years old; that means I'm much bigger now. So, you don't scare me one little bit!"

A small hand reached up behind Sam, tapping the small of her back.

"AAAAGGGGHH!"

Turning, she immediately started running back toward the porch.

Out of the corner of her eye, as she ran, Sam saw her sister giggling, holding her sides. Sam stopped, turned slowly, put both hands on her hips and stared at her.

"Sarah, that wasn't funny." Sam's face exuded irritation.

"Yes. It was." Sarah continued to giggle, swaying side to side, her dress blowing in the breeze. "Momma says we shouldn't mess with that cow."

Sam replied, "It's not a cow, it's a bull. Mom's scared of everything and I'm not. I'll be eight soon. Besides, all *she* ever does is take care of babies. *We* get to have adventures."

Sarah was gazing at her as only a younger sister could, with complete, unconditional adoration. Not only was Sam sure that Sarah believed every word she said, but she was also convinced her little sister would follow her anywhere.

Sam said, adding the greatest fanfare any eight-year-old could muster, "Today, we will stand on top of the world and view our great domain!"

Sarah giggled. "What do you mean?"

"Today, this morning, we'll get on top of those hay bales! See them over there? You can climb on top and see the whole world from one of those."

Sam pointed across the cow field to five round bales stacked next to each other.

"Nooo, I won't go through the pricker bushes, not again!" Sarah looked as though she had eaten sour berries and would be sick for a week.

"We won't go through the prickers, though; we'll be heading straight through. We can get under the fence and run across. It's not far," Sam said as she nudged her sister.

"I can't. That cow is scary … and besides, I'm only five. He'll catch me."

Sam's gaze wandered across the field again, looking back at Sarah several times.

She measured the space with her forearm, and again with a make-believe ruler. Meanwhile, the bull had wandered off to the other side of the field.

When Sam finally spoke again, it was with the greatest authority. "I believe we can do it. I've measured it." Nodding, Sam slid under the fence.

Sarah paused, her voice small, almost as little as she was. "I don't think we can, and—"

Sam interrupted, "I'm going on an ad-*ven*-ture; you can stay here if you like. Besides, that 'cow' as you call it is very far away."

Sarah slipped under the fence to follow, quietly as she could.

Almost to the round bales, the girls heard the 'thud, thud, thud' of the bull's hooves quickly striking the ground. Sam yelled at the top of her lungs, "Hurry!"

Poor Sarah tried to stand up and start running again.

The bull was closing in on her, gaining speed with every thud.

Sarah stopped, too scared to run anymore, fixated on the bull charging toward them.

Sam ran back to her sister and threw her toward the bales. Then, running in the opposite direction of the round hay bales, Sam screamed and yelled at the top of her voice, waving her arms and puffing up her body to try to look big.

The bull turned, pausing, looking at Sam for a fragment of a second.

That was all.

When it happened, it was all at once.

The bull charged the center of the round bales, sending Sarah toppling off into the mound of hay somewhere. Even Sam, panicked, couldn't see; she screamed so loud her voice sounded as though it belonged to someone else. "Sarah, run, run!"

The bull charged the bales again, hitting it hard with its head this time, shaking the massive bales side to side.

Sam screamed as she threw rock after rock at the bull, yelling something about how unscared she was. The bull paused. Blowing out of both nostrils, it turned, squarely staring at her.

It seemed to have all but forgotten about Sarah.

Complete silence filled Sam's world, only about thirty feet separating them. Sam wiped away tears, standing as tall as she could. Yelling in a loud voice, she said, "Leave her alone! Look, I'm not scared of you. Not. At. All!"

She stretched out both hands and screamed, "Soweeee!" And again, "Soweeee!"

Then the bull gave two big hoofs at the ground, blowing ferociously.

Sam swallowed hard, only to find there was no spit left in her mouth.

In slow motion, Sam saw the bull start toward her at a gallop.

She ran as fast as she could, veering right, not back toward the house but in the direction of the fence line next to the pricker bushes. *Thud, thud, thud.*

The ground shook underneath her feet, and too scared to look back, she ran for her life.

She imagined the bull's hot breath just behind her, and zigzagged like her mom had said.

"Always zigzag if you're being chased; it makes you a lot harder to catch." Sam was about to find out if Mom knew some stuff or if she was simply full of herself, just like Daddy said.

Just about at that second, Sam veered right, sliding under the electric fence into the bushes.

The bull stopped just short of the fence, and Sam met eyes with a very angry giant beast. She said, "Told you I wasn't scared."

She could just hear Sarah crying down the fence line. Sam spoke quietly this time.

"Just stay put. I'm coming to get you."

Sarah replied, "You can't."

"I can, I'm coming!" Sam said.

Her sister's plaintive small voice came again. "You can't get me. Because I'm stuck."

A loud indistinguishable yelling began on the other side of the field.

Sam finally got to a standing position as the bull ran off toward the noise.

Walking through pricker bushes was her least favorite activity and she was glad when she cleared them. Glancing in the direction the bull was heading, she saw the farmer.

He had a pail and was yelling, striking the tin bucket with great ferocity.

The bull quickened its pace, thundering through the gate and into another field. The farmer quickly closed it behind his bull. Looking out across the field, the farmer then stepped out a bit, slowing. Sam thought she saw him shake his head but wasn't sure.

He hated them all anyway, the whole family of 'outsiders.'

He even hated the babies, and no reasonable person could hate those.

Sam made her way through the bushes toward the center of the round bales, sliding under the fence and around toward the front.

"Sarah?" she called out quietly, looking around the other side where the bull had charged.

There, she found her sister wedged between the second and third bale in a little triangle opening at the bottom. "Sarah, it's me."

Sarah replied, "I'm scared!" She was almost crying, her voice trembling. "I'm too scared to come out. I don't like ad-*ven*-tures anymore."

Sam threw her head back and landed on her bottom.

Laughing, she said, "It's gone. I took care of it. You can come out! It's super-duper safe."

Sarah crawled out, and the first thing she did was leap on top of her sister. "I thought you were dead!"

Sam replied, "I can't die, remember. I'm *eight.*"

The girls hugged each other, both crying and not crying at the same time. "Daddy says we can't cry, so stop it and let's climb on top of the world."

Sam grabbed the rope holding the round bale together. She began to scurry up. Sarah grabbed Sam by her belt, following.

Both girls soon stood on top.

Blood covered Sam's legs, her arms too, and a single drop slid down the front of her face.

Sarah looked at her sister. "We better go get Mom."

"No way. Besides, it doesn't hurt after—"

"Yes, it does. I know it does!" Sarah was not being denied. "Look at your pants, mom's gonna be so mad!"

Sam took in the sorry sight of her pants, not wanting anyone knowing she'd wet them.

"I fell and slid under the wire. I just need to wash off in the river, and dry, good as new."

But their mom certainly was going to kill her for ruining another pair of blue jeans, she was sure of that. The two sat there, just looking around until the sun tipped past the first set of trees.

Sam pointed into the sky. "We really are on top of the world."

The girls examined the fields around, even able to see past the farmer's house, all the way to the chicken houses. They could see the old two-room shack, so small next to everything else.

They could see the roof of their own ranch house, too, but nothing of its front.

The woods on that side were also concealed.

Hearing a hissing sound, both girls looked up.

A vulture flew just over their heads, then circled back, repeating its terrible hissing sound.

Sarah's eyes were wide.

Sam said, "No worries. It only eats dead stuff, and we're definitely alive. It's just a turkey vulture."

With low nasal hiss, it landed on the first big round bale. Sam turned to Sarah. Their eyes were huge, and neither girl seemed to know what to say, stunned into silence.

The bird was huge. The girls just held eye contact, nodding at one another.

They slid off the bale and slipped into the woods, scurrying toward the river.

What they called 'the river' was more like a small stream, but to Sam and Sarah, it was huge and tumultuous. When it rained, the riverbanks filled.

This week, it had been raining hard, so the banks were full of treasure. Jumping into the water, Sam got as clean as she could. When she was sure she'd done a good job, she stepped out and sat on a big rock beside the water.

Sarah was wide-eyed. "We can't go home till you're dry ... but I'm really hungry."

Sam gave a sad look. Sarah was right, though; she had to get dry first.

The worst sin ever would have been to track mud into the house just before Daddy got home.

Sam jumped up. "Follow me; I wanna show you something!"

Sarah followed, up past the big rock, up the deer trail, taking a turn to the right, then left.

Sam lifted several tree branches and revealed an opening.

They slid underneath, into the space. Sam put her fingers to her lips, letting Sarah know to be very quiet. When Sam pointed, her sister couldn't help but gasp. Off in the corner, underneath the lowest branches, was a young doe curled up with her tiny fawn.

Sarah caught sight of Sam, seeing wonder crossing her sister's delighted face.

It was as if she believed Sam could conjure up all the magical creatures of the woods, that there could be no other explanation for the deer being right there, right now.

Sam smiled. Sarah was the gentle one.

She moved gracefully and ever so slowly up to the doe, then sat down next to it.

Sam stayed off to the side, near the opening. Sam was tough and brave, but grace, she possessed very little of. She watched her sister and thought the world needed more of the kindness she saw there. There were very few places for kindness in Sam's world, but her sister's world seemed to be full of it. Sarah put out her little hand, brushing the side of the doe.

Only a second later, Sam felt a twinge of jealousy.

Hadn't she been trying to pet that doe for about a week now?

Watching her sweet sister Sarah do it in minutes kinda made her eyes water. But as she looked at little Sarah, she really couldn't be that mad. Sarah saw the world through eyes filled with sweetness and joy, whereas Sam never saw things that way.

Mom said they were just made different.

Today, Sam had been made abundantly aware of that difference.

She slipped quietly outside the enclosure.

Walking a couple of hundred feet, she found the cornfield.

The ears of corn, only just beginning to ripen, seemed to be begging to be picked. She snuck through the wires and grabbed two ears covered in silk, the color of gold. Underneath the golden hairs were kernels as sweet as Sarah. Sam knew her sister would love them.

Arriving back at the enclosure, she found Sarah still sitting next to the doe. Easing as close as she thought she could get, she sat down next to her sister.

Peeling back the silk, Sam marveled at the beautiful rows of corn.

She handed Sarah one of the corn ears. "I wonder why they call them 'ears'?" Sam commented. "They don't look like ears to me."

"Shhh," Sarah replied.

Breaking her ear in half, Sam put it down right by her sister, also near the doe.

When the doe reached out, Sam laid her hand on its neck. The doe 'maybe' smiled back, and Sam just couldn't be sure because it had happened so fast.

There they sat, eating and smiling and petting the sweet mama deer.

Sara whispered, "We can't pet the baby, it says so in the *en-cyclo-pedia* Momma read to me. And there were pictures."

Sam asked, "Why not? I mean why can't we touch it?"

Sarah shrugged. "Not sure why. We'll have to ask Momma."

Moving out to the riverbed again, the girls collected treasure, fish, bugs, and all kinds of crab-looking things that were living there. Both girls marveled at bringing them home, trying their best to find their 'treasures' in the en-cyclo-pedia.

Mom said it was important to know things, explaining that the things you knew depended on what was important to you, and what you were interested in.

She never tired of explaining anything, over and over.

Yes. They would definitely ask her. Tired, full of corn, finally dry and holding her sister's hand tightly, Sam headed home as the sun began to drop from the sky.

Chapter 3

Mom was just finishing dinner when the girls arrived.

"Go back outside and play while I finish dinner."

She smiled as she chased both girls back out.

"Wait, Momma, I need to ask a question ..." Sarah asked as if desperate to know something.

Just outside the sliding glass back door, Mom paused. "What question?"

"Why can't I pet a baby deer?" Sarah looked at her mother with wonder, dancing side to side, waiting for an answer. Sam stopped too, listening just as intently.

"Hmm, first of all. It's not called a baby deer; it's a fawn." Mom peered at both girls to ensure they were listening. "Secondly, you shouldn't pet it because you will leave your smell on it. Fawns don't have a smell so they can hide from predators."

Sam chirped, "Predators? What are those?"

"Predators are other animals that will chase it, kill it, and eat it. So, if we pet baby wild animals, we are putting their lives at risk."

Sarah gasped, "Mommy! We can't let that happen, never, ever. The animals can't die."

"Well, sometimes, they do. It's part of the world. Remember the dead animals you've seen in the forest?"

Sarah seemed about to cry.

Sam nodded, and said, "Sarah, you're such a baby; animals die all the time. Everything eats everything else. And *we're* gonna eat a cow, tonight!"

"Stop it, Sam," their mom said. "It's a tough thing to learn that animals kill and eat each other. There's always a purpose. If nothing ate the deer, we wouldn't have any trees or grass. And there'd be so many deer that they would start to die of disease and starvation."

"I don't like it." Sarah crossed her arms now, stomping her small foot.

Mom laughed and patted her daughter's head.

Sam was considering everything.

"I understand, Momma. Everything that lives also dies, and everything that survives has purpose, right?" She said it slowly and carefully.

Momma had spent hours explaining this to Sam already.

Sam thought she might still not quite understand but didn't want any more long discussions. Sarah could ask her 'thinking questions' later.

"Yes, Sam. Now, like I said, you girls go play; I've got work to do."

Sarah tapped her sister on the shoulder and started a game of tag through the trails by the house. Weaving in and out, both girls giggled, and ran.

Sam wasn't sure who ever won the games they played; if you asked her, she would swear it was her, but it never mattered. She just loved playing with her sister.

"Look," Sam said, pointing up into the tree.

The turkey vulture sat there, surveying its domain. Sarah gasped, "It's so big."

"Yeah. but remember it only eats dead things; if you see them circle, it means there's something already dead on the ground."

"Don't they kill anything?"

"Mom says they aren't bad. She says we need them to keep everything clean. I don't think they actually kill anything. Or maybe they kill stuff that's already dying. I don't know."

It seemed that between the girls, there was always a new question being born.

Sarah tagged her sister and started running again. They ran and ran, dodging in and out of their yard. Sam ducked under a tree limb and ran straight for the house, veering left, and around the house they went. She then ducked behind a bush and held her breath.

Stooping below the bushes, she saw Sarah coming around the corner.

Sarah ran by at top speed, hurtling past her sister twice before she stopped, signs of confusion lining her face. Sam started moving. *Careful, easy,* she thought as she slid from behind the bush.

Sam was never quiet. As she neared her sister, Sarah turned, pushing her into the grass.

Both girls went rolling down the hill toward the woods.

When they stopped, they both giggled, unable to stop till it hurt to breathe.

From behind them, the woods snapped.

It was Sam who saw the stranger first. Dirty, wearing overalls and no shirt, he stepped out of the woods and stopped. A bag hung from his shoulders. He just stood there, watching them.

The girls gasped and jumped up, fixing their clothes, brushing off the dirt. They stood up to greet this unpleasant looking stranger who was still slightly hidden in the trees.

Sam was first to talk. "Whoever you are, you can come out. Mom always has a gun."

Sarah pushed her sister, almost knocking her over. "You're not supposed to tell people that."

The voice replied, "I ain't looking for trouble. Besides, you two girls look like you could take care of yourselves."

The man stepped out of the wood line, his face covered by the brim of a wide dark hat.

"Get here, girls," Mom yelled from the porch. Her voice was anxious.

Sarah and Sam ran up and stood right next to Mom, each trying their level best to look tough.

It was always so scary when Daddy was gone and something—or someone—came up through the trees. All kinds of stuff showed up. Once, even a mountain lion had wandered out, but Momma said there weren't many of those so they needn't worry; it wouldn't stay around there.

Usually, Sam thought it was interesting stuff, but when it was a man, it was different.

Momma walked slowly toward the man.

He was very dirty, and very big. His floppy hat hung down, covering his eyes, and he smelled like the guys who worked over on the pig farms. Sam could smell him from the porch, and it made her nose crinkle; she pinched it shut to keep from coughing as he got a little closer.

"Don't mean to cause no bother, ladies. I just stopped here for a little rest from the rails. Ain't bathed yet, but I'll get to it soon."

So, the man must have known that he stank to high heaven.

He sat down just on the edge of the woods, against a crooked dogwood tree.

Somewhere inside the house, a baby started crying.

If Sam were to be honest with herself, it was a screaming baby. She whispered behind her mother's pants, "That's gotta be one of the boys."

Sarah said, "I know. Why are boys so loud?"

Sam rolled her eyes. "I have no idea, but they're still annoying when they get older."

"Isn't Daddy a boy?"

"No. He's a man. That's totally different," Sam said as she shoved her sister.

"Shh. You girls go inside for a minute." Mom sounded very serious. "Sam, please go take care of the baby. I'll be right in."

Going inside, Sam quickly got the screaming baby. Unfortunately, by now, there were several screaming babies to be comforted. She put the first on the floor next to Sarah, grabbing a second one, huffing to herself as if the babies were endless. Walking to the window, she searched for Mom, seeing her still standing there, talking with the man for what seemed like forever.

Sarah said in a whisper, "Can you tell what they're saying?"

"No. Can you?"

"No," said little Sarah's timid voice. "I don't like the man."

"Me neither."

Sarah asked, "What do you think this one wants?"

"I don't know. Daddy says she should just shoot them. Then they'd stop coming outta the woods. Reckon he'd be right."

"He sure is big and dirty. He's *really* filthy."

Sam went wide-eyed. "She left her gun."

The long rifle rested just inside the door.

Sam placed the baby back in the crib and ran to grab the rifle. The Remington Model 10 was heavy and unwieldy, so Sam groaned as she lifted it, barely able to stop it dragging on the floor.

Sliding the glass door open, she stood watching her mom from behind. The man had eased out of the woods by this time, and now, he was standing right in front of Momma.

Sam was going to stay standing just where the man would be sure to see her.

Sure enough, he caught sight of her, but he started laughing.

"Girl, that gun is as big as you are."

Sam stood up straighter. Was he really laughing at her? He was stupid! After all, she did have a gun, and a big, loaded one at that. They were all afraid of the gun, especially her. Daddy had shot a deer with it once; Sam almost didn't recover from the shock of watching it die.

It was something she had tried to forget, but it always came back.

Mom turned. "Oh, my God, Sam, what did I tell you?"

Sam just adjusted her stance and lifted the barrel of the gun.

Momma sighed, then yelled out, "Sam, you'll go put that back inside. He's just hungry. We all get hungry. Don't be stupid."

Sam didn't budge.

The man lifted his head just a bit. "Ma'am I think she's serious. I can wait back here."

He had stopped laughing. The man turned, walked back to the wood line, and sat again on the crooked dogwood. Sam lowered the barrel, a satisfied look on her face.

Mom turned, and Sam immediately knew she was in serious trouble. "What on earth do you think you are doing?!"

Sam moved quickly inside the house. Mom was close behind her.

"Really, Sam, what were you thinking!" Mom appeared bewildered. "Sam, you're always overreacting. You have to stop. Not everyone's going to hurt you, and those who will are the ones you least expect. You have the biggest heart there is; it's your imagination that runs away with you. Now, stop messing around and get the baby. He's still crying."

Sam rested the gun in its place.

Sarah walked up behind her, carrying the smallest baby. "He *is* a scary man," she whispered.

Sam peeked over her shoulder, checking to see if her mother was listening. "Yes. He is, and big too." It was a shame Momma didn't see the problem. But what could Sam do?

The girls changed diapers on all the babies, careful not to pin the cloth diapers to an actual infant. Sam had done that once and was in trouble for a week.

She was sure her own bottom was still sore from the aftermath.

After they had rinsed the diapers in the toilet and washed their hands, they bounded into the kitchen. It was a magical place; Momma could make good food out of more or less anything.

The yeast was the best.

Watching the bread rise, Mom had said the dough was alive because of the yeast, and soon, warm fresh bread sat on the counter.

Momma sliced thick pieces and placed them on a cloth napkin. Smoothing peanut butter on a few and sliced cheese on some others, she made sandwiches. Sam only meant to put her finger in the peanut butter but somehow managed to get her whole hand covered.

Mom laughed, saying, "What a mess! You know better."

Momma play-swiped at Sam's small outstretched hand, at the same time giving her a piece of bread. After giving Sarah one too, Mom wrapped all the sandwiches in parchment paper.

Handing Sam the wrapped sandwiches, her momma said, "We must always feed the hungry because we never know when God will show up. If you're scared, you share anyway. Now take these sandwiches and those old clothes out to that man on the tree line."

Sam shrugged.

She would rather not go and see that unpleasant smelly man again, but Mom had told her to.

So, she set off, slowly walking toward the tree line, all the paper-wrapped sandwiches clasped in her hand. The old clothes were draped over her shoulders, threatening to slide off.

The man was waiting patiently, leaning back on the dogwood. Sam thought he might have been sleeping, the broad-brimmed hat pulled way down. *You can tell a lot from looking in people's eyes,* she thought, but she couldn't see his. As she moved closer, he shifted his weight.

Sam cleared her throat, afraid to get any closer. "Where do you guys come from?"

He answered without even hesitating, "We ride the rails. They call us hobos but we're really just regular folks trying to earn a living and to get someplace."

"Where is someplace?"

Sam could tell he was thinking by how long he paused.

"Well, it's different than where you are."

"Why would you wanna go someplace? You don't have a home?"

"Some do. Some don't."

He pulled out a pocketknife, beginning to pick out the dirt from under his nails. "That was a big gun you had. Anyone teach you to shoot it?"

Sam almost dropped the sandwiches.

She lied, "Of course I know how to shoot it! Almost shot you, didn't I? And don't you think I won't! Just you try anything, and you'll see!"

"Hold on there; I was just making conversation. You girls are too pretty to be way out here playing all by yourselves. You're both as beautiful as little butterflies."

Sam crossed her arms. "Butterflies aren't tough, though," she insisted, repeating her earlier point. "I can handle myself."

"Who told you that? I once knew a beautiful butterfly like you. She was beautiful *and* strong. In fact, butterflies are super tough. How do you think they travel around the world?"

He started cleaning under the grimy nails on his other hand.

He glanced up at Sam, smiled, and said, "You disappoint me. I thought you were smart?"

Sam stomped her foot and huffed. She looked at the man, truly annoyed, and crossed both arms across her chest. Sarah peeked out from behind her.

He was about to ask something else the girls would not like.

"Do you have a daddy?" This man was full of questions that were none of his business.

"Doesn't everybody have a daddy?" Sam said, squaring her shoulders again to be sure he saw how tall she was this time, in the absence of the rifle.

"Well, daddies are kinda like everything else. Not everybody has 'em."

Sam set the clothes down as close to the man as she dared go. She still couldn't see his eyes, and all this talk and his familiarity made her uneasy.

He was big, dirty, and his teeth were bad. She then set the sandwiches on top of the clothes, and his big hand reached out, steadying them. He eyed the food as though it was precious metal.

"What's your name?" the man asked.

"What's yours?" Sam replied, quick as a flash.

"Girl, isn't there anything that doesn't put you on guard? The name's Thomas, and I better get headed somewhere. Looks like it might rain tonight. Tell your mama thanks for the sandwiches, and the clothes. I sure do appreciate it."

He turned to move away with his haul of garments and good food.

"Samantha, my name is Samantha. But everybody calls me Sam."

He turned back, smiling. "You're way too pretty to be a Sam, so Samantha it is."

And with that, he was gone, disappearing into the woods.

Chapter 4

The Buick Estate station wagon eased onto the gravel drive leading up to the house. Both girls had done their chores, helped Mom with dinner and the babies, bathed, and put on fresh pajamas.

Their reward every night was getting to see Daddy pull down the long gravel drive while Momma got all the babies ready for bed.

Tonight was special for Sam; it was the day before her birthday. Daddy always took her out, just the two of them, and it was the only time all year she got her daddy all to herself.

"Where do you think he'll take me this year?" she asked Sarah. "What d'you think?"

Sarah smiled. "I went to Dairy Queen for ice cream on my last birthday!"

Sam huffed. "Dairy Queen! That's baby stuff. I'll get to do something special; that's for sure."

Sarah frowned at her sister.

She suddenly smiled, pointing out the window to the station wagon. "It's Daddy!"

The station wagon was kind of cream colored with trim like wood across the bottom. When Daddy had bought it, Sam had serious concerns about *her* Daddy driving a car covered in wood. They burned wood every year and she had quite the collection of spots on her hands, evidence of her not-so-kind experiences with fire.

Her dad had finally convinced her that it wouldn't catch fire because for one thing, it wasn't even real wood; he'd explained this after a full day of discussion and inspection. Now the station wagon, safely inspected regularly by Sam, was successfully driving her dad safely home again from work. It pulled to the end of the gravel, Dad driving around to the back beside the patio.

As he parked, both girls pushed through the door to be the first to greet him. Sam was so excited; she jumped and grabbed her dad around the waist. He picked her up and swung her around, tossed her in the air and skillfully caught her. Sarah already had her hands up when he put Sam down. Grabbing his smaller girl, he twirled her around and around.

Kissing Sarah on the cheek, then doing the same to Sam, he said, "How are my girls doing?"

The chatter from both girls came at once as they tried to update Daddy about their whole day.

"Wait a minute, you two little ones." Daddy was grinning. "Let me get inside before you wear me out." Throwing his briefcase back into the car, he took both girls by the hand, and they walked across the patio and into the house.

Chatting away mindlessly, Sam chimed in, "And there was this man …"

Sarah added excitedly, "And you should have seen Sam with the gun!"

Then, a deafening silence permeated everything.

Dead silence. Heavy silence that you could almost cleave in two with an axe and never recover from. Sam knew at once they had suddenly changed the mood inside the house.

Sarah had said the wrong thing. Like always.

Dad was probably mad at her now. "Gun? What were you doing with the gun?"

Sam inspected the floor, scuffing at it with her shoes.

She stayed silent for a moment before he said again, "Sam, I've said a hundred times, you are not to handle the rifle. What were you doing with it?"

"Mom was outside talking to a man who showed up from the trees. She forgot to take it with her."

"So, you took it to Momma?" He frowned, his brows knitting, thinking.

"No. I held it in case the man hurt Momma."

She spoke loudly and fiercely, like the warrior she evidently believed she was.

He sighed, visible annoyed.

"Why was your mother talking to yet another man who came out of the woods? They aren't ever going to stop coming if we keep feeding them.

They're like pigeons. They'll keep coming back for-ever if the food's plentiful. Seems I'll have to talk to your mother again."

Mom stuck her head out from the kitchen, leaning on the bar separating it from the dining room. "I heard you. But you worry too much. He was just passing through; all I gave him was some sandwiches."

Dad appeared to be very serious.

"Why would you need the gun if he wasn't someone to worry about?'

"I actually didn't need the gun. You know how Sam is, always stressing about nothing. If I'd needed the gun, I would have gotten it for myself."

Mom made a rolling motion with her hands, signifying that it was nothing of consequence.

"You have got to stop feeding those men. Really, you could be hurt. Or worse, the girls could be hurt or taken from us. Or the babies could." Dad's face was beginning to turn red at the edges.

Sam had already started moving toward the hallway. He was right.

Sarah popped up, nudging her Dad's hand. She could always calm him down when no one else could. "Daddy, did they bring the new TV in today?"

He smiled, taking in his adoring daughter. No matter what he did, however he behaved, little Sarah would always seek the goodness in him.

"Yes! They did, and guess what?"

"What?"

"You have to guess," he replied. "That's why I said *guess what!*"

Dad sat down at the dining table, pulling Sarah onto his lap. She began to giggle and looked at her dad with wide eyes. "Is it big?"

Dad shook his head yes, then said, "And that's not all; it's got color."

Sam immediately understood and was stunned. She knew he sold appliances for the power company but somehow, she had missed that they might get a color TV out of it.

Her excitement was barely contained. "Daddy, can we get one? How big is it?"

Sam was standing right next to him now.

"Well, that depends on how good my girls are."

Mom interjected, "No, television is bad for their eyes."

"You worry too much. It's the newest thing. All the kids want to see it." Dad scruffed Sarah's hair. "We'll get one soon, you girls just wait. We'll replace that old black and white with a full-color console! I'll work on convincing your mom."

Mom brought dinner out while Daddy changed.

They all sat down at the table. One of the babies sat next to Mom in a highchair and another in a seat on the floor. The food smelled amazing. Sam especially loved the baked chicken.

The vegetables, not so much, but tonight was green beans and potatoes. Sam sat in her seat, squirming in anticipation. She kept looking at the chicken, then at her plate.

Holding hands, Dad prayed.

"Good food, God bless, let's eat." Clapping his hands and rubbing them together, he smiled wide. "Sam, I know you don't like this chicken at all, so we might just skip your plate."

Sam sat up completely straight and said, indignant, "Dad, no, I really like it! It's my favorite!"

Everyone laughed but Sam. "Really? We'd never have guessed. But since it's your birthday tomorrow, I tell you what: we'll give you the first portion."

"Oh no, Daddy, I can wait. You're the one who works for us all. You always should get yours first, Momma says so." Sam bit her lower lip just a little, sitting on her hands.

"Well, tonight, you can go first," Mom said, nodding and smiling at Sam.

Mom passed the food to Sam. She got a piece of chicken, followed quickly by the biggest spoonful of mashed potatoes that she could manage, then she picked out three green beans and put them on her plate. The hardest part for Sam would come next.

No one ever ate until everyone had a plate of food, then Daddy took the first bite.

Sam watched every single person filling their plate, waiting while Mom helped Sarah with her napkin. She stared at her dad, sure he saw her, and he very slowly lifted his first forkful.

Again very slowly, he took a bite and they all let out a laugh as Sam literally dived into her plate.

Sam had a mouthful of potatoes, but she still managed to say, "What?"

Mom replied, "Sam, watch your manners! You're a young lady, and we don't want to see your half-chewed potatoes going around and around like they're in a washing machine. Birthday or no birthday, remember your table etiquette."

"*Eti ... what?* Plus, what if I don't want to be a lady?" Sam replied. "It's boring." She swung both her feet under the table with an attitude that swept through her entire body.

Sarah made eye contact, sweetly grinning.

She said, "*Everyone* wants to be a lady! They're the most beautiful!"

Mom smiled, and said, "That's right, Sarah, and a very beautiful lady you will be."

Dad scowled at Sam. "Speaking of being lady-like, the farmer called me at work; seems someone has been running in his field again."

Sam slid down in her chair. Sarah couldn't take her eyes off Dad.

"Well, we climbed up and saw the whole world!" Her eyes were wide with wonder. "Daddy, we could even see the shack." The shack was where Matthew lived with his brothers.

He did some yard work sometimes. Mom liked him, and she said he couldn't help being that poor. Sam liked him too, but he was always getting beaten up and she couldn't figure out what was happening. He never liked to fight with anyone, as a matter of fact; he was always there to keep them safe if they wandered too far up the roads.

"Oh my, you could see that far, huh?"

"Yea. That's all the way past the chicken houses, and the field."

Sarah was standing in her chair now, pointing the way.

"I heard the bull charged you, is that true?" Dad lifted an eyebrow as he asked. Sarah hadn't learned to lie yet and if Sam's ability was any indication of family traits, she may never learn.

"Kinda. It was scary, but Sam saved me." Sarah recounted the story, and bit by bit, Sam slid further and further down in her seat until barely her forehead and eye were above the tabletop.

Silence.

Dad persisted, asking again, "I said is that true?"

No answer. Sam seemed to be finding something fascinating under the table.

"Of course it's true," Mom said. "You can tell by how she's behaving."

Silence. "Hush. I was asking Sam." Daddy could get serious so fast.

Sam had nearly disappeared under the table by the time she answered, "Yes, sir. Yes, Daddy."

Dad replied, "Well. I'm glad you were there. He's gonna keep his bull in the upper field from now on. But you two just stay away from his cows, understood? Cows and bulls. They can do a lot of damage to a child."

His expression seemed to say, *they can kill you in a heartbeat,* but he stayed quiet about that.

Sarah, still standing in her chair, said, "Yes, Daddy."

Nodding as she said it added extra emphasis.

They ate and chatted about nothing else important. Sam was glad. She really didn't want to ruin her birthday that was coming soon. Birthdays were the best days, and hers was tomorrow.

After dinner, Daddy said he and Mommy needed to talk, so both girls hurried to brush their teeth and settle into bed. "Maybe they're gonna talk about my birthday?" Sam said to Sarah as they brushed their teeth. "I think they bought me a really big, important present. Do you?"

Sarah didn't say anything. She just shrugged her tiny shoulders.

When Sam turned away to return to her bedroom, little Sarah mumbled, "How would I know? No one tells me *any*thing! They always say, 'Shut up, Sarah, you're too young to know.'"

She put her toothbrush back into the little pot with the toothpaste.

Sarah slept with the babies, while Sam now had her own room. The smallest bedroom, it was on the front of the house, nestled between the foyer and the bathroom.

She loved it. Her canopy bed had a cover Momma had sewn just for her, and her covers matched it. She also had new sheets today because it was Saturday, so everything was almost perfect. Almost. Sam slid into bed, worried about the serious look Daddy had shown when he'd said they needed to talk.

Just then, Mom opened the door and walked over to tuck Sam into bed.

Sam said to Momma, "I'm so sorry about the bull and my pants."

She gazed down into her covers, ashamed of always ruining her clothes which Dad had worked so hard to buy in the first place. It wasn't as if he had lots of money to spend.

Mom held her hand and smiled.

"That's all right, Sam. Of all my children, I don't know if you'll understand but you 'belong' to us the very least. Sometimes, children are born who don't really belong at home. These kids are stronger, more inquisitive, and just so wonderful; their light burns so brightly that they can't hide it anywhere. You are just one of them. It makes you special."

It was nice to hear Momma's words, but Sam didn't agree. And besides, what did any of this have to do with getting dirty pants when playing outside? It didn't make much sense.

"I don't feel special," Sam said as she swallowed hard.

Mom met her gaze for a long time, then clearing her throat, she said, "You're my brave girl. The world isn't ready for you, that's all. You are gonna have to make a way for yourself."

Sam's face crumpled. She had no idea what her mother was talking about.

"What about Sarah? And the babies?"

"Well, they aren't my first-born baby girl, are they?" Mom smiled and swooped Sam up into a hug. "You just have to remember it's your job to keep them all safe. If you did anything wrong today, it was putting your sister in danger. You can't do that again. Understand?"

Mom stood and headed for the door. "Mommy, what do I do when I'm scared?"

"Little one, that's what it means to be brave. If you aren't scared, you're stupid, not brave. And you're not stupid, not one little bit." Mom grabbed the basket of laundry by the door. "You look confused. Think about what I said; you'll get it soon enough. Goodnight!"

"Hhhmppfff …" Sam let all the air out of her lungs.

Mom could be so confusing sometimes.

She was a trained special education teacher; she actually had a college degree, so sometimes, she said things Sam knew were important, but she just couldn't make heads or tails of any of it.

This was certainly one of those times. The sheets were amazing, fresh pressed. Sam was sure mom had ironed them, just for her. As she nuzzled into her bed, sleep overtook her.

Chapter 5

S he felt him staring, felt his gaze boring into her. As Sam opened her eyes, the figure of a man appeared silhouetted in her window. She was sure he was looking right at her through the window, but darkness covered his eyes. Sam felt terror for the first time.

She didn't move at first, just trying to focus, really focus. She saw him just enough to think she might still be asleep. She rubbed her eyes. *Nope, still there.* She sat up.

He tilted his head.

"Daddy, Daddy!" Sam screamed as she scooted back, up against her headboard. Grabbing the headboard with both hands, she held on and closed her eyes tight.

Daddy rushed in and turned on the light. "Sam, what's the matter? Are you having a nightmare?" He sat down on the side of the bed, and she climbed into his lap and started to cry.

At eight years of age, she hardly ever crawled onto her daddy's lap for protection anymore, usually insisting she was all grown up.

But now, she was shaking and crying and couldn't even say what was wrong.

Sam tried to sit herself up and talk, but her throat closed.

She shut her eyes, reopening them over and over, staring at the empty window. At long last, Sam finally said, "There was a man. Daddy, there's a man out there." She pointed, too.

Her dad rose from the bed and walked toward the window.

Sam screamed, "Don't, Daddy, he'll get you! He's still out there, he is. I just know it!"

"Calm down, Sam, I got it. Try not to overreact. It was probably just a dream." Sam stopped breathing as her dad approached the window, raised the glass, and stuck out his head.

"Nope, nothing here." He glanced up and down, then right and left before pulling his head back inside. "Nothing's there, Sam. You must have had a dream. Take some deep breaths; dreams can be very scary."

Mom was at the doorway to her room now, looking at her with great sympathy.

Dad said, "You've had bad dreams before; it will be just fine."

Sam asked, "Can you pull the shade down, Daddy? I mean all the way."

Her dad pulled the green shade all the way down over the window. The shade was a plastic green and covered most of the opening. You could see the silhouette of the moonlight but nothing else. Sam began to relax into her bed.

"There really was someone out there, really, really."

Mom sat on her bed. "Honey, you've had bad dreams before. I thought they had gotten better. Is this happening a lot?"

"Mommy, I didn't make this up; it was a big man. Big enough to stand outside and look in through the glass." Her throat was closing again in fear.

"Are you sure?" Mom asked as her dad slipped out of the room.

All Sam could get out was a soft whisper. "Yes."

Mom got up, staring outside.

The window was on the front of the house, in the middle; the dirt road could be seen about 150 feet straight ahead, and the wood line was off to the right.

Mom studied the scene.

Sam thought her mom might have seen something when she walked over to let the blind up, then opened the window. Mom stuck her head out and looked to the right, just like Dad had done. But she abruptly closed the window and dropped the blind again. "You're okay now."

'You believe me, don't you?" Sam's question was more of a statement.

"I always believe you."

"Daddy doesn't."

"How do you know?'

"Because I'm almost eight, that's how I know. I'm so big now that I know things no one has to tell me."

Mom sat up against the headboard. Sighing, she said, "My brave sweet little one, some things, no one really knows. What you need right now is someone to believe you and I do."

Sam flopped against her bed, turning her back on her mother. "But you don't really, do you?"

Mom stroked the curly hair on Sam's head. "I know you've had night terrors before, mostly because you let your wild imagination run away with you; remember when you were sure there was a ghost in your room? Or the time a lion was in the hallway?"

"Those were really scary."

"Yeah. Your dad had to take away the National Geographic magazines for a few months."

Mom laughed just a tad.

Sam crossed her arms, looking back over her shoulder at her mother.

She said, "Those were silly baby dreams. This one … this man … was real."

"You thought those were real too." Mom sighed.

"Can I come sleep with you?"

"Not tonight, Sam. You just need to calm down a minute. And like you just said, you're a big girl. You don't need to sleep with Momma anymore."

Her dad walked in, placing a glass of cold water by Sam's bedside.

"Your mom and I have a few things to discuss, so are you calm enough to get some rest? We have a big day planned tomorrow."

Sam smiled. "It's gonna be my birthday!"

Dad smiled back. "Yeah, but it won't get here if you don't go to sleep."

Sam drank her water, handing the glass back to Daddy. Her parents tucked in her covers; each kissed her forehead, clicked off the light and closed the door as they left, heading back into the hallway. Sam turned to see her shade, studying it, sure she'd seen something.

Whatever it had been, nothing was there now.

She pulled the freshly ironed covers over her head.

***

This time, Sam was awakened by the sound of dishes being broken.

"No, stop!' she heard her mom screaming.

She got up and ran to the door, bumping right into Sarah. "Can I stay with you?" Sarah had immediately wrapped both arms around Sam.

Pulling her sister inside her room, Sam closed the door. She knew what was happening.

She heard her daddy yell, "You should have cleaned them!"

"Please, that's my mom's china!" her mother's voice sounded so small.

The crashing stopped.

"Please," her mom sobbed.

"I don't care! And you've got to get Sam under control. She almost killed her sister today. The farmer came to see me at work! Came *into* my work, for God's sake! We have to have my job, you know that, right? Things are hard enough as it is! If she loses me my job, then ..."

He broke off, and Sam was glad about that.

"She's just an imaginative little girl. You can't blame her just because that old man had a bad attitude."

"Bad attitude? She was in the fields with a bull, for God's sake. She could've gotten her sister killed, if not also herself! He said if he hadn't called the animal back, both girls might have died, and then who would also have been in trouble? He would. He wants to charge us because he can't use that field anymore for his bull. Says it's not safe if we can't control our kids. I said we can. But it's too late."

Mom was choking out words through her tears, Sam could hear it, hearing the choking sound as if not enough air was passing through Mom's throat. Sarah was holding onto Sam under the covers. Sam kissed her little sister, saying, "It's gonna be all right. It won't last much longer."

Daddy walked down the hallway, and back again. Sam always knew his footsteps when he was angry because they were so heavy. Then, glasses clinked.

Mom sobbed, "Stop drinking, please; let's go to bed."

"I'm not done yet. Besides, you haven't told me how you're gonna handle Sam; you have to reel her in. She's feral."

Sam heard him hurl another piece of china out onto the patio.

"She has to know she can't be causing so much trouble; you have to teach her to control that crazy imagination of hers ... and you have to stop feeding those hobos, something else I keep saying till I'm blue in the face. They won't stop coming till you stop feeding them. For God's sake, woman, we can barely feed our own kids, let alone the whole world."

"She's just a little girl finding her way though."

"Then you have to find her another way! That man—your visitor you seemed keen to keep around—scared the hell out of her today. She actually picked up my rifle and brought it outside!"

She said softly, "Then maybe you should teach her to shoot it."

"Christ, woman, that would be awful. With an imagination like that, she'll kill someone. Thank God I finally have sons; they'll at least bring some sense into this house."

"There is nothing wrong with the girls." Mom said it with such furious intent, Sam could feel her rising up in the other room. She shuddered in fear, tucking Sarah down further under the covers, then she pulled them up over her head, squeezing the pillows around their ears.

"Damn you! You don't know anything about the real world. You sit around the house all day doing nothing, absolutely nothing. You're useless."

Something banged into the wall.

Sam hated it when her mom fought back; it only made things so much worse.

More dishes crashed into the patio, and this time, there was no sobbing. This was worse. Her momma must have been standing, now, shoulders squared.

"You can't continue to treat the girls like they're 'less than' just because they're girls and then work them like boys!"

"Shut up, woman, you've got no idea. Sam's only gonna find suffering if she keeps her attitude up. She can't fight the whole world."

"And *you* can't say what she can do or can't do. She's my eldest daughter and I will not let anyone break her like some animal to be ridden! Screw that old man and his field."

The crashing sound that followed was deafening.

Sam was sure she heard the dining room table turning over, too. Then silence, which was even worse. Her dad said, "I'm going to bed; you get this mess cleaned up. You created it."

His heavy footsteps lasted forever as they headed down the hallway.

Sam didn't realize she had been holding her breath till he closed the back bedroom door. She heard a baby cry. Sliding toward the edge of her bed, she was intending to go fetch the little one.

Sarah grabbed her hand. "Stop, Sam. Don't go. Mom will get him."

Just as Sam was pulling away from her sister, she heard her mom's footsteps heading for the back bedroom, and then the babies stopped crying. Little Sarah had been right.

She concentrated on her.

"Are you still scared?" Sam asked as she wiped her sister's tears away. Sarah had been sobbing the entire time, nuzzling closer and closer.

"Is it over? Why is Daddy so mad?"

"I *think* it's over, but let's just stay quiet." Sam adjusted the covers around her sister.

The door opened. Mom popped her head inside. "Sam, is your sister in there?"

"Yes. Momma, I'm right here," came the small voice, timid.

Sarah couldn't help her sobbing, which had gotten considerably worse.

Mom eased the door open, a baby on each hip. "Sam, take care of your sister; it's all okay now. He's just stressed out about work. It's nothing to worry you two."

But it *was* something to worry them both, Sam especially, because just as Daddy had said, she'd caused this mess today, the mess and the anger, all about that great big bull in the field.

She exhaled hard, holding back emotion. Anger. Hurt. Tears …

Sam couldn't see her mom's face but she could feel the emotion there, too.

She got up and took the older baby. "Momma, there's room for one more here."

Her mother had given up the baby so easily that Sam knew immediately she'd done the right thing. "Sam, make sure you keep the baby from falling off the bed," Momma said. "Don't take your eye off him while he's so little, not even for one second."

Sam replied, "Yes, ma'am," and her mother closed the door, heading into the kitchen. Sam's eyes fixated on the infant, almost as if he would implode if she looked away.

Now, she was so scared of getting things wrong again. And with a baby, she just couldn't.

Sam kissed Sarah. "We gotta move to the floor! The baby will fall off. I can't watch him."

She actually could watch him, and she was doing it, too, but the stress was too much.

"If we're down there on the floor, he can't topple off. He can't go *any*where."

Sarah rubbed her eyes and helped as they pulled the freshly ironed sheets off the bed, making a comfortable area on the floor for the three of them.

The baby wasn't crying anymore, and Sarah was curled up under Sam's arm.

Sam couldn't sleep this time. She just lay there on the floor, staring rigidly at her window, at the green blind. Suddenly, the crickets stopped, and a shadow appeared. The silhouette behind the shade moved side to side, finding a small opening on the side of the blind.

Sam was terrified, too scared to speak, too scared to move, yet too scared to lie still, all at the same time. She wanted to scream, to run, to hide, to get the gun again, to call for her father ... who was too drunk to control himself, let alone anyone else who was hanging about.

And Momma had far too much to deal with already. No, she couldn't worry her.

She lay there with her arms around her siblings, staring back, silent. Fiercely intent, she willed herself to not be afraid, making a promise to never look away again.

I am eight years old, she told herself adamantly. *Old enough to protect Momma and the babies. And old enough not to keep scaring Sarah all the time. I am eight. Well, nearly.*

***

The man had left hours before the sun came up. Sam knew he was really gone when the chirping started again. The crickets eased her fear with their rhythmic song, and Sam had heard the roosters in the distance announcing the sun as the light rose against the green shade.

It wasn't long after the sun rose that she heard her father easing into the babies' room, then into the kitchen. The smell of bacon soon began to permeate the whole house.

Sam loved bacon.

Sam also loved her birthday—usually—but there was no smile left in her this morning.

When her father walked quietly into her room, she closed her eyes. She felt him get the baby first, then come back and pick up Sarah.

"Daddy."

"Shh, Sarah, you'll wake your sister. It's her birthday, so let her sleep."

"Okay," Sarah said, barely audible, obviously still intimidated after the night before.

Daddy spoke again, saying, "Anyway, I bet you kept Sam awake half the night, talking like you always do!"

"I didn't, Daddy," said poor Sarah, so subdued that it was sad.

And he didn't even seem to notice it, either.

Sam thought, *no, what kept me awake was my daddy hollering and yelling, throwing Momma's best china, smashing stuff. And threatening her. And complaining on and on about me and that bull. That's what stopped me sleeping.*

That's what she thought, but she would never dare to say any of it to her dad.

Sarah nuzzled her dad lovingly and they both made their way to the dining room.

When Sam was sure they'd both left, leaving her alone, she got up, walked over to the blind, raised it, and opened her window.

Quietly, she said to herself, "I'm not afraid of you … I dare you to come back."

If she could face her father after all that shouting last night, she could face whoever the shadow was. Inside herself, though, she knew she wouldn't pull the shade down again.

She willed herself to raise the window and to look outside and down; and sure enough, just as she expected, there they were, big footprints in the dirt. It wasn't her imagination.

Rain began to fall, and she closed the window as the droplets got fatter and heavier.

She backed up and sat on her mattress with no sheets, still staring at the window.

There, she waited till she couldn't anymore. She had to use the bathroom. As she went down the hallway past the kitchen, the smell of bacon called to her, her stomach growling.

She visited the bathroom, brushed her teeth, and smoothed her hair as much as she could. Sarah came bouncing in behind her.

"Happy Birthday!" Sarah said, all giggles. "Guess what? Daddy's made pancakes and bacon! and *french* toast!" Sam looked at her sister, trying to form a smile.

She couldn't. But she ruffled Sarah's hair.

"You eat it, I'm not hungry."

Sarah huffed and led her sister in by the hand into the dining room.

The table was set, the babies all bathed and lined up in highchairs, ready for breakfast. Dad placed the food on the table, a delighted look on his face as if he'd made a five-course meal.

"Where's Momma?" Sam asked flatly, looking directly at him.

"Still dozing. She had a long night with the babies. But you girls wouldn't know; you'd have been long asleep."

Sam thought, *yeah, as if.*

He smiled at Sam. "It's your birthday! Happy eight years old! You're a big girl now."

"Yeah. Old enough to know stuff."

More than that, she didn't say, but reluctant tears stung her eyes. She didn't let them fall.

Her dad seemed to ignore her statement.

Smiling, he said, "Yes, you are. Won't be long now and you'll have a family of your own."

They sat down, saying grace. Dad said, "Sam, you want first dibs again this morning?"

Sam sat up and did not answer at all. She put a pancake on a plate and mixed it up with syrup, then butter, then began feeding one of the small babies.

Sarah giggled. "This is the best breakfast ever … ever."

Daddy smiled at her, enjoying her flattery. "You think so?'

Sarah nodded her head vigorously. "Sam, guess where you're going today?"

"Nowhere. I'm staying home."

"But it's your birthday; no one stays home on their birthday!" Sarah seemed very puzzled, then said, "Daddy says you're going to Woolworth's! For ice cream and to buy new blue jeans!"

Dad cleared his throat, smiling. "You've given my secret away!" he said to Sarah, chuckling. "But yes, that's right. I planned a special trip."

Sam didn't smile back. "I'm not going." She kept feeding the baby, then stood to take him out of the highchair. Gently placing him down, she put another one into the highchair.

Her father's expression was now annoyed. His voice was the same.

"You don't get up from the table without permission."

Sam didn't even look at her father, she couldn't. All she could hear was her mother's choked response, "Please, don't." Then her dad grabbed her arm, pulling her into the present reality. Sam was hungry, but she felt something else: fierceness was piercing her soul.

"Stop this. You do not leave the table without being excused. Do you hear me?"

This time, it was Sarah who was sliding down her seat underneath the table.

Sam couldn't bear to see her sister so scared yet again. "Yes, sir." Emphasis was placed on the pause between the two and it was not lost on her father.

"Make yourself a plate and eat up, right now."

Sam strapped the baby into the chair, made her plate, and began to eat. Silently.

"You're just like your mother, disrespectful, moody, and never satisfied."

"You can't make me go."

He leaned in across the table. "I have a belt that will. You go get dressed."

Sam sat still, shaking inside, but she kept feeding the baby, her plate of food barely touched.

"I mean it, get up." This time, he was serious—and loud.

Sam put down the spoon, tilting her head. "Please may I be excused?"

"Yes, you may. Go get dressed." His voice had softened quite a bit at her politeness.

Sam rose slowly. She was exhausted, and she wandered into her room. The sheets lay in shambles on the floor. She picked them up and made her bed. Put on her clothes from yesterday.

When she re-emerged into the dining room, the babies had all been fed and Sarah was standing on a step stool, helping Daddy with the dishes. Her plate was still on the table.

Sarah was thankfully still young enough that the sun shone when Daddy was around. But it wouldn't be too long before even she would realize what was happening in their house.

"I left your breakfast for you; you didn't eat much," Daddy said to Sam, smiling.

Sam thought he was charmingly handsome … But she still wasn't going anywhere.

"Come on now, Sam, let's drop the attitude," he said. "You don't want a bad atmosphere for your sister, do you?"

Shame you never thought about that yourself, she thought, saying not a word again.

She slumped into her chair and slowly began to eat.

The bacon was perfectly cooked, and she ate it first. On a nicer day, the crispy edges would have made her smile and thank him. But not today. Today, there was nothing worth smiling for.

As she nibbled her cold pancake, Daddy said, still trying to change the mood in the room, "I can heat that up if you want. I have your mom's in the oven on low, so it's no trouble."

Sam just shrugged and kept eating in total silence.

She finished, depositing her dirty dish in the sink.

Her father grabbed her arm, pulling her up hard. "Drop that attitude, right now!"

Sam went limp in his grip.

"I don't want to go anywhere with you!" she screamed at him. He lifted her up by the arm to his face, then changed his mind, lowering her to the ground and letting go as if he realized …

This time, he scoffed, "Fine, I won't make you go. Sarah, how would you like to go get a special soda at Woolworth's with your dad?"

Sarah's eyes lit up. "Me? Really?"

Dad laughed. "Yes, really. Just go get yourself all dressed, and we'll go. We'll spend on you today what your sister would have had."

Sarah clearly didn't like that.

"But it's *Sam's* birthday, Daddy. I can't spend her money!"

"Not her money, is it, sweetie? Daddy's money," he said pointedly, but her lips turned down.

Was Sarah going to cry? She was staring at Sam, her lower lip wobbling. "Sam, what are you going to do?" Sarah was worried, probably feeling very mean and nasty all of a sudden.

The girls loved each other so much, nothing could come between them. Not even ice cream, but Sam couldn't let this go.

Sam glared at her father, then said to Sarah, "You go. I don't want to."

With that, Sarah smiled, chuckling. "I want to go." Sarah ran out of the dining room. She could be heard getting dressed, singing, "I'm going to Woolworths! I'm going to Woolworth's!"

A few minutes later, she emerged with her Sunday dress on, and sandals to match.

Sam sat on the floor, playing with a baby, looking up just enough to grin at Sarah. She did not want to play a part in spoiling her sister's day too. "You look so pretty!" she enthused.

Sarah hugged her sister. "Thank you for letting me go."

She took her father's hand, and she danced all the way to the station wagon. Sam watched from the patio as Daddy opened her door, bowed and extended his arm for her to get in.

"For you, m'lady!"

Sarah jumped in.

Daddy closed the door, and looking back, he said, "Sam, you can still change your mind."

Sam walked to the patio door. Just as she was about to change her mind, she saw pieces of china shattered by her feet. She shook her head no, and closed the door.

After she had watched them go all the way down the drive and turn down the big dirt road, Sam checked the babies and turned on the radio.

'Our love we have to re-arrange, and move on to something new ... Oh, but it's all right once you get past the pain; you'll learn to find your love again ...'

With the music playing, she grabbed the broom and swept the patio.

Mom had gotten most of the pieces, but Sam was determined to keep some. She put the pieces into the small mason jar she found under the sink. Once she was certain the patio was clean and the babies settled, she made her way into her momma's room in the back.

"Momma?" Sam said quietly.

Her mother lifted up on the bed, sitting up against the pillows. "Sam, Why aren't you with your dad? I just heard them go. He didn't even tell me they were leaving."

"It's Sunday. Why aren't we going to church?"

"Woolworths is only open for a little bit on Sunday. Plus, we're Catholic and the daily struggles are more important than a one-time trip to church. Father O'Flaherty will understand. Besides, it's a long drive and your father didn't want to be late. So, tell me why you didn't go?"

Sam pulled her hand from behind her back.

She handed her mother the small mason jar. After rolling the contents around, opening the jar and inspecting the inside, Mom said, "Oh, little one. Come here."

"I swept it all up, but I saved you this," Sam said as she climbed all the way into her momma's lap.

"I thought I got it all last night." Thunder clapped loudly outside. "Oh boy, there's a storm brewing out there. You can feel it in the air as well."

Sam smiled but she could tell her momma was even more exhausted then she felt.

Mom smiled back, tickling her eldest daughter. "Yup, God's moving more furniture."

Sam loved the storms and the rain.

Every time the thunder rolled, she could feel its power in the very air around her; even on days like today, it filled her veins with excitement. She hugged her momma.

"Your dad said he was making you a special breakfast. Was it good?"

"I like bacon."

There, I avoided the question, Sam thought cleverly. *And I didn't even have to tell lies.*

"I know you do; I do too. Any left?"

"Oh, yes!" Sam jumped up and saw her mom wince in pain.

As she looked back, Momma smiled.

"I'm fine." Mom reached over and lit a cigarette. She was so beautiful sitting there. Sam always thought her momma's red hair shone as bright as the sunset. She always wished she'd got more Irish from her mom than just a head full of chestnut brown curly hair.

Sam went into the kitchen and carefully got warm pancakes and bacon from the oven. She reached in one more time to get two pieces of french toast to put on top. She topped it all with syrup and butter. Careful as she could, she brought it back to her mom.

"Oh my, that plate is full. You kept all that for me, and I bet you could've eaten it all!"

As her mother said this, Sam frowned; she'd spilled syrup all the way from the kitchen. A trail of golden stickiness marked her path.

"Mom, I'm sorry. Dad'll be annoyed again."

Her momma smiled. "Come here, I want to talk to you. We'll clean it up together later."

When Sam realized she'd forgotten the fork, Mom giggled and said she preferred to eat with her fingers sometimes, saying it added character to her meal.

Momma ate the whole plate, commenting several times on how well Sam had done, putting it all together and bringing it to the room. But Sam watched her seriously the whole time.

"You seem sick, Mom," she said at last. Sure, her mother had just eaten a huge breakfast but even so, she appeared pale and somewhat sad. And more downbeat than Sam had ever seen.

"I'm all right, just a bit tired," Momma said, putting the plate on her bedside table.

"You don't look all right, and you didn't get up this morning."

"Why don't you tell me why you didn't go with your dad? He was gonna buy you new jeans. And why didn't you wear your birthday outfit? I laid it out last night for you, last thing."

"I couldn't find it." Sam stared at the floor, her usual habit when she thought she had landed in trouble. "We messed up my sheets and I don't know where it is."

"I bet it's under your bed."

"My dress will be wrinkled anyway if it's under there." Sam looked out at the raindrops as they slid down the windowpanes. She appeared to be carrying the weight of the world. "Momma, I'm really sorry about the bull, and I won't touch the gun again."

"Sam, this isn't your fault, none of it."

"Yes, it is. I don't listen."

"How can you listen to something you weren't told about?"

"But Daddy told me not to mess with the bull!"

"Sam, no one told you not to climb up and look at the top of the world, now, did they?"

Sam couldn't look at her mother. "No."

"Then how would you know not to do it? And how would you have known that the angry bull would show up? He's not always there, in the field, is he?"

Sam cocked her head, thinking. "No, sometimes, he's not."

Momma went on, "Besides, I wanted you to show me that very spot, so I could see too. I bet you can see all the way to the horizon and back again. And to the sea."

Of course, her mother knew that the hay bales were really not that tall, but a little exaggeration made it so much more fun. "And I bet we could see all the way to the moon!"

Sam giggled; at last, Momma had cheered up her daughter.

"Mom, that's silly!" she cried. "You can only see the moon at night!"

They burst out in laughter, giggling until their stomachs hurt.

"And just imagine Daddy's face if we go to sit on the hay—with the bull—at night!"

Her momma fell back leaning on the head-board, laughing so much she couldn't stop, and her eyes were watering.

"Oh, you are funny, Sam."

Sam answered, "So, no, we can't see all the way to the moon … but we could see all the way down the road! The bales are so tall!"

"See, I said they nearly reached the sky," her mother said, laughing again. Then, she turned serious. "Daddy was very mad last night, but you do understand that you just gotta be careful with your sister, don't you? She's not as strong or as big as you are. But no one was hurt in the end. Remember what I said about 'near-leez!' You do remember, don't you?"

Hope was filling Sam's eyes. "That they don't count?"

Mom smiled. "Yup. Near-leez don't count. Oh! I have a present for you, just for your birthday. We nearly forgot all about it, didn't we!"

"What is it?"

Mom emptied the matchbox by the bed, pulled out the inside box, brought a pen out of the drawer in the bedside table and wrote something inside the tiny box.

Putting the box back together and pushing one side open, she said, "Smiley face!"

Inside the box appeared a smiley face.

Mom was giggling so vigorously that Sam couldn't help but grin too.

Pushing the other side through, Mom said, "Sad face."

When Sam peered in, there appeared a tiny sad face in this side of the box. She giggled, staring with wonder. "That's so funny, Momma! What is it, though? Did you make it?"

"It's a game of sorts. The kind of game that makes life better, even when it's a hard day."

She handed the matchbox to Sam. "You try it."

Sam pushed the box open, and a sad face appeared on the bottom, inside of it. Then she pushed the other side through, a smiley face appearing.

"How is it played?'

Mom reached around Sam's shoulders.

"On days when you're having trouble getting by, this helps you. You get to choose how you feel. You get to pick your feelings." Sam was puzzled. "Your job is to try and pick which one you want; that's the biggest struggle in this life. Once you master how you feel, everything else is so much easier. Ready? Let's play."

Sam squared herself. "Ready."

Together, they pushed out the box. "Smiley face!" The other side … "Sad Face!" They did it over and over, from side to side, and Sam ended up laughing so hard she fell over onto the bed.

"See," Mom said. "Doesn't it make you feel stronger? You always have a choice. It will help you to decide how you feel, so people don't know when you're scared, or angry."

Sam giggled. Leaning back against her mom, she popped out one side of the box. "Smiley face." Her mom kissed her forehead as one of the babies started crying.

Sam jumped up.

Her mom held her back. "You just rest here, birthday girl; it's your day off. I got it."

Sam settled into the big bed, pushing the box inner back and forth, gazing at it. "Magic!"

She was smiling, whispering, "Smiley face, sad face," over and over as she drifted into sleep.

Chapter 6

Sam was woken up suddenly. Sarah was jumping up and down on the bed, singing, "Happy Birthday to Sam, Happy Birthday to Sam! Happy Birthday."

Sam rubbed her eyes and sat up, still in the big bed; she must have been asleep a long while. She felt the matchbook in her hand, and as she got up, she shoved it in her dirty pants pocket.

Sarah ran ahead. "Can we eat now? Sam's awake!"

"You didn't wake her up, did you?" Mom was smiling as Sarah wiggled into her chair.

"Not on purpose." Sarah looked down at her hands.

Momma giggled and it gave Sarah permission to laugh too.

Dad came from Sam's room, screwdriver in his hand. "Of course, it was on purpose; we've all been working hard, waiting for her to wake up."

He patted Sarah on the head.

Sam heard them from the bathroom, washing her hands and doing her best to smooth down her curly hair since the rain always made it wild and unruly.

She walked out to join them but was still in no mood to be happy about anything.

As Sam entered, Dad announced, "There's the birthday girl! How does it feel to be eight?"

He said this as he placed a fork under her chin as if it was a microphone.

Sam's glance lifted in surprise; she couldn't help but smile as she took her seat.

"It's okay," was all she actually said.

Dad never wavered with his smile, not giving up. He reached out and tickled Sam, who giggled in almost involuntary response.

Sarah even joined in. "We can have cake when you feel better!" her sister said, smiling.

Sam gave in and smiled back.

"That's my girl." Dad smiled wide. Her mother carefully put a beautiful yellow cake with fresh fudge icing on the table. Sarah immediately bubbled with delight, saying, "Sam, we had the best time in town. Wait till you see the surprise in your room."

Dad interrupted her. "Now, don't you go giving away the surprise."

Sam's eyes gazed around, for the first time noticing her dad was covered in dirt.

"What surprise?" She smiled back at her daddy.

"Oh, *now* the birthday girl is interested!"

Sam asked, "Are those the surprise?"

She was pointing at the jeans sitting folded on the table.

"Nope. Those are the jeans your dad promised you for your birthday. Sarah picked them out," her mother commented with a tilt toward Sarah.

The little girl had obviously spent time considering which pair to pick out.

Sarah eyed her sister with wonder, putting her hands up to her face and whispering behind her hand, "The lady said they're belly pants."

Both her parents burst out laughing.

"No, Sarah," her dad interjected. "Bell-bottom pants, the newest thing. Sarah thought you might want something stylish to wear to school."

Sam stood and wiped her hands on a napkin before gingerly picking up the pants. They had a strange flair at the bottom, a stark contrast to the dirty jeans she wore.

Sam enthused, "Sarah, I love them."

Sarah smiled super wide. "That's not the only present."

Truthfully, Sam didn't see the need for anything fancy but she didn't think upsetting her sister was worth another disaster like the morning had been.

She smiled and climbed back into her seat at the table just as everyone started singing, "Happy Birthday to you, Happy Birthday to you, Happy Birthday dear Sam, Happy Birthday tooooo yyyooouuu."

Dad had lit the candles while they were singing.

Sam stood by her seat, closing her eyes to make a wish, blowing air as hard as she could to be sure she blew out all eight candles. Sam looked down, seeing one remained lit.

Mom blew it out and said, "You still get your wish. I helped. I always will."

Sam was grateful for her mom, but she knew the rules: you only got a wish if you could blow all the candles out on the birthday cake.

Sam thought, *I don't need wishes anyway; wishes are for babies.*

Irish Catholic girls were superstitious to the core. The implications of a lit candle on a birthday wasn't lost on any of the three females at the table.

The few seconds of silence that followed were just enough to recognize the loss.

Sarah almost completely bounced out of her seat. "Cake," she said. "CAKE!"

Sam took the knife and cut the first piece for herself. Actually, she took almost half the cake, and sheepishly put it on her plate, waiting for someone to say something.

She scanned around. No one said anything about it. Nor did anyone say anything about eating real food first. Mom just smiled and began cutting everyone else a piece.

The cake was delicious, but 'Mommy' cakes always were.

Sam looked on the counter, where cupcakes were packed and ready in Tupperware. "Do I get to take those to school?"

Mom smiled. "Of course you do!"

Sam didn't have many friends at school. They were not from around here, and by that, it meant she didn't have a thousand cousins everywhere like everyone else.

Bringing cupcakes always made her feel a little bit more as if she belonged; the kids always loved the cupcakes even if they didn't like her.

Just as things were settling down a bit, Sarah whispered to her sister again, "Don't you want to know about the surprise?"

Sam smiled. Her sister was really excited. Sam said, teasing, "I don't know. Do I?"

She was trying desperately to finish her huge piece of cake.

Dad got up from the table, everyone grinning and looking at Sam.

She thought it must be a big surprise by the way they were acting.

Daddy said, "I'll be ready for you in a few minutes; you'll know the surprise when you hear it."

"Hear it?" Sam said, truly confused.

"Yes!" Sarah smiled. "Just wait till it happens."

She jumped out of her seat and followed their dad into the back.

Sam jumped up.

Mom put a hand on her shoulder. "Give them a minute; they've been working all afternoon."

Sam sighed.

She'd really wanted another dog.

The farmer had killed hers when it had somehow got into the chicken house and Mom had said it wasn't wise to get another. Tears welled. She couldn't help but hope … maybe.

She wished she could hate the farmer, but she couldn't even do that. Something about him made her believe he was just trying to get by. Mean as he was to her, she saw pain hidden behind his eyes and recognized her own every time he spoke.

Momma said that her Irish blood had been passed down, meaning she had to beware the 'evil eye' and say "God bless" every time the farmer came around. But Sam knew the farmer wasn't possessed by the evil eye. She'd seen men with it, but he wasn't one of them. Her daydreaming was interrupted by a very loud ringing sound coming from her room.

"Go on, it's your surprise!" Mom said as they both followed the noise.

There, sitting on her dresser, was a bright red phone.

"Pick it up," Momma said as she pointed at it.

Sam picked up the receiver and said, "Hello?"

"Hey there, little one!"

"Daddy?"

"Yup. You got a phone of your very own now."

"Who can I call? How does it work?"

"You just pick it up and it rings right next to my bed."

"Really?"

"Yes. Really. Go ahead. Hang up, give it a minute, then pick it up again."

Sam put the phone receiver down on the phone base, on her dresser. She looked at the rotary phone and wondered, would she have to dial? He hadn't told her the number.

Mom surely must have noticed the confusion. The phone rang.

Mom said, "Just pick it up."

Sam picked up the receiver and put it to her ear.

"Hello, birthday girl! There is someone here absolutely dying to talk to you."

"I want one too, Daddy," Sarah said in the background. Honestly, Sam didn't need a phone to hear her sister just up the hall. Sarah really was excited.

Her dad must have handed the phone to Sarah because there was a giggle on the other end.

"Heeelllooo."

"Sarah, how did you do this?"

"Daddy climbed under the house, saying there's a special rope that ties it all together. He says he can wake you up now without yelling anymore."

"I am not hard to wake up!"

"Heellllooo. Heellloo." Sarah laughed so hard. Sam laughed too. There they were, both laughing on the phone till Sam's side hurt.

Dad picked up. "That's enough for now." Sam could hear her dad laughing. "I want you to know if you're ever scared again, your mother and I are right here."

"Yes, sir."

"I mean it. We're right here. I checked outside your window and didn't see anything out of the ordinary. It rained, so anything there might have washed. Just know that we believe you and you can always call on us to help."

Sam swallowed hard; he was trying, but the problem was, she just didn't believe him.

One look at the bruises on her mom's arm was enough 'truth' for any eight-year-old girl.

"Okay, Daddy," was all she actually said, but her tears garnered her a big hug from Mom, and soon Dad was there too, also Sarah, all three of them caught in one big hug.

Sam sobbed big elephant tears, so much so she was ashamed of herself.

"You know, we all get scared," Mom said when she finally sat back on the bed.

"Even me," Dad interjected.

"Really, what are you scared of?"

"Bears. Your mother is always talking about sending the men inside a cave first, just in case there are bears. And I am scared of bears."

"Yup. You always let the men go first because there might be one." Mom smiled.

"That's why Daddy always walks by the road, with us on the inside," Sarah added.

"But if you're so scared, why do you do it?" Sam looked directly at her dad. She wasn't sure she expected a real answer, but she expected to wait for it.

Surprising her, Dad didn't pause with his response. "Because you always protect what you love the most, and I love you, and your mom, and Sarah—and the babies—the most."

Chapter 7

The phone rang. Sam answered. "Hello?"

"Good morning! The morning girl and I are here, trying to invite you to breakfast."

Dad hung up.

Sam hated Sarah being called the morning girl.

Mornings weren't anything short of awful and Sam couldn't sleep much. She was too preoccupied, staring at the window, waiting for the sound of silence that never came.

She'd promised herself to never lower that window blind again and she'd meant it.

She just hadn't realized it meant she was going to stare all night, looking back and forth from the phone to the window. She put the matchbox in her dresser drawer.

She'd finally gone to sleep pushing it side to side, saying, *happy face, sad face* in her head. Mom was always right. It was true; it was a magic box.

She got up, went into the bathroom, and brushed her hair and teeth. As she walked out of the bathroom, Mom was walking down the hallway with a baby in her arms.

Sam asked, "Can I wear my dress to school today?"

Mom smiled. "I thought you might be feeling better. It's ironed and folded on my bed."

Sam ran into her mom's room. There it was, with beautiful spring flowers on the fabric. She'd picked out the material herself, and Mom had measured every inch of her to make it.

The pattern she'd picked was McCall's 3401 A. The sleeves puffed just a little and the skirt stopped at her ankles, just high enough to walk. "Mom, can I wear my sneakers with it?"

"Sure. That's actually a great idea. You won't ruin your sandals during recess. Just be sure you get a bath this morning; the tub's ready for you in my bathroom."

Sam's smile faded. *Ugghh … a bath.*

She walked into her mother's bathroom, slipping into the tub.

"Don't get your hair wet! I don't want you getting sick in this cool spring air," Mom called out from the kitchen.

"Yes, ma'am."

Sam was done almost as soon as she slid into the bathtub, jumping back out to towel off.

She thought it was strange that there was a bathroom in her mom's bedroom at all; what was that all about? She had spent a whole summer when she was little asking her mom about it. She still didn't understand what privacy meant but grown-ups needed a lot of it.

She ran, almost giddy across the room to put on her dress.

It was gorgeous! She admired herself in her mom's full-length mirror.

Twirling around, she felt like the most beautiful girl in all the world. She smiled, then giggled like little girls did when the delight of the moment became too much to hold inside.

"Oh, my goodness, you look like you could win all the beauty pageants in town wearing that." Mom had appeared in the doorway behind her.

"But I didn't win any pageants, did I?"

"Well, you won't if you don't smile. If you smile, it lights up the room for the judges."

"But those are always such fake smiles. I like real smiles."

"We all do. Now let me look at you."

Mom pulled a beautiful purple ribbon out of her drawer, tying Sam's hair up in a perfect ponytail. Her curls fell around her face and Sam thought it was the absolute perfect thing to finish her dress. "Oh, Momma, that's beautiful. What if I lose it? What if I mess up my dress at school?"

"Nice things are for using. Life is for living. Wear the dress, play in the dirt. I can always make you another one. I still have the pattern."

Sam knew that her mother couldn't buy her more fabric, not expensive fabric like this.

"But Momma, it took you a week to make it."

"And I would love to spend another week making you another one, as long as you smile. Now quit being so serious and enjoy your day."

She hugged her mom. It was going to be the best day ever, Sam could feel it in the air. Something exciting was going to happen. She smiled all the way into the dining room.

"Now look at you!" Dad was smiling too as he said it and Sarah peeked out behind him, wearing a huge smile of her own.

"It's so fancy," Sarah said.

Sam just smiled and twirled around before she jumped into her seat.

"It's technically still your birthday till you take your dress off," Dad commented as Mom put eggs and toast on the table.

Mom sat and they all held hands to bless the food.

"Good God, good food. Let's eat," Dad recited.

Mom smiled and winked. "Good Catholic prayer, and you're getting better at it."

They ate quickly. Then Sarah grabbed her lunchbox from the counter.

Sam delicately picked up her own lunchbox, and at its side was a Tupperware container.

There, all the cupcakes were, on the counter, ready to take off to school.

Sam licked her lips and looked at them with cupcake-filled excitement.

Bundling them up, she grabbed her book bag, lunch, and the cupcakes, quite the balancing act for an eight-year-old. Walking out to the bus, Sarah toddled behind her.

"Can I have one?" she asked.

"No, Sarah, these are for class. I get to share them."

Sam, eyeing her sister, emitted a long, plaintive sigh. It was pointless to insist to herself that Sarah wouldn't get a cupcake; already, she was weakening. She knew that as soon as they reached the end of the yard to wait for the bus, well, she'd have to give her just one.

Sam put her backpack and lunchbox down in the dirt and gently opened the Tupperware, taking out one cupcake and giving it to Sarah. She was careful to close it back tight.

Sarah handled the tiny cake as though it was made of gold, her eyes alight.

Sam got almost as much pleasure from watching Sarah eat that cupcake than she would have had by eating one herself.

Sarah suddenly stopped eating, mid-bite.

"Did Momma make any extra? There won't be enough for everyone now."

Sarah was always worrying about everyone else, a generous little girl at school and at home.

Sam patted Sarah on the shoulder. "I ate almost half of my big cake. I don't need a cupcake after all that, do I? So, there'll be enough." Frankly, Sam hadn't even thought that she was giving her sister her own cupcake, but one look at Sarah shoving the last bits into her mouth and then wiping her face on her sleeve convinced her she'd make exactly the right decision.

Making the right decision didn't stop her from counting the cakes.

Seventeen. Fifteen kids in her class, one for her teacher, and ... one spare!

So, Sam could have one, after all.

She sighed in relief. Mom had made eighteen, knowing she'd share one with her sister.

The bus pulled up, the door opening. The driver's face was alight with glee today. "Don't you look happy! And dressed up! What's the special occasion?"

"It's Sam's birthday," Sarah said as she jumped the steps to get inside.

"My, my, don't you look beautiful."

Sam smiled, and nodded, too embarrassed that someone had noticed and was talking about it; she hated being the center of attention.

She felt the redness creep up her neck and that just made things worse.

"The best response is, 'Thank you.' It always is."

The bus driver was an older woman with short brown hair, and she was smiling at her in a way that said she understood exactly what Sam was feeling.

Sam smiled back. "Thank you!" she said at last, though reluctantly.

She bounded onto the bus with renewed confidence. Sam and Sarah were always the second kids to be picked up. The first were the Leiven kids.

There were eight of them in all, but only a few were old enough for school.

Mom said Sam shouldn't be scared of them because their name meant 'friend' but she only really liked one of them. Sam sat next to her sister, across from the next to the eldest brother, who was named Matthew. She liked the name Matthew better but they called him Matt.

"Those look like cupcakes," Matt said, leaning across from the seat. Next year, Matt would begin at high school. He was an eighth grader and bigger than any of the other boys.

He had dirty blond hair and skin that had turned dark brown from working outside. Either that or he was very dirty and needed a bath, urgently. But Sam thought it was a suntan.

"So, are they cupcakes in that box?" he asked, trying again.

"They are." Sam smiled. End of conversation as far as she was concerned.

"What kind are they?" He was obviously intending to get one for himself. Sometimes, just by mentioning things like cupcakes, other people would say, "Well, would you like one?"

But it wasn't Sam's way. It never would be, either. People had to ask her something directly if they expected to get something out of her. "They're yellow and fudge," she said.

"What're they for?" Matt appeared genuinely puzzled.

Sarah popped up, hanging over Sam's shoulder. "It's her birthday."

Sarah bumped against Sam's back as the bus bounced up and down the dirt road.

"Wha'? How old are you, then?" Matt asked, a sly grin starting to form.

"Eight. I'm almost grown up." Sam felt the air tighten and straightened her spine. She prepared herself for the teasing that was sure to follow.

Matt laughed. "You know you ain't really grown till ya get boobies."

Sam was very confused. What did boobies have to do with being grown?

"You stupid boy. That doesn't have anything to do with being grown up. Those are for when you get the babies." Sam wasn't about to let anyone make fun of her.

Matt's brother stuck his head out from the seat behind. "We all know that's what your mom uses 'em for."

Everyone but Sam and Sarah burst out laughing. Mom had always said to let them laugh. Sam's mom was breastfeeding in public all the time, something that was especially embarrassing in the grocery store. She carried a baby on her breast more or less constantly, and as soon as one grew big enough, well, there was another.

Mom said it was fine to be seen breastfeeding as long as she covered herself with a shawl. Sam didn't think anyone else agreed about the 'fine' part.

It was pretty obvious they didn't because all they ever did was laugh and make fun of her.

Sarah had slumped into the seat beside Sam, but Sam was prepared for a fight.

As she squared her shoulders, Matt's laughter became contagious, Sam smiled too.

"Quit it. It's 'er birthday," Matt said, shoving his brother back behind the seat.

His brother immediately launched himself back over it, shoving Matt into the aisle of the bus.

Both boys started to punch one another, fists flying as the vehicle pulled to a hard stop.

The stopping of the bus had thrown both boys forward, right next to the driver.

Sam had barely saved her cupcakes from flying off her lap; they would have gone sailing right underneath the seats in front.

Sarah was now standing in her seat, trying to watch all the excitement.

The driver stood with the door open. She was tired of these two boys messing about like that, so she wasted no time in throwing one boy outside, then the other. Matt was now standing outside the bus door, holding his brother by the scruff of his shirt.

His brother wiggled around, trying to free himself.

Matt didn't let go. He shook his annoying sibling, yelling, "Ya know Ma will kill us."

His brother responded, "Shit, Lemme go, idiot!"

The bus driver hollered, "Look, you both have a choice. I am gonna turn this bus around and take you both home to that rathole you live in—and we *all* know what will happen there if I do—or you both get back in and take your seats like the Christian gentlemen I hope you can be."

Both boys gazed at her, silent and wide-eyed, though still jostling one another.

It seemed like forever before they climbed back onto the bus and took their seats.

As they passed by the driver, she said, "And for God's sake, take a bath this week."

Like the rest of the Leiven children, Matthew was always dirty. His family drew water from a well. Sam was jealous because he didn't have to bathe *all* the time. Sam also knew a little about what the driver meant. The part about what had happened 'there.'

Matthew had shown up at the river one time, blood pouring from his face.

He'd been upset, sullen and silent, refusing to answer when Sam asked what had happened.

At the time, Sam wasn't sure what had gone on but it had obviously been so terrible that Matt had run away when she and Sarah called out to him again. Finally, he'd returned, claiming he had nowhere to go, so Mom had fed him for over a week while he'd slept in one of the farmer's shacks. Eventually, Matthew had said that the guy who lived at the house wasn't his dad.

Sure, he looked like a dad, but he wasn't one, only a stepdad. Sam's mom said Matt's house wasn't safe at night and if the girls ever went up there, they couldn't stay long if 'not his dad' was there.

Matthew came down the aisle and flung his brother.

Sam heard a thud as the boy hit the window of the bus and slid down into the bus seat. Matt sat down next to the aisle, trapping his not-so-happy brother in. He looked across the aisle at Sam, putting his hand up so his brother couldn't escape, and fixed his eyes up front.

The sound of the bus starting and the jostling as it lurched forward made Sam realize her sister was staring at the boys. "Don't stare, Sarah. It isn't nice."

Sarah immediately stared down at her feet.

As the bus filled with children, Sam would occasionally glance over at Matt. He kept his eyes fixed forward, sitting straight up, and didn't speak or move again till they reached the school.

As they were getting off the bus, Matt got up and let his brother out. "Don't start nothin' today. I ain't takin' your beatin'." He shoved him down the aisle, exiting just behind.

Sam waited till everyone was off before she and Sarah dared to exit. She couldn't risk the cupcakes getting thrown by those boys. Sarah said, "I can't believe you still got 'em."

Sam smiled at her sister. "Of course I do. I'm guarding them with my life."

"Just like you look out for me," Sarah said, looking up at Sam with big wide eyes.

"Yeah, just like that," Sam said, grabbing her little sister's hand. "I look after you as well because you're so little, anything could happen to you."

The girls laughed.

"Am so not little," said Sarah.

"You so are."

They jostled with their elbows, having fun.

Sam walked her sister to class. The school was just a big building with a long hallway down the middle. On each side of the hallway were classrooms, and separately were Sarah's classroom and the cafeteria. Sam loved to eat in the cafeteria, mostly because she wasn't supposed to.

The food they served there was nothing like Momma's. Sam took a left just before the first-grade classroom down a hallway, outside toward the cafeteria.

Kindergarten was a new thing.

Kids didn't go to 'proper' school until first grade when Sam had started.

As they approached Sarah's classroom, Sam could see a cage just inside the doorway. It was the home of their classroom squirrel, and the girls could hear him crunching nuts.

Sarah had the coolest teacher; no one else would have allowed them a squirrel!

Sam's teacher, Ms. Manny was the exact opposite of Sarah's young energetic teacher, and she certainly would never have allowed a squirrel or anything else in the classroom.

Sarah had even said that when they closed the door, her teacher would let the confident little squirrel out to run free in the classroom, all the kids giggling and watching him go up and down desks, climbing the blinds, stealing pencils and pieces of fruit the kids laid out for him.

Sam smiled at her sister when she told that story; Sarah was so sweet. Sarah's friends ran up to her, all yelling out questions about the weekend.

Sam swallowed. No one cared what *she* had done on the weekends.

As she turned to walk back up to the big building, Sarah came running out.

"Want me to help you with the cupcakes?"

"Nope. I got it."

Sarah hugged her sister around the waist, just like little kids would.

Sam tried to step away but Sarah moved so fast. "You really are the bestest ever sister."

Sarah's teacher stepped out, saying, "Sarah, did you learn your numbers? We are practicing because today, we count to from one to a hundred, remember?"

"I remember, ma'am. I think I know them. Well, some of them."

Sarah left Sam standing there and ran inside to practice before school started.

The teacher took three steps toward the door and then turned.

"I love how you protect your little sister, Sam. I notice these things, but you know if you ever need anything, my door stays open. Sarah isn't the only kid that deserves protecting."

Sam smiled, mostly because the teacher was smiling too.

Sarah's teacher was always smiling as bright as the sun, just like Sarah, who was always grinning in the mornings especially.

Sam thought maybe these people had gotten some kind of special something that she'd missed. Even though she was still smiling, Sam took a bit of offense to the 'protecting' part.

That was kinda weird; what on earth did the teacher think she needed protecting from?

So, she chose not to reply to that bit.

She simply said, "Sarah's my sister, and that's what sisters do. They are supposed to love each other and keep each other safe."

She jiggled from foot to foot, eager to leave.

The teacher's face was all aglow, as if Sam had said the most brilliant thing ever.

But Sam felt there was something odd about this conversation deep in her stomach, like when the boys gave her that 'evil eye.'

She adjusted her heavy box of cupcakes and book bag.

The teacher was still going on and on about things. "I know you walk her every day, all the way to my door. She says you're the best. I think I agree!"

"Momma says I have to …"

"Oh," she said, still smiling as Sam turned to go. The teacher seemed a little disappointed to hear that the way Sam took care of her sister was just something mandated by their mother.

Sam took advantage of the moment's silence to start to turn. "Nice talking to you. Bye!"

"Sam, wait. Let me walk you in. I have a student teacher today."

Sam sighed. She was way too big for anyone to walk her to the classroom.

After all, it was her second year at school, and she knew the way.

"No. I mean thanks, but it's all right."

She turned again to try and make it back to the building before this lady cleared the doorway. But in her haste, she tripped on the sidewalk.

Her arms flew upwards, the cupcakes slipped, and Sam watched on in horror as her cupcakes toppled! But the teacher grabbed the Tupperware box's handle just in time.

Quite literally, the day and the precious cupcakes had been saved.

Sam fell on top of her book bag. The teacher had somehow grabbed Sam too; Sam looked around. She didn't think anyone had seen it. *Well, I hope not. That would be embarrassing.*

At school, you could never be sure. In the countryside, on the other hand, everyone saw everything. The teacher squatted beside her, reached up and adjusted the ribbon in Sam's hair.

"This sure is a beautiful ribbon."

Sam leaned in to whisper in the teacher's ear.

"It will be embarrassing if you follow me in. I'm in second grade, and I'm now eight."

"Oh, my goodness, I didn't remember that about being eight. It's been so long since I was eight that I forgot how important it is." The teacher stood, still grinning. "Well, I'll just stand here and watch you get in safely, then. How's that?"

Sam gave her a grateful smile. But she was still wondering, *why is she so worried about me being safe all of a sudden?* It made no sense. She shrugged.

Turning, she walked inside the school, and turned left in the hallway. The second-grade classroom was at the very end on the left. So, she walked along the left side, almost leaning against the wall to keep her cupcakes safe. She sighed when she made it to the doorway, walked inside and safely deposited the container on her teacher's desk.

Ms. Manny was the oldest teacher in the building.

In stark contrast to Sarah's teacher, Ms. Manny almost never smiled.

She focused on Sam, saying as she inspected the plastic box, "Ah. These must be those cupcakes you talked about all last week. You can pass them out at the end of the day."

"Yes, ma'am. My momma made them."

"Yes, we know all about it. Now, take your seat." Sam almost thought she saw her teacher grin but she wasn't completely sure. It would be very rare if so. Like seeing a live dinosaur!

Ms. Manny was odd. Sam didn't think she had any children of her own, so why had she chosen to be a teacher, of all things? They called her an old spinster in town.

Sam wasn't sure what a spinster was. She couldn't find it in the encyclopedia, and because she thought it might be terrible, she hadn't asked her momma.

But she sort of liked Mrs. Manny despite everything, mostly because she didn't lie.

Most grown-ups did, but not Ms. Manny.

Even when the boys tried to lie, Ms. Manny always knew the truth, and you *had* to tell her. She just looked at you and you knew you had to tell no fibs. Sam thought it might have been a magical power. She'd tried it with Sarah and her mom but the stare wasn't the same; she'd even practiced in the mirror and couldn't quite get the 'truth-telling' glare to work.

Sam put her lunchbox on the hook in the coat room, which was a hallway that ran the width of the classroom. There was a sink, and a doorway at each end.

Walking into the classroom again, Sam took her seat, right next to Theresa Bickell. Sam had once been shocked to see a roach crawl out of Theresa's shirt collar.

The Bickells were the poorest family in town, and not very smart either.

Sam always leaned her paper over so Theresa could see her answers. She knew cheating was wrong, but so was Ms. Manny when she announced the lowest grades in the class and always embarrassed Theresa.

Theresa leaned over. "Are those real cupcakes on the teacher's desk?"

Sam whispered back, "Yes. Momma made them."

"Did you really bring enough for everybody?"

Sam filled with excitement. "Yes!" She knew she'd said it too loudly.

Ms. Manny glared right at Sam. "The lesson starts in just a few minutes. Use up all your loudness now. I expect you to pay attention."

"Yes, ma'am." Sam looked down at her desk. Each kid had one, and there was a basket underneath. She pulled out a pencil from her backpack and the notebook labeled 'math' from under her desk. Sam thought math was so terrible, and it just *had* to be first thing in the morning.

Ms. Manny droned on and on about 'times tables' and numbers, and Sam had to keep picking up her head to keep from falling asleep. Oh, she hated math!

Couldn't she tell stories instead? Sarah said her teacher sang songs and told stories all day about numbers and letters. Finally, it became time for recess. The bell rang.

Sam loved recess as the playground was the most amazing place. There were swings, and a merry-go-round in the center, flanked by monkey bars and a see-saw. It all came into view as she bounded out the back door right by her classroom. The best part about second grade was the extra recess she got by not having to walk right down the hallway.

As she made it out of the building and down the steps, Sam stopped.

She remembered her dress. Smoothing it down, she looked at the play yard. Nope, nothing to do safely there. Mud was everywhere, from all the rain.

Momma had said it was okay to play in her special dress, but Sam knew she was lying.

She couldn't replace this dress.

She meandered around beside the one building in the yard. She leaned on it, dreaming of riding the merry-go-round, and swinging her dress from side to side. She looked up at the school.

There he was, staring at her again from just inside the door.

His stare made her stomach hurt, her heart race, and somehow, it also made shame move through her. 'His' name was Kevin, and that was the 'evil eye' her mom had told her about.

He looked at her as though he was salivating over his dinner.

Sam said, "God bless," over and over as he stared.

She glanced away and back. She didn't see him anymore. Sam didn't know what was worse, him staring or her not knowing where he now was.

Kevin worked at the school, and was Theresa's older brother.

He was slow, so he didn't go to school anymore; he ran the mowers and swept up the hallways. Sam had never actually talked to him herself but everyone knew who he was.

As Sam looked at the doorway, she realized she was standing right next to the shed that held the lawnmowers. She heard a shuffle behind her.

Kevin appeared, unlocking the door just to the side of the building.

He looked at her, and she looked back just long enough to say, "God bless!" and to run inside the school as fast as her legs would carry her.

She sat at her desk, carefully arranging her special dress's skirt. Ms. Manny followed.

"Recess isn't over, and I can't watch you and fifteen other children with you inside."

"I am not going back outside today."

Sam lifted her chin just slightly in a look of petulance.

"You are, and you'll have to because I'm going to lock up the classroom, Sam. I'm very sorry if you want to be diligent and study, but I have orders to lock up if I'm not in here."

Mrs. Manny stood right by her desk.

"Please, I'll ruin my dress," Sam pleaded. Ms. Manny just stood there with that *you will do as I say and tell the truth* stare.

She was pointing outside. There was no sense in arguing, Sam thought.

So, she stood and walked outside, but she stood by Ms. Manny the rest of the recess.

The teacher gave her a strange look when Kevin came along too, taking to leaning on the side of the shed, resuming staring right at Sam.

She had tilted her head, squaring her shoulders too, as if to ward off evil spirits.

In her head, she said, "God bless, God bless, God bless," over and over, and was grateful when Ms. Manny moved in between them and she couldn't see him anymore.

Just before the recess bell rang announcing the horrors of continuing an education, Ms. Manny looked down at Sam.

"You shouldn't wear that dress to school again, Sam. You're distracting the boys."

Sam was immediately ashamed of herself, but she didn't really understand.

Weren't girls supposed to look pretty? Wasn't that what all grown-ups said?

She didn't dare ask Ms. Manny. The look the teacher gave was one of finality. Ms. Manny had made a statement, not asked a question. She just made a note in her head to ask her momma.

The bell rang, ending recess. All the kids ran into the classroom, taking their seats.

Chapter 8

Ms. Manny droned on and on about things Sam wasn't the least bit interested in. Spelling and practicing their cursive over and over, they wrote the words. Sam was so bored. Momma said that because she spoke correctly, spelling and writing wouldn't be a problem. But cursive … The very tediousness of it made Sam want to jump up and run away.

If the words made sense on the page and people could read and understand them, what point was there in making them look all fancy like that?

Like, when people spoke, they all said the same words, and no one's spoken words formed cursive in the air, did they?

So, knowing cursive could not make one child better than another!

Nevertheless, because the teacher said they had to, she furrowed her brow, sticking her tongue out to one side of her lips, determined to get it right. Moving her pencil, she carefully wrote the words without picking the pencil off the page. The secret to cursive lay in not picking up your pencil at all, or that was what everybody said. Sam was sure it was another magic trick that needed the one thing she'd never had an interest in—patience, and plenty of it.

The bell rang, finally. Sam jumped up and got in line to wash her hands in the coat room.

Theresa carefully washed her hands too. "The soap here is so fancy."

Sam smiled. "That's ivory soap; my momma sent it, so we'd have the good stuff."

Theresa smiled back. "You buy it at the normal store?"

Sam nodded and stepped forward to wash her hands too. Somehow, the soap felt different, even fancier now, just because Theresa had said it was.

Sam stepped out into the hallway, just catching a glance of her cupcakes through the small glass pane on the door, giggling. She was so ready for the end of the day to just get here.

She did her best to stay still in line but couldn't help bouncing in place, jiggling.

Ms. Manny led the line straight up the hallway. Turning to the right, they headed outside past Sarah's classroom. Upon arriving at the lunchroom and sitting down, Sam frowned.

She raised her hand.

Ms. Manny cast her gaze all the way down the long table. "Sam, what's wrong now?"

"I forgot my lunchbox." Sam looked as though she'd failed miserably. She had lost her thoughts again and waited for Ms. Manny to embarrass her publicly. Sometimes, because she was scared of this teacher a little because of how she reproached students in front of others, Sam found herself wondering why she even liked Ms. Manny so much. But she just did.

Ms. Manny frowned, sighing, but all she said was, "Well, go get it."

Sam stood up and headed back to her classroom.

As soon as she entered the long hallway, she felt him. She turned left, and he was right there, across the hallway on her right. She glanced over her shoulder, making eye contact.

Her stomach turned. Kevin leaned into the wall across from her, sliding along it.

She started walking faster, sure she could sense him following.

She just had to get her lunchbox from the classroom. She was so stupid for forgetting it.

Fear started pooling in her neck, but she didn't know why. "God bless," she whispered as she picked up her pace into a slow trot down the hall.

She didn't want him to know she was scared, so she slowed. Looking back, he was still there just a few steps behind. He licked his lips. Why was she so afraid?

She remembered the deer, and the word *predator* screamed in her head. "God bless," she said louder, but still just under her breath. *Oh, my God,* she thought, *he's hunting me.* Sam didn't know what to do or what he wanted, but she knew she had to grab her lunchbox and get away.

He was still across the hallway when she turned left into her classroom.

Kevin closed the space quickly behind her. She darted to the back of the classroom, putting the desks between her and Kevin. She had barely escaped his grasp.

If she could just get her lunchbox and get back, it would all be over. She weaved back and forth through the desks, only just faster than he was. She saw his long arms reaching for her.

He was tall, dirty, with dark blond hair that sat just above his shoulders. She held firm, holding a desk between them. In the pause, she simply stared at him, while he stared deep into her, but in a very peculiar way, one she had never known before.

His eyes reached into her soul, trying to pull out pieces and devour them.

Sam was officially terrified. Her breathing quickened and she realized she'd lost control. She tried to scream, but no sound came out, only the rushing of wind past her vocal cords.

She darted to the left, still trying to get to the coat room.

She could see her lunchbox from where he had her pinned against the windows.

Two desks sat between them.

Several desks lay on their sides where Kevin had pushed them over, in frustration. Sam had lost all concept of time. It stood still. There was nothing but her and this man.

She saw her opening and moved through it, slipping between the two desks and under his right arm. She entered the coat room, and he raced in behind her—then disappeared.

He entered again, cutting her off at the other end.

She turned; he disappeared again, and cut her off, back and forth. Then silence.

Sam stopped at the opening to the coat room, looking behind to the other opening.

She knew he was there waiting, but which side? The one closest to the hallway was her best bet but wasn't that his, too? She tried to calm her breathing, but couldn't.

As she looked at her lunchbox, she saw her hands shaking. She was standing in the middle of the coat room, trying to decide which way when Kevin made the decision for her.

He rushed in, grabbing her by the waist. Sam dropped her lunchbox. As she tried to scream, he covered her mouth with his, pushing her to the floor. She tried to scratch him, and he leaned back to look at her. She scooted back on her elbows, realizing, with more horror, that she now rested up against the wall. She tried to scream again; no air, only terror. He was so strong.

He flipped up her dress and leaned hard into her. He said, "Easy in."

Covering her mouth with his, he pushed again against her. Her head slammed into the wall. He smelled like mud just days after a storm, rancid. Sam tried to move. She couldn't.

Suddenly, for what seemed like eternity, that was her whole world.

That terrible smell as he adjusted her underclothing. The searing pain.

He pushed his fingers into her, hard. She struggled, then somehow slid her face away from his mouth and she screamed. Then, it was over.

Kevin was gone. Sam stood up, disoriented. For what seemed like forever, she stood in the coat room, trying to understand why she was even there. Her lunchbox.

She picked it up; she thought for a second it might belong to someone else.

Someone she once had known, but didn't anymore.

She reached up and touched her hair. Her ribbon was gone.

She searched around the floor for it, then realizing where she was, terror again filled her chest. What if he came back? Sam walked quickly up the hallway to the principal's office. She'd tried to go to the lunchroom, but tears had welled in her eyes. She was too terrified to walk outside.

Gripping her lunchbox with all her remaining strength, she opened the door.

The lady at the desk smiled.

Sam didn't know where to look. "The Bickel boy threw me down and put his fingers in me."

The woman's broad smile disappeared from her face, and she left Sam standing there, saying hurriedly, "Just a minute. Just stay there, Sam."

Sam sat down.

Disoriented again, she didn't even notice when the lady came back and took her seat again.

As hard as she tried, she couldn't stop the silent tears that welled in her eyes. She just stood there looking at the lady at the desk. Someone gave her a glass of water, and a tissue.

She had nothing else to say. Not to the principal, or the lady at the desk.

Not that they asked about anything. She heard the principal call someone.

"You shouldn't send her to school in her Sunday dress; this isn't an all girls' school."

Silence, then, "Oh, no. She's not really hurt. I think he just scared her. Well, if you can't come right now, I'll have to call your husband."

She heard him put the phone down on the receiver, hard.

Sam felt something even more terrifying enter her world.

Shame, the kind you could taste.

The principal came out, and then Ms. Manny was in the room too.

Ms. Manny gently offered her a napkin, which Sam accepted. "Thank you, Miss Manny."

"Did you eat your lunch?"

Sam realized she was still gripping her lunch-box. "No, ma'am."

"Well, you can eat it now. It looks very good! I bet your mom makes those lunches."

Sam just stared at the food, then mumbled, "But I can't eat. Don't want to eat, Ms. Manny. My hunger's gone ... somewhere."

"Sam, this is important. Tell me what happened," Ms. Manny said, putting a gentle hand on Sam's left shoulder, completely out of character for her.

Sam's eyes welled with tears again. Ms. Manny said, "Sam, you don't have to tell me but you will have to tell your mom and dad. Are you hurt?"

Sam shook her head no.

"Why don't you sit here and eat your lunch? You need something in your stomach before cupcakes." Ms. Manny tried to smile, but it looked strange and twisted. "You just wait here; I will be right back."

Sam watched as Ms. Manny entered the principal's office, closing the door behind her.

She heard whispering, then a slamming noise.

Ms. Manny was yelling, "No, you *will* fire that boy. I don't care who you're trying to help. Sam's a lot, but it's no excuse for what he did. And don't you dare call her dad; I'll keep her safe till it's time for the bus. It's bad enough without you making things worse for her at home."

When Ms. Manny exited the office, she paused, squared her shoulders, and tipped her head back. Sam wondered what could be so scary that Ms. Manny had to stand straight to bear it.

Sam hadn't told her anything.

"Are you finished with your lunch?"

"No, ma'am. I'm just not hungry."

Ms. Manny leaned down, took Sam's hand, and patted it with her other hand. "This will be all right. Just, next time, save your dresses for church."

Standing with Ms. Manny, holding her hand, Sam walked back to her classroom. The desks were back in perfect rows. She sat in her seat. No one seemed to know anything had happened.

Sam was unsure anything *had* happened, as even her cupcakes were sitting there, perfect.

Theresa leaned over, genuinely concerned. "Were you in trouble?"

Ms. Manny interrupted, "Theresa, you need to go upfront. Your mama's here to get you. Says she wants all her children home."

Theresa looked directly at Sam. "What's ya tell 'em? Mama never comes here, 'cause gas costs too much."

"That's enough," Ms. Manny said as she directed Theresa into the hallway.

All the kids in her class were talking in hushed tones, but no one spoke directly to Sam.

Ms. Manny tapped her ruler hard on her big desk, and everyone just stopped, gazing upward.

Sam's world blurred. Time stood still. She kept trying to remind herself where she was, but her thoughts kept wandering, almost as if she was dreaming. Sam thought she heard Ms. Manny talk about a map, then maybe something else.

It was so blurry, the next thing Sam heard was a bell ringing.

Ms. Manny took her by the hand again, and now, Sam understood why Ms. Manny was someone she had really liked all this time. Because the teacher knew exactly when to be nice.

The room was empty; everyone was outside, and she was just sitting there.

Embarrassed, but finally getting her bearings, she walked with Ms. Manny this time, not protesting about being accompanied because she was eight. She said not a word.

Her teacher didn't say anything either. It was afternoon recess. Sam loved recess.

She saw a group of kids playing a game of marbles.

She loved watching marble games, and sometimes, she played but hers were still in her desk.

"Can I get my marbles? I wanna play too."

"Not today, and you won't be playing with the boys again anytime soon." Ms. Manny didn't look at her, but she didn't let go of Sam's hand either.

She didn't even understand herself when she heard her own voice say, "But I like playing marbles, and I like playing with boys. Girls are no fun, and the girls don't like me."

"You better get used to the girls," Ms. Manny said. Sam knew it was a statement and not a question. She didn't understand any of it. She wiggled a bit because standing still wasn't ever her best option. Ms. Manny just tightened her grip on Sam's hand.

"Can we still have the cupcakes?" she whispered, hardly daring.

"You and those cupcakes. Of course. I'll pass them out as everyone's leaving. How could I ever forget, what with your every-two-minutes reminders?" She chuckled.

Sam smiled, feeling herself coming alive again. And she wanted to chuckle too but couldn't.

The bell rang. She entered the hallway, glad that Ms. Manny was still holding her hand. The fifth graders were going out as they were coming in.

Sam even thought one of them pointed at her.

She was so confused, not able to understand anything about today.

Chapter 9

By the time the bell rang, Sam was so excited she could hardly keep her seat. It was the time she'd finally get to share her amazing cupcakes. Usually, the teacher gave them out after lunch and Sam could watch the other kids smile, nodding at her in appreciation. Today, they single filed out of the classroom, each person getting one cupcake each. Sam was last, savoring every moment. Ms. Manny snapped the lid tight. There were two cupcakes left.

"One is for you too."

"Sam, I don't eat sweets, don't you know? I am an old lady. I have to watch my figure."

Ms. Manny sighed as Sam looked at her, confusion clearly displayed in her eyes.

"Everyone loves cupcakes."

Sam seemed so sad.

"Well, then, I would love one too. But may I save it for later?'

Sam grinned. "Of course."

Ms. Manny reopened the Tupperware and carefully took out a cupcake. Sam was so surprised to see it. *Perfect,* she thought. *They're still perfect.*

"Here you go. Thanks for the cupcake." She handed Sam the Tupperware with one cupcake remaining. Sam smiled and grabbed the box before going outside, through the play yard to the bus. She was sure Ms. Manny would try to make her go up the long hallway, but her teacher didn't even try to stop her. Ms. Manny Just watched her carefully as she walked.

Sam climbed onto the bus, so excited to see one of her classmates sitting up front, chomping away at the cake. The girl gazed up at Sam, then looked away.

Sam was so confused. She took her seat. No one sat on in front or behind her. The seat across from her, Matthew sat, stoically staring frontwards.

His wayward brother was trapped next to him. Kindergarten was the last to get on the bus. Sarah came bounding on board, jumping across Sam to get next to the window in their seat.

Sarah giggled, then whispered, "We got to play with the squirrel for extra time today. And Kevin locked himself in the shed. The principal had to get *tools* to get him out."

Sam's throat was so dry all of a sudden. "Sam, Sam!" Sarah was shaking her.

"Quit that."

"What's wrong?"

Sam looked at her sister, then around at the kids on the bus. No one made eye contact with her, except for Matthew's little brother. He had a weird sneer on his face, and was leaning over his seat to get a look at Sam and Sarah. Matthew elbowed him hard, so hard he hit the window and the bus driver called out. No one looked at her again, and no one spoke even one word.

Sam could hardly breathe by the time they almost got to her stop. She was glad only the Leiven boys remained, but she had to walk past them to get off the bus.

Sarah had been talking nonstop about squirrels, squirrel food, squirrel fur, squirrels' tails, and even squirrel eyeballs.

Sam was glad that, for once, Sarah didn't have any questions.

Sarah didn't even seem to notice anything might be wrong.

Sam chuckled at Sarah; it was so easy being little. The bus pulled to a stop, and Sam gathered her backpack, lunchbox and her one remaining cupcake snapped safely in the Tupperware.

Sarah was puzzled. "Aren't you gonna eat that? *I* could still eat one."

"Come on," was all Sam could get out. She just *had* to get off this bus.

As she exited past the boys, they started giggling. "Nice dress."

Sam knew which one had said it because Matthew was glaring at them.

She also knew what it was like to be the eldest, responsible for everyone.

She looked at him. He surprised Sam and stared back, then down. Shame was still foreign to Sam but she felt it anyway. Why was no one looking at her? Why wouldn't anyone talk to her?

Sarah pushed her, and Sam realized she had stopped walking and was just staring at Matthew. He was looking straight ahead, back straight, eyes fixed.

Sam walked Sarah to the steps at the front of their house. The babies were crying, but she just couldn't be bothered. Sarah ran inside yelling for Mom, saying something else about squirrels.

Sam put her backpack and lunchbox down on the steps, clutching her perfect cupcake, safe inside the Tupperware. She started to run, tilting her head back, running harder.

She ran and jumped through the woods so easily it surprised even her.

She darted right, then left, past the old oaks, deeper, heading up past the farmer's cornfield.

She burst into the river, letting the cool water fill her soul. Her dress caught on a tree limb somewhere under the water. Keeping her cupcake safe above water, she pulled.

She felt her dress rip, sadness creeping in, but the water washed the sensation away.

The water washed everything away, and Sam let it, welcoming it.

She walked out of the river, head held high, resting her precious Tupperware under a nearby tree. Sam began to squeeze the water from her dress.

She had to dry it or she'd be in even more trouble.

She heard her mom call, "Soweeeeee!" It was the hog call. Momma couldn't whistle so she'd invented this call so Sam would know when she needed to come home, but Sam wasn't coming.

Not with a wet, ripped dress. A ripped dress, yes. A wet dress, yes. A wet, ripped dress, no. She frantically began to squeeze, the water falling to the ground around her.

"You need to take it off to get it really dry, you know."

Sam tried to scream, but only air came out. She looked across the river. It was Thomas, the hobo, wading across. The river barely came up to his knees, and he was laughing.

"No need for all that mess, girl. I ain't gonna hurt you. Besides, ain't that your mama callin'?"

Sam dropped her dress, stood up straight, "I thought you said hobos were just passing through?"

"Well. Those sandwiches were so good, I thought I might stay a while."

Sam panicked. She ran back into the woods. Her mom called again, "Soweeeeee!"

Sam stopped. Her cupcake. She turned fast and ran right into the hobo. "I thought you might come back for this." He was holding the Tupperware container out for her.

He was still laughing. How dare he laugh at her!

She snatched the Tupperware and ran. This time, she ran as fast as her lungs would let her. When she reached the special spot, she literally threw her legs underneath, coming to a sliding stop. Breathless, but glad she was safe, she looked at her cupcake; it hadn't survived the slide.

She sat up and backed up as far as she could in the space—and bumped into Sarah.

"Are you trying to give me a heart attack?"

"Everyone is looking for you. Daddy's on his way home from work, too, to look for you."

"I really am in trouble." Sam let all the air out of her lungs. She was breathing harder than she meant to.

Sarah started to talk again, but Sam held a finger to her lips.

He was still laughing. The tree branches surrounded them, but they had to be quiet. Sarah pointed to the corner. The fawn was gone. Sarah looked so sad.

Sam whispered, "The mama deer just moved it. I'm sure it's okay."

Twigs snapped just a few feet away from the opening. He had stopped laughing.

The girls could see his dirty boots stopping at the opening. He pushed leaves across it with his boot's toe, then he just stood there. Sam realized she was holding Sarah and her breath. She eased the air out as slowly as she could. The girls saw his hand reach down and rub the ground where Sam had slid underneath, then Thomas just walked away.

Sarah sighed. "Momma says we shouldn't be afraid. They just want food."

"That's *not* all they want. He might hurt us. Maybe Daddy's right."

Sarah smiled at Sam, then nudged her.

"I knew I could find you." Sarah looked as though she'd won the Publisher's Clearing House sweepstakes, and her smile made Sam smile too.

"I can't go home just yet; my dress is wet *and* I tore it."

But Sarah, distracted, seemed to ignore everything Sam said.

"What's that?" Sarah was pointing, and smiling.

Sam's eyes followed to where Sarah's fingertip jabbed. It was her cupcake, toppled upside down, still in its big container. All the icing was splattered.

"It's ruined."

Sarah seemed puzzled. "Why? Does it taste different?"

Sam giggled. "Let's find out."

For the next few minutes, the two girls sat safely in their special place, protected by the trees, and ate one smushed and toppled cupcake.

They smeared fudge icing all over their mouths just to get the very last bits out of the container, then Sam used her dress to clean her sister's face.

Sam giggled. "Nope. It doesn't taste any different."

"Soweeee, Soweeee!" The call was loud and sounded frantic.

Sarah met Sam's gaze. "We better get in before Daddy shows up."

They both scooted out from under the trees, and hand in hand, they headed home. By the time they reached the tree line, a group of neighbors had gathered around Momma.

The farmer, Mrs. Leiven, and 'not his dad' were there.

For Sam, the world stood still.

Sarah let go of her hand and ran up to Mom, yelling and smiling, "I just knew I could find her."

Momma scooped Sarah up into her arms. "Sarah, you scared me to death. Don't run off like that and not tell me where you're going." Tears ran down Momma's face as she then eyed Sam standing just outside the tree line.

Sam gazed at the crowd. Shame was becoming her constant companion, and she couldn't figure out why she felt that way. Sam thought she might stay confused forever.

Mom ran over with Sarah in her arms. She pulled Sam tight.

Sam was so startled, she didn't even know what to do in the moment, so taken aback by it.

Momma was crying even harder now. "I am so glad I found you!"

Sam wanted to burst out laughing to stop herself from crying endlessly, her soul hurting so much. If she started crying right now, she might never stop. Not ever.

"But Momma, I wasn't lost. Those are my woods, so how can I get lost there?"

Sam looked at the crowd and made eye contact with 'not their dad.' She took another step back from her mom and tilted her chin up, squaring her shoulders.

'Not his dad' was giving her the evil eye!

And now that she knew for sure what it meant, she didn't say 'God bless' because God wouldn't dream of blessing anything like that. She tilted her chin forward.

Her mom frowned, then smiled, sadness filling her eyes.

Momma said, "I swear, girl. Not everything is out to get you. You're Irish for sure with that stance. Suspicious of everyone!"

Sam was standing straight, chin tilted high into the breeze, the wind just barely pushing her wet, torn dress backward. Mom smiled.

Sam saw tears in her mother's eyes, but she saw something else too. Pride. And love.

The neighbors laughed and joked for what seemed like forever about Sam 'not getting lost' in 'her woods.' Sarah ran back and forth into the house and back out again, grinning as if company was a wonderful thing. She was bringing everyone something to drink.

Sam just sat on a rock in the tree line, watching, listening to everyone. She was suddenly so tired. The crowd slowly dispersed. The farmer lived the closest and was the last to leave.

He handed Sarah his empty glass, then took two steps and turned.

He tilted back his old hat, looked right at Sam and said, "I never could get lost in those woods either. You sure are something. I'm not sure what yet, but something."

He smiled at her, and it warmed her, and Sam wondered what he meant by 'something.'

The farmer walked up the driveway, Sam following him with her eyes.

He waved at her daddy as the station wagon pulled up the drive. Daddy pulling to a stop behind the house. Sam just sat there, so utterly tired.

***

The shadows were getting longer when Sam awoke again. She had leaned her head against the tree and fallen asleep. Her dad sat on the ground beside her.

Sam gasped and sat up, straightening her dress, running her fingers across the rip.

"Daddy." Sam couldn't really talk; she just started crying.

Her daddy pulled her into his lap, and just let her sit there, her eyes spilling over as she took great inhalations, barely able to catch her breath.

Sarah showed up with a wet washcloth. "Momma said this will help." Sarah shoved the washcloth into Sam's hand, then ran back up to the house.

Sam tried to keep herself from sobbing even harder, but she just couldn't stop.

Daddy said softly, "Hold it up to your mouth and breathe through the cloth. It will cool the air you breathe. You're okay. You have nothing to be ashamed about."

Shame. How had he picked up on that?

Sam did as she was told, finding that breathing through the cloth helped her calm her sobs. She still wasn't sure what 'shame' really meant, though she knew the word, of course.

But she could only think that maybe that was why she was so upset.

Daddy just kept patting her, saying, "You're okay, it's gonna be okay."

It's not, Sam thought. *Nothing is ever okay, not when you say it will be. I don't believe you.*

Daddy was lying like grown-ups did when they didn't have any answers. It wasn't okay, and wouldn't ever be okay!

And now, she realized something else she would sooner not acknowledge, which was that even Ms. Manny had lied too, when she'd said this would be all right.

It wasn't all right, was it? And it never would be all right! And Ms. Manny was a liar, after all.

Her dad pulled her into a hug which Sam was just too tired to push away.

When her sobbing slowed to a soft whimper, she felt her daddy lift her up and take her across the yard into her own room. He tucked her in. Momma came by and kissed her head, stroking her soft hair, helping her drink some water and leaving the glass at the side of her bed.

Sam closed her eyes.

The crickets stopped.

She opened her eyes, then closed and opened them again.

She looked at her window, seeing only shadows there. Yet again, the crickets were chirping away. Sam thought for sure she must be dreaming, but was she? The crickets stopped again.

Sam was sure this time: it was a dream.

She pushed up on her elbows, her pajamas clean and dry. Sam thought about her ruined dress, reaching out for the glass of water. There was a shuffling sound on the floor, and she gasped, suddenly frightened, trying successfully not to drop the water. There, on the floor, was Sarah, wide-eyed, looking up at her. Lying down, her sister was wrapped in a blanket.

"You didn't scream! You always scream when you have those dreams," Sarah said.

"Well, I don't scream anymore. I'm big enough to take care of myself."

Sam truthfully couldn't scream anymore. She didn't know why; she just knew she couldn't. The feeling of not being able to scream, and the smell of mud were burned into her mind.

"Mom said I could stay here tonight but that I couldn't get on the bed. Daddy said, 'Call if you get up.' Please can I use the phone?" Sarah said it as if it was the most important announcement in all the world, with both her hands up. Sam couldn't help but smile at her sister.

"I will make a deal with you; if you don't call, I'll let you sleep up here. How's that sound?" Sam moved over just a little and made room for Sarah.

Sarah smiled and jumped up. "Deal."

Sam felt relieved as her sister snuggled into the bed. Normally, Sarah was just irritating but tonight, she was welcome company. Nothing in the world was making sense anymore.

Something had happened, something terrifying. But Sam wasn't sure what.

As she drifted back to sleep, she remembered something about her lunchbox.

Chapter 10

S am ran up through the farmer's field. She could slide under the electric fence now without getting stung by it, so she easily managed to traverse it this way. It was worth it to see the bull.

The sun hadn't come out yet, but she had to get close to him. Why she had to go every morning before dawn, she couldn't fully understand, but the sheer power of being near the animal filled her with courage. The bull was so tough and strong.

The trip there always seemed like forever, walking at night through the shadows outside her house, under the first fence, and more shadows through the field. And a dog, a dog that usually stayed in the tree line. She was sure it was the biggest she had ever seen, feeling it watching her as she crept through the field. She fancied it was her friend, but it never got close.

She'd crept out into the darkness that first night, with her mom's butcher knife, planning to make the darkness yield. She refused to stay scared. She wouldn't just do 'nothing.'

In her mind, something—anything—was so much better than trying to not be afraid.

To her surprise, her eyes adjusted easily, the darkness wrapping her in a kind of warmth.

As she slipped under the first fence, she saw the dog in the middle of the field.

Sam stood very still, gripping the knife at her side.

It looked almost regal in the last of the moon's glow. As she'd stared, trying to get a better look in the darkness of that first morning, she had felt a presence, and her grip on the knife loosened. She felt an essence, like a long-lost soul, attempting to get close but it moved purposefully into the brush by the field. After that first morning, she might have seen it briefly, and she'd heard it follow her, but the dog had never come out in the open field again.

In her mind, Sam had made it into a wolf, her spirit animal there to guide her safely.

Since that first night, she'd always left some of her dinner from the night before, placed carefully on the ground. A 'thank you' for being her only friend in the world.

This morning was the same as every other. Sam pulled a piece of chicken from her pocket and placed it in the very spot where she'd first seen the dog.

"Thanks for being there." She said it softly and tenderly as she left the food on the ground.

Passing through the field, under another fence, she slid past the farmer's hog pen, and then she was standing right beside the round pen. A rooster crowed, and Sam jumped. She was late this morning. The bull greeted her, stomping the ground with its front hooves, Sam marveling at the steam escaping from its nostrils. She stared back at it, wishing deeply for the courage to enter the round pen. She walked around it, the bull following, rushing in and out but always stopping at the fence. Fierce and powerful, Sam tried to absorb its strength.

Watching its muscles twitch as it moved, she continued to walk back and forth.

Sam stopped, stared, just watching, staring into the eyes of the bull.

She felt the ground shake as the bull shifted its weight side to side.

The shaking of the earth vibrated her feet, and she imagined it rising through her. She breathed in the fresh air, out and in, courage to face the day filling her.

"I wish you weren't so mean."

Sam said it with a certain sadness; she had become so lonely since that day at school. Months had passed, months when no one would talk to her. The boys wouldn't let her play marbles at recess, and her mom was sick. Something had happened when Mom had birthed this last baby. Something Sam couldn't quite understand. The baby was so tiny, smaller than any of the rest had been, and her mom had stopped talking almost completely, spending her time with the infant.

She looked at the bull. "We could be friends. Real friends, you know?"

"Yes. You could if you weren't so intent on scaring him with that stare of yours." Sam almost jumped out of her skin. Later, she would swear she saw her own soul that morning.

The farmer laughed so hard he had to lean on the gate at the round pen, clutching his belly.

"How long have you been there?" Sam was not amused in the slightest.

"Which morning?"

"Do you get your thrills from spying on people?"

"Only little kids who sneak on my property in the wee hours of the morning. Your father told me you shouldn't be coming here now. He's sure you don't come to this field anymore."

Sam wasn't really upset; she was glad for the company but very aware she shouldn't be there.

"How long have you been watching me? And why are you still laughing? Scaring me wasn't all that funny." Sam stood taller, trying to show him she wasn't frightened anymore.

"You ain't exactly the quietest."

The farmer laughed harder, a full belly laugh that was almost contagious, but Sam wasn't giving in that easily. She just stared at him, trying to look irritated.

"He's not mean," the farmer said. "Actually, he's the tamest bull I've ever owned."

The farmer tossed a large carrot at Sam. To her surprise, she caught it. "Give him that. If you're determined to come every morning, you don't have to always scare him near to death."

"Scare him? Have you seen him?"

Sam made a waving motion with her hands, mimicking the presentation of an award.

"Not everything is the way it looks, girl. Just give him the carrot."

And with that, the farmer opened the gate to the round pen.

The bull stood in the opening but didn't step out. Sam gasped.

"Geez, don't scare him again. Just step up and make friends, will ya? Hold the carrot out with an open hand. Like this." The farmer pulled another carrot from his pocket and held it out. The bull took the carrot gently from the farmer's hand, then pulled its head up and blew steam from both of its nostrils. Sam stepped forward slowly. The size of the bull still gave her pause.

"I swear, I don't know who's more scared, you or him."

As Sam stepped forward, time stood still. She held out her hand, just as the farmer had. The bull stepped forward, the ground shaking with each step. By the time the bull took the carrot, Sam was shaking so hard her teeth were chattering. Then just as the bull swallowed the carrot, the biggest tongue Sam had ever seen erupted from its mouth and licked the whole side of her face. Sam fell backwards with shock, then was grounded to reality by the farmer's laughter.

"I guess if you're gonna come by every morning, we have to give you a job. We ain't seen your mama come out of the house since she had that last baby. The wife and I have been figurin', since you're wanderin' and we ain't seen her, she's got the baby blues."

"What's that?" Sam was genuinely confused. Momma had been sick since this last baby was about a week old but they hadn't told anyone. Sam and Daddy had been bringing her the baby, but it'd now been two weeks since she'd even bothered getting out of bed.

Sam's Dad had said she would get better, and they had to just keep taking care of things till she did. The truth was Sam didn't think her mom was improving.

That morning before she left the house, after Dad left for work, Sam had to latch the baby onto Momma's breast to nurse. They couldn't afford formula, and the baby had to eat.

Her mom had opened her eyes, but Sam wasn't sure she'd even seen her.

"I'll let the wife tell you. Go on up to the house. You're gonna get our eggs every morning from now on. In payment, you'll get a few eggs, and breakfast. Now, go up there and knock on the door. My wife knows you're coming."

Sam swallowed hard. No one was even supposed to know Momma was sick. Daddy had said the social services would come if they knew. Sam began to panic as she approached the door. She paused, then took the three steps up, and knocked. Sam had never seen the farmer's wife up close, and she was still mad at them both for shooting her dog a few years ago.

The woman who opened the door was graying, slightly heavier than she should have been, and was looking at Sam as if she was the most precious child in the world. Her relaxed, open posture gave Sam another reason to pause. She'd always thought they were both mean.

But this woman was anything but mean. Sam stood there, waiting for the lady to punish her for trespassing and causing them to get up super early, but the woman just smiled at the child.

"Good morning. So, you're the little birdy that's been riling up old Willie every morning? Why are you lookin' so angry?"

"I am not little and I'm not a birdy. Besides, we can't have a dog because you shot mine."

"Well, girl, the dog was eating the chickens. The chickens are our livelihood. You should have kept the dog at home."

"You can't keep dogs locked up," Sam said furiously.

"If you don't take care of your own, what happens is left up to the world. Having any animal comes with lots of responsibility." She smiled kindly at Sam, who was having trouble being mad.

This woman had such a disarming way about her.

The farmer's wife held out a big basket.

She huffed, a nice huff but a huff all the same. A second passed, and she shook the basket. "Time you started earning your keep. The chicken coop is behind the round pen. Check underneath all those hens, and in the nesting boxes. Bring me all the eggs."

"Under the hens? Nesting boxes?"

"Yes. You'll be okay. They peck but it won't hurt. Just stick your hand underneath, and a nesting box is just a wooden box. You'll see them. Now shoo; get to work."

The way she waved her hand made Sam stiffen, but she took the basket.

She hated it when people told her to do stuff, especially when they were all but strangers!

Sam walked back down the three stairs, past the round pen.

The farmer was putting hay out for the bull. He glanced up as she passed him, but he didn't speak. Sam reached the chicken coop about the time the sun crested the trees.

She hurried to get the eggs. The chickens did peck but the farmer's wife was right. It didn't hurt. The rooster crowed again when Sam reached the farmer's door.

Sam was scared she'd miss her bus to school. It was the last week, and she had to get Sarah ready, make breakfast and take care of the babies or she couldn't leave.

Sam was almost frantic when she finally knocked on the door. She didn't know what scared her more, Momma being sick, the work she had to do before she left or Daddy finding out she'd been there, messing with the bull. She was holding the basket out with two hands.

The farmer's wife opened the door and took the basket.

"Wait right here. I have to pay you for your work. My husband is gonna call your daddy and tell him we hired you this morning."

Sam gasped, saying, "No! Don't do that. He'll be mad."

"No. He won't, men have a way of talking with each other. Now, wait right here."

Sam peeked inside the front door of the small farmhouse. She watched as the farmer's wife picked up six beautiful fresh biscuits, a pile of bacon, and a jar of something orange.

"What's that?"

"What?"

"That orange stuff?"

"Why, it's the best stuff in the house. I make it every year." The woman smiled brightly at Sam. "It's called orange marmalade and because you're our first worker this year, it's yours. Put it on the biscuits. You got any butter?"

"Yes, ma'am, Daddy got groceries last Sunday."

She wrapped the food in brown parchment and put it in the basket, then laid two eggs on top.

"Now, you bring this basket every morning and get those eggs, then bring it back and I will fill it. Understand?"

"Yes, ma'am." Sam couldn't think about anything but bacon.

Her mouth was already watering.

"I suspect your mama's real sick, so I'm gonna start checking on her today. Your daddy's been leaving early for work and coming home twice during the day. We figurin' he's exhausted."

"You can't do that."

"We can and we will. We ain't the government. We are your neighbors."

She smiled at Sam and tapped her on the shoulders. "It's gonna be all right, girl. Is there anything you don't worry about?" She handed Sam the basket, pointing her toward home.

Sam left at a run. The sun was up, and the bus would arrive all too soon.

Chapter 11

S am took her seat in Ms. Manny's class. Theresa sat at her desk next to her.

Her face was swollen, as if she'd been crying a very long time.

Theresa made a choking sound as if she'd still have tears if there were any left.

Sam pulled a napkin from her lunchbox, walked to the sink in the coatroom and turned the water on. As she walked back by Theresa's desk, she placed the napkin on the edge.

As quietly as she could, Sam said, "Put it over your mouth and breathe through it. It'll make it easier." Theresa didn't move, and Sam wasn't sure she even heard her.

Sam took her seat again and the bell rang.

Ms. Manny started talking about how important Mother's Day was. Out of the corner of Sam's eye, she saw Theresa pick up the napkin, put it to her mouth, and inhale.

Sam wondered why no one ever seemed to notice when girls cried.

Theresa cried a lot. Sam knew Kevin had lost his job.

She knew Theresa's daddy had lost his job too; she also knew Theresa had repeated first and second grade, and she'd watched in horror one morning on the bus as a roach had crawled across the collar of Theresa's shirt. If no one talked to Sam, then absolutely no one talked to Theresa.

The bell rang for recess, and Sam waited for the room to clear.

Ms. Manny waited for Sam to get up. Sam reached into her lunchbox, pulling out a biscuit with bacon and orange marmalade on it, wrapped in parchment. She laid it on Theresa's desk.

"You don't owe her anything, Sam. You've been leaving her lunch for weeks, and I can't help noticing you're getting thin. You need to eat your own food."

Ms. Manny had developed the habit of giving Sam all kinds of unsolicited advice.

Sam tilted her chin upwards, and responded, "You always feed the hungry because you never know when God will show up."

For once, Ms. Manny had nothing else to add.

She took Sam's hand and patted it, leading her outside. Sam thought for just a second she might have seen Ms. Manny's eyes water. Maybe even Ms. Manny cried like all the girls did.

Sam didn't have any tears left, and she wondered if Ms. Manny might.

Sam had tried as hard as she could to play marbles with the other kids but usually wound up playing by herself. Besides, Ms. Manny oddly got way nervous if Sam left her for long.

Sam had five marbles in her pocket today. Drawing a circle on the ground, she tossed her marbles inside it. All but her big shooter lay before her, in the circle. Sam lay down in the dirt.

With Mom sick, no one paid attention to her clothes when she came home, so she no longer worried about being dirty. It was truly freeing for a little girl in expensive jeans.

She pushed her arm forward, eyeing which marble would be first.

Nestling the shooter marble between her index finger and her thumb, she prepared to shoot.

Four more marbles dropped in the circle, and Sam lifted her gaze from the ground.

Theresa shrugged.

Sam adjusted her aim, letting the shooter marble fly across the dirt, crashing into Theresa's marble. Sam smiled as the marbles crashed together, one careening out of the circle.

Taking aim again and pushing her shooter marble out again with her thumb, Sam sent another marble out of the circle. Only two left.

Theresa huffed.

Sam aimed and missed.

Theresa squatted when she played, holding the marble on top of her thumb and sending it into the circle with her middle finger. Theresa's shooter clattered against two others, then rolled Sam's marble outside of the circle. The bell rang, and both girls collected their marbles from inside the circle and their winnings from outside the circle.

Sam had six marbles.

She felt terrible for taking Theresa's marble, and she wanted desperately to be sure she played with her again. Sam held out the extra marble to her.

"You won that fair and square, and I don't take no charity." Theresa looked furious.

She kicked up dirt, turning and running back up the stairs into the school.

Sam stepped into the classroom, Ms. Manny close behind her. Sam gazed out of the corner of her eye again, straining and struggling to not appear as if she was looking.

The biscuit was gone.

Sam smiled to herself. She took her seat, the smile working itself into her chest.

She'd got to play marbles with someone else.

Playing marbles had pushed the world back for half a day. Sam had forgotten just how unwelcome she was until she walked toward the bus. Getting into the bus, into her seat, was a daily walk with the shame that lived inside her.

She saw it in everyone's eyes.

The bus driver glanced down, and Sam saw it immediately. She began her ascent up the stairs into the bus. Turning the corner into the aisle, she felt shame wrap around her, squeezing tightly.

Sarah had bounded in front of her, unaware of the eyes that followed them, jumping into her seat and looking out the window, watching the other buses load in the school yard.

Oh, how Sam wished to be unaware again!

She'd given up trying to talk to anyone.

She tilted her chin as she climbed the last step and entered. Looking down the long aisle of the school bus, she tried to focus on Sarah, and on the delight living in her.

Every day for months, time almost stood still as she began her walk down the aisle to her seat.

Someone stuck a foot out to trip her, but she dodged it.

Matt threw a book and hit the boy square in the head.

"You don't run this bus!" the boy yelled out. He was rubbing his head, immediately throwing the book back at Matt.

Matt caught the book with ease; after all, he was the best baseball player in the school. He rarely missed any opportunity to show his prowess.

"Ya think I don't?" Matt stood.

"She ain't one of us; why you protectin' her? Her ma's not from around here. Who knows what crap they brought with 'em?" The boy was still rubbing his head.

Matt just glared at him.

The bus driver hit the horn. "Sit down, boys, and hold on."

Sam just made it to her seat as the bus pulled out onto the street in front of the school.

Thankfully, Sarah had missed the whole thing, too busy waving at her kindergarten classmates on another bus. Sam was too tired from the day to explain anything to her little sister, especially something she didn't completely understand herself.

"God bless." Sam knew he wouldn't answer.

She said it anyway. During the first few weeks after what she now called 'the event,' Matt had remained, always just sitting there and looking ahead, never changing seats.

Everyone had changed seats, packing into any space they could get except for the seats around Sam and Sarah. Sam told Sarah they were working on the bracing of the seats.

Sarah had smiled, believing every word Sam had said.

She hated lying to her sister but sharing the truth was not an option. Sam wasn't even sure what that truth was, and on that day, she'd understood why grown-ups lied so much.

Matt had even stayed there when *all* the seats around her were empty.

When the ugly boy had sat in front of her seat, sticking his head up and looking backwards, sneering at Sam, Matt had snatched him up and re-deposited him in the seat behind.

Matt had thrown two of the other boys down the aisle.

The driver hadn't ever yelled at Matt, she'd just blown her horn, telling the boys to take their seats. Through it all, Matt said not a word to Sam.

He just sat there, moving quickly to keep her and Sarah safe. Every time, Sam had said, "God bless." She had always said it quietly, but she was sure he heard her, every time.

Sam had learned to save her "God blesses" for those who actually deserved it.

The bus emptied one stop at a time, droning on through the dirt roads. Theresa's stop was next, and Kevin and two of her younger brothers would be waiting.

Theresa's head was down.

Sam noticed she didn't make eye contact with anyone as she walked down the aisle. Maybe she knew what shame was too. Something was happening. She stood in her seat, stretching her neck to see. As the doors to the bus closed, Theresa yelled.

Kevin lifted her up by her hair. "Mama told you not to go to school today. We got work to do." He threw her back down.

Sam didn't hear anything else. She watched the boys walking back toward the one-room farmhouse, tossing fake punches and laughing, as boys did.

They left Theresa lying there where Kevin had thrown her.

Theresa stood, ran to catch up, and her younger brother pulled her into a hug. The bus pulled around the corner. Try as she might, Sam couldn't see anything else.

Sarah turned to her sister. "What happened?"

Sam shrugged as if she didn't know and smiled at her sister.

Sarah pointed at a marker on the road.

"Only one mile to go, then babies. I love the babies."

Sarah giggled and jumped in her seat.

Sam had taught her sister about mile markers, and Sarah was right.

Only one mile left till their stop. Three miles after Theresa's house, and almost one mile before the Leiven house. The babies would be waiting, their diapers needing to be changed, and there'd be crying, always crying. Sam felt her chest tighten as she remembered a time when it seemed they'd never cried, and the newest baby had been so little.

She was worried but had no idea what to do.

The house was full of sadness, dark with curtains pulled. Sam had tried to keep up with the house cleaning but had failed miserably. Daddy was always tired now.

The bus stopped in front of her house.

Sarah jumped up. "I can't wait to see the babies!"

Sam drew in a deep breath. She stood, walked past the Leiven boys, and got off the bus. Her sister rushed into the house. Sam gathered herself and walked toward the front porch.

The farmer's wife poked her head out of the front door.

"Come on, girl, don't dawdle. We have lots to do." She waved at Sam to hurry.

Sam started to run. She couldn't be in the house.

Daddy would be so mad. This was terrible. What had she done?

Sam had been so excited about the biscuits and bacon that she'd forgotten they were going to call Daddy. By the time Sam reached the front door, panic had completely taken over.

"You can't be here! You have to go."

Sam was so out of breath, she was gasping to finish her sentence.

"I can and I will," the farmer's wife answered without even a second glance at Sam. "Sam, wash your hands. Stop yelling, or you'll wake the babies. I just got them down to nap."

Sam realized there was no crying. It was the first time in weeks that she'd heard quiet. Sam immediately lowered her voice to a whisper. "Really, you can't be here. Daddy will be so mad."

"No, he won't. The men talked at lunch when your daddy came barreling down that long driveway of yours."

Sam followed as the farmer's wife walked into their dining room.

Sarah was seated, enjoying a rather large plate of spaghetti.

"Does no one explain anything to you?"

The farmer's wife cocked her head and waited for Sam to answer.

Normally, this would send Sam into a defensive position, but there was something about the kindness that lived inside this woman.

Sam relaxed. The house was clean, and the window curtains were open. She swallowed hard.

"Mom tells me stuff, but she's stopped talking. And we have encyclopedias," she answered.

Sam just wanted spaghetti. She put her book bag and lunchbox down on the table, pulled out a chair and slid up to the table as the farmer's wife placed a big plate of spaghetti in front of her.

Sam immediately started eating.

Kindness radiated from the farmer's wife as she sat leaning across the table. She was looking directly at Sam when she said, "And regular stuff? Do they explain regular stuff to you?"

Sam just looked puzzled. All of a sudden, she was aware they hadn't said grace. She hadn't checked on her mom either. She stopped eating and jumped up from the table, running back to her mom's room. Her momma was sleeping. The babies were too.

Sam jumped when the farmer's wife tenderly put a hand on her shoulder.

"My babies didn't live to see their first birthdays, but that doesn't mean I can't run a household." She smiled lovingly at Sam.

Sam turned. "You had babies too?"

The woman looked at Sam, turning her head to the side, looking at Sam as if she was a giant puzzle. "You go eat your spaghetti, then we are gonna talk."

The 'gonna talk' part scared Sam, but, frankly, she was far hungrier than she was afraid.

She ate the whole plate.

Sarah went to take a bath. Sam felt guilty because it had been several days since she'd been able to put Sarah in the tub. She heard the farmer's wife explaining to Sarah that she could run her own bathwater if she wanted to, telling the girl it was part of being five years old.

Sarah giggled as she dried off; she actually liked bathing. Sam gave Sarah a blanket, and Sarah curled up in it right next to their mom, very quickly falling to sleep.

The farmer's wife tapped Sam on the shoulder. "It's time we had that talk."

"What talk? Daddy will be home soon."

"Yes, he will. The house is clean. The wash is done, the linens changed. The babies are all dry and fed. Dinner is ready, and my husband has mowed your grass. Your sister is resting comfortably. So, what you got left to do? Besides getting clean yourself and talking to me?"

"I don't talk much."

With that, the farmer's wife erupted into the kindest laughter Sam had ever heard. She knew she was laughing at her, but it didn't hurt. "Oh, my. You are anything but quiet. Besides, you already told ol' Willie everything, so I know it all because he tells me."

Sam started to push her shoulders back, and the woman stopped laughing. "Now don't get your shoulders all up around your ears; we don't have that long to talk. You're the eldest, and your daddy won't let me come but once a week. You're gonna have to keep this together till your mom gets better. Thankfully, it's not as bad as I thought."

"It isn't bad at all. We are fine." Sam was defiant, standing tall now.

"That's the girl I know." She smiled and led Sam outside where ol' Willie waited at the fence line, huffing and puffing. "I'll take him home when I go; we're still scared he might step on Sarah, but he wouldn't miss a chance to see you."

The farmer's wife handed Sam a carrot.

Sam looked at the bull. He was still huge; he still huffed and puffed, too, steam blowing out of both nostrils, but despite it all, despite how fearsome he could be, wasn't he her best friend?

She gave him the carrot, stroked his neck, and absorbed his strength.

She rested her head on his haunches.

"How well can you read?"

"Well enough to read encyclopedias no one else around here can."

Fierceness was gleaming from Sam's eyes.

"That's cause they ain't got them. We have Bibles instead. Is there anything that doesn't scare you?"

"I'm not scared of anything." Sam stopped hugging the bull and squared her shoulders. The wind caught her hair and the farmer's wife smiled wide.

"You sure are a pugnacious one. I'll give you that."

"What did Daddy say?"

"That it's none of our business. He's quite stubborn. The conversation was long enough that your daddy won't be home till late to make up for it. My husband told him, the yard is our business because it buttresses our fields. Oh, and he told him he ought not be throwing things like plates out the back door in the middle of the night."

"You know about that?" Sam took an interest in the ground again, shame filling her. When she felt her skin turning red, she immediately looked up, determined to defend her father.

"Why are you watching us?" Sam stepped back just a bit.

"Hey, easy does it! We can't help but see—and hear—some things. We know how to mind our own business. Besides, my house is on the hill, and we see the whole back of this house."

She smiled at Sam again, patting her shoulder. Sam relaxed just a bit.

"Remember, I'm here to help. Okay?"

Sam felt helpless as she responded, "I don't know what to do. Mom won't get up."

"I think she will tomorrow. I talked to her. Right now, you're gonna have to feed that new baby. I know your dad and mom are against formulas 'cause they cost so much, and your daddy won't take charity. So, I hid some under the sink with a bottle and directions. You gotta feed that baby once before you leave for school, then again when you get home and once again before your dad gets home around 5.30 p.m., you understand?"

"But it's so little, and anyway, Momma feeds it."

"No, *you* gotta feed it. Just until your mom starts getting around again. You don't have to feed it much, just till it stops sucking, understand?" Sam nodded as the woman continued, "She's sad because there were two babies, and she only got to bring one home."

Sam gasped. "Two babies? How? Momma never had two babies at one time."

"You need to look up twins in them encyclopedias your family is so proud of. Sometimes, one of them dies, and it just happens."

"But how?" Sam was genuinely puzzled. "Mom is so good at having babies. I didn't even know she was pregnant this time."

Sam was mortified. It was true; she hadn't noticed. She'd been so busy trying to stay awake when the man stared into her window that it seemed she'd been blinded to everything else.

"Of course, you didn't; she wasn't but just past five months when them babies was born. That's why it's so little. it wasn't ready for this world. Now, we gotta get ready, and gotta get your mom movin'. I don't envy you, it's a big job. But you gotta do it. And hide that formula."

Sam wondered why the woman cared so much when no one else seemed to.

She had so many questions, but couldn't think of any of them as the woman quietly hugged her. Emotion filled Sam's throat, the hug making it hard to breathe and she was grateful when the woman finally pulled away. It felt like forever.

The woman held her by the shoulders. Looking squarely into her eyes, she said, "There's another thing. That big ol' dog that's following you around."

Sam's eyes widened. "Don't shoot it!"

"We ain't gonna shoot it. It ain't concerned with nothin' but you. Walks right past the chickens an' anyways, ol' Willie likes it."

"Have you really seen it?"

"Like I told you, the house looks right down over that field into your yard. I think it won't be long before the dog's sitting on your doorstep. When a dog chooses you like that, it's usually 'cause you need it. And if anyone needs a friend, you sure do. But to be sure, it's the biggest dog we've seen around these parts that wasn't a wolf."

"Are you sure it's not a wolf? I think it might be."

Sam said it like it was a huge secret, making the farmer's wife laugh.

"No, there ain't been a wolf 'round here in a long time. It's just a dog. A big ol' scruffy dog but just a dog, even so. So, let's go over your work again. Do your job and get my eggs early, give yourself enough time to feed that baby, then get your mom a wet washcloth and tell her to get up. Make sure it's cold. Cold washcloths do miracles when you're upset. I'll send enough breakfast for you and your sister, and your dad will feed the other babies while you're gone gettin' the eggs. Be careful to wait till he's gone to feed the littlest one. Your mom knows she's gotta get up, a'right, but don't expect her not to be sad. You got it?"

"Yes, ma'am," Sam lied. She was terrified. Terrified about getting caught with a bottle, or formula. Terrified about lying to Daddy. To her dad, nothing was worse than lying.

"What's worrying you, girl?"

Sam said sheepishly, "I can't lie to Daddy."

"I ain't asking you to lie. Just don't tell. You ain't gotta tell everythin' in this world."

The farmer's wife made a clicking sound with her mouth. "Come on, Willie, let's go home."

Sam watched them walk all the way across the field and into the round pen.

The kind woman in a long dress being followed gingerly by a fierce, humongous beast seemed so odd to Sam.

She thought deeply.

What if the things that scared her were not really the things she should be fearing?

Confused, but very tired and with a full belly for the first time in days, Sam turned and walked back toward the patio.

Chapter 12

She thought she could feel the dog following her, but when she turned, nothing was there, just the shadows of the night. Sam wanted a dog so badly, her bones were aching for it.

She walked in the darkness toward the tree line.

The crickets stopped. The fear jolted her awake from her dream world.

Lying in the bed, eyes closed, she knew he was there.

Even in the deepest sleep, Sam had trained herself to wake when the crickets stopped. She saw him, shrouded in darkness. He stared back through the window, the same as he usually did.

She no longer looked away. He had a strange habit of bouncing up and down before he disappeared, too, always suddenly leaving, as if he had somewhere important to go.

Sam was determined to make out his features, to put a name to the dark force that visited.

She propped herself up on her elbows, able to see the shape well enough to know that when she did this, it gave him pause, and he'd tilt his head.

She narrowed her eyes, unable to make him out but she was positive it was a man. And she knew he was tall and that he never came around until all the lights went out. She also knew he came from the woods to the front of the house, where no one would see his approach.

Sam had tried hunting him with her big kitchen knife, sure he'd followed her that night in the woods. *Someone* had followed her, anyway. She'd hidden herself away behind a massive great oak, waiting, but he didn't come that far down the center trail. The next day when she investigated, she'd seen his footprints, heavy booted, pushed deep in the ground.

Sam followed the boot prints, walking down the center trail. Then just before the oak tree, they veered to the right. She'd followed them till they disappeared, heading away into the river.

She lay back into bed, while he finished bouncing up and down.

As usual, he ran off immediately afterwards. She was astonished by how quickly the crickets started up their song again, thinking that maybe they were getting used to him too.

She couldn't get back to sleep, wondering.

Maybe he's like ol' Willie and not scary at all, just misunderstood.

But something about the way he loomed in her window still caused terror in her.

***

She got out of bed early as she had a big job this morning. Running up to the chicken houses, she cleared the nesting boxes. Thirteen eggs, still warm!

"Has to be a record," she told ol' Willie as she passed his round pen, throwing him his usual carrot. "Gotta go this morning, no time to visit."

She jumped up the stairs, knocking on the door.

"Good morning, my fierce little one."

The woman smiled, took the basket, and emptied all the eggs.

She then filled the same basket with parchment-covered goodness.

Handing it back to Sam, she patted the girl's shoulder and smiled but said nothing else.

Sam couldn't help herself from peeling and eating a boiled egg on the way through the field back to her house. She dropped her offering for the dog as she jogged.

She stopped, convinced she could feel it just behind her. She turned her head. Nothing.

Something.

Fear crept up her spine. She saw him, just there in the tree line. A man, or a woman, standing there. Sam gasped. She ran. Sliding under the fence and looking back … No, there was nothing.

"Stop being silly; you're not afraid of anything in the dark. The dark is your friend." Sam wasn't sure when she'd started talking to herself, but it seemed way too normal this morning.

She checked her pocket. The smooth outline of her matchbox gave her courage, and checking the contents of her basket made her smile.

She took one last glance at the tree line, too far away to see anything, then she darted away into the house. Sarah was up, dressed, and ready for breakfast. Sam opened the parchment paper and handed her sister a boiled egg, and a piece of fresh-baked bread.

"Is it hard work?" Sarah looked wide-eyed at her sister. "Are they really nice?"

"You met her; you can tell for yourself. Why do you always ask me silly questions?"

A tear formed in her small sister's eyes, tumbling slowly down one of Sarah's cheeks.

Sam hadn't meant to be harsh but she could still feel the man's piercing gaze.

Truthfully, Sam thought she might be getting used to being permanently terrified like this, but taking it out on Sarah was not allowed.

Her mom entered, from the hallway.

Sarah lifted her head, another tear falling down the other cheek.

Then came a whole river.

Sam watched as her mom scooped up Sarah. More tears, a cascade of them, a torrent.

Sarah dropped the egg and let it fall to the floor. Sadness enveloped everything and Sam stood in silence against it all. She would never cry again. She saw that it didn't help anything, ever.

She put the basket down on the counter.

Unnoticed, she passed them both, heading to the bathroom to brush her teeth.

Looking in the mirror, Sam felt alone, eying her reflection as if there was a stranger living there, inside her body. Truthfully, Sam wasn't sure she would ever be herself again. She stared into the mirror. "Mom hasn't been out of bed for weeks and the first thing she sees is you barking at Sarah. You gotta do better."

Sam walked back to check the babies.

All was well. She had fed the little one before she'd left, terrified she would be caught.

The baby had only taken a little, but it was sleeping so soundly, Sam was sure she'd done the right thing. A hand touched her shoulder. Sam had heard her mother's footsteps.

Her mom turned her, putting both warm hands on her arms.

Looking at Sam, she said, "I'm so sorry, but I've been lost. I promise I'm back now."

Sam shrugged, looking down, ashamed at herself for feeling lost too. Hope pushed its way in.

"Mama, are you sure? We're okay; we just miss you, that's all, but we've been alright."

It was a lie, but Sam hoped that she could be forgiven for it. It was to make Mom feel better.

Her mom pulled her close, but Sam was stoic, holding back, afraid to let hope seep too far into her. Then she threw both arms around her mom.

"We really miss you. We love you, Momma."

For several minutes, they just stood there. Sarah was there too, holding her mother's leg.

Then Mom held Sam by the arms again.

"Well, suppose we better see what's in that basket! I heard you got a J-O-B."

Mom didn't smile but it was enough for Sam.

There was a semblance of spirit in her tone.

They all ate boiled eggs and buttered bread.

Sam wanted to believe Mom was all better but as she left for the bus, she saw a broken boiled egg on the floor. In her heart, she knew that broken things just never came back the same.

Chapter 13

The last day of school went by fast. Sam was ready to be done with school, in fact, ready to be free. Summer promised long sunny days without everyone's beady eyes on her.

On the bus ride home, Sam's sister was talking about her new crayons, which Sarah's teacher had given them all. Expensive Crayola crayons that came in every color imaginable.

In truth, Sam was eyeing the big box with envy, hoping Sarah would share. Sarah always shared, but she might not give Sam the newest colors.

There was a new purple in the big box, and Sam already had her eye on it.

Sarah was turning it around in her little hands when Sam saw it.

It was a big pile of dirt was next to a massive hole, right in front of their house!

She watched as a shovel head appeared out of the hole, throwing more dirt out of it, onto the pile. Well, Sam didn't know what to think. She didn't even know what might be happening. Why would anyone dig a big hole right there, in front of the house?

Sarah exited the bus at a run, jumping on the pile of dirt, giggling as she did.

Sam, on the other hand, walked slowly toward the pile, the hair on her neck standing tall.

She felt the wrongness of it all as she approached.

A rectangular hole, it was, and one so deep that Sam had to look over the edge to see her mom who didn't seem to see them approach. A baby cried from down inside the hole.

Digging furiously, with the baby crying and strapped to her chest, was her mother, her eyes glazed and intense. Sam watched as her mom shoveled the dirt.

One shovel full of dirt, then two, three. The third shovelful came flying out of the hole and hit Sarah, covering her head with brown dirt. Sarah cried out, beginning to sob.

Sam yelled, "Mom! What are you doing?"

Her mom didn't answer, just looked at Sam and threw another shovelful of dirt out of the hole. Sam stood at the precipice, leaning over.

"Momma! What *are* you doing?"

This time, her mom made eye contact.

Glazed eyes, red and swollen, looked back at Sam.

When Momma spoke, her voice was clear, and startlingly frank.

Her mom finally replied, matter of fact, shrugging. "I'm digging my own grave, wanted to know if I could do it. That's all."

Sam felt her eyes widen. "Mom, you aren't dying, are you? Why are you doing this?"

Her mom didn't answer, just kept on digging.

Sarah was at Sam's side and grabbed her hand. Sam looked at their hands coupled together, and the world seemed to wobble. What was happening?

The other babies were in the hole with her mom. She had to get the babies out of the hole!

"Mom." Nothing. "Mom." Nothing. "Mom, hand me the babies!" she shouted.

Sam watched as her mom laid the shovel down without answering, picked up the babies one by one, and handed them to her. Their clothes were covered with soil and debris.

There was even soil around their eyes and noses. Mom seemed oblivious.

All she cared about was that hole.

Sam told Sarah to take the infants into the house and change their diapers.

Sarah said, "What do I do with the dirty ones? The basket's full."

"Rinse them in the toilet, like always, and lay them next to the basket. I'll wash them later. Sarah, I know this is a lot, just try, okay?"

Sam thought of getting the farmer's wife to help; if the basket was full, those cloth diapers hadn't been washed for several days. Sam immediately felt guilt climb up her spine; she hadn't been paying attention. This was all her fault. She stood to go get the farmer's wife.

Her mom cried, "Oh no, you don't!"

Sam stopped, peering down at her mom. Her mother continued, "Don't you dare go get that woman. If I wanted her to know my business, I would have dug this hole in the back, wouldn't I? She's making your father furious with all her meddling."

The baby at her mom's chest was screaming and screaming, only occasionally stopping to take a breath. Mom was furious, but why?

Sam tried to calm herself. She said, "The baby's crying, Momma. Hand me the last baby."

Sam's mom looked at her chest, confused.

Had she forgotten the little baby? Several seconds passed.

Sarah appeared, kneeling next to Sam.

Sarah said, "Momma, give Sam the baby."

Momma gazed at Sarah. "You are always my sweet one, Sarah. Don't worry. I'm fine really."

Sarah tried to smile but didn't succeed. "Please, Momma."

Sarah held out her little hands as her mom untied the swaddle and handed it upwards.

Sam helped Sarah lift the little one safely out of the hole, then said, "Take the baby inside, but after that, don't come back out."

Sarah started to answer, but Sam stared straight into her sister with warning in her eyes.

Sarah quietly took the crying baby inside.

Mom had a mean look. "You always are the busybody, aren't you? Always thinking you can fix things. The world is a cruel place. When will you just accept that?"

Her momma said it in a way that pierced Sam's soul.

As her mom began to scold her, Sam had seen her neck.

Clearly lined, purple fingerprints ringed her throat, while yet more purple and blue peeked out from under her mom's shirt, suggesting more damage.

Sam took a breath, the squeezing in her chest almost unbearable.

Dad was furious.

Sam said, "Mom, you're hurt. Let me help you."

"Sam, get away from me. I have to finish this. Go make yourself useful and take care of the babies. I can hear them crying. Don't you care? Haven't heard them all day till now."

Sam backed away from the hole as shovels full of dirt quickly flew out, one after another. Her eyes burned, but Sam refused to let tears fall. There was far too much work to be done.

Sam ran into the house, babies crying everywhere. Sarah had changed them and was washing the cloth diapers in the toilet, sloshing water to the side, and making.

"Sarah, where's the basket?"

"It's full, so full." Sarah was crying too, gasping for air in between sobs. Sam caught sight of those little, red-raw hands wringing out the diapers, and she hugged her sister tightly.

"Sarah, I got this. It's gonna be okay."

"No. It isn't. You can't fix Momma. No one can, or she'd be better."

"Oh, you think I can't? I can and I will. Because I love you enough."

Sarah just sobbed in her sister's arms, finally pulling away to start wringing diapers again. Sarah didn't look at her sister again. She wouldn't. Not when she had Momma's work to do!

Sam squared her shoulders, stood and walked into the dining room. Sadness crept through her as she saw the table toppled over. Dad had been home for lunch, and he wasn't just mad; he must have been furious. She tried to lift the table, but it was too heavy for her. She strained but only managed to tilt it a little and have it fall to the ground again.

The chairs were scattered, stuff everywhere.

The crying babies caught her attention. She started doing what she knew. She fed the babies, starting with the smallest and a bottle of formula.

Chapter 14

Her mother finally stopped digging as darkness fell.

Sam had washed and fed all the babies by then. Sarah had stopped crying, and with reddened swollen eyes, she had helped Sam pick the table up.

As her mother entered the house, she'd fallen against the doorway, exhausted.

Sam and Sarah helped her into the bathtub.

As Sam washed her mother, she noticed every bruise, anger welling inside her like a volcano. Sam held it in. Sarah was there, like always, gentle ... but even her sweetness had faded.

Mom wasn't talking again, and now neither was Sarah.

Sam lifted her sister into the bath with their mom, washing both of them at once. Her sister appeared so tiny to her; why hadn't she ever noticed before how little Sarah was?

Sweet Sarah; the world was just too big for her too.

Sam thought she would have to try harder to protect her.

When Sam finished drying her mother and her sister, she helped them into pajamas, resting them both into bed together. Amazed at how easily Sarah curled into her mother's arms and drifted immediately into sleep, Sam stood at the bedside.

Her mother was looking directly at her.

"Momma?" Sam said quietly.

"Bring me the little one, it has to be hungry."

Her mother's breasts had started leaking, and Sam obliged.

When she finally left the back bedroom, her mother was asleep with the tiny baby in her arms. She glanced backwards, and despite all that had transpired, her heart warmed at the scene.

Sarah cuddled next to her mom, and a baby lay safely swaddled in her mother's other arm, all sleeping sweetly as if the carnage of the wretched day had never been.

Sam walked into the kitchen, aware she had to somehow fill the hole.

Her dad would be so mad. They had picked up the mess, washed the diapers, and the table and chairs sat neatly where they belonged. Only the hole remained.

She sighed, taking a close look at her clothes.

She was filthy. No time for cleaning up now, though. Besides, she kinda liked being dirty. Sam walked out front, the porch light illuminating the giant hole.

A daunting task, Sam thought. "How could it have gotten any bigger?"

She grabbed the shovel and started moving dirt, shoveling furiously at first, her anger bursting forward with each swing of the shovel. Her breath quickened; she tired quickly. The shovel was heavy and so was the dirt. She paused, resting on the handle, sweat pouring from her forehead.

She smelled cigarette smoke. She didn't have the energy to be surprised as she noticed Matt take another drag off his lit cigarette. How long had he been there?

"That's a big 'ole." He hadn't spoken to her since 'the event' months ago, and Sam wasn't the least bit glad at that moment to see anyone.

"*And?*" she said fiercely, as if defending her whole family with a single word.

"Why are you filling a hole after dark? Nobody's gonna see it till tomorrow. It's stupid."

"I just have to. Anyway, why are you here? And why don't you mind your own business?"

"I was doing. Had to go to the store for Ma, and here you were, throwing a shovel around. Ever had anyone teach you to shovel?"

His country accent always shocked her at how terrible it was. Momma would say he should pronounce his words better, but he was missing too many teeth.

"I shovel just fine. But thanks anyhow."

"You gonna fill that whole thing by y'sel'?"

She didn't answer him now, completely out of patience.

Sam just turned her back and started shoveling again.

At some point, Matt had left but she wasn't sure when.

Each shovelful seemed to peel the anger away. Tears stood just behind her efforts, so she couldn't stop. She just couldn't, or the flood gates would burst. Then the tears were gone, and only the anger remained, pure, cold steel filling her veins. She knew she could fill this hole.

The anger propped her spine and the shovelfuls became rhythmic.

A shovelful of dirt flew past her.

"Why we gotta do this again, Matt?" The youngest Leiven boy was standing in the darkness to her right, holding a shovel of his own. He didn't look so happy to be there.

"Just shut up and use that shovel for somethin' better than a lean post," Matt said as he stood behind his brother.

As Sam glanced around her, five of the Leiven boys stood around the huge pile of dirt and started throwing it back into the hole. Sam felt one tear fall before she furiously added more dirt to theirs, metal filling her spine and willing it straight.

No more words were said as the hole was quickly filled. Stomping the ground down, it was the youngest Leiven who finally broke the silence. He was in the class just below Sam, and he was kinda odd looking. Wide-set eyes, and none too smart.

"Can we go home now, Matt?" He lit a cigarette. Matt took the lit cigarette from his brother.

"You ain't near old enough for that." Matt's other brother pushed him from behind.

Matt started to speak to Sam but stopped.

"A'right, let's move on home now, boys. Looks like it's filled." He turned to Sam. "Don't be lettin' yer ma dig another one."

She silently nodded, then whispered, "I won't."

Without another word, the boys left.

Sam watched them until she could no longer see the lit cigarette in the darkness. She was too tired to be grateful, but she knew she should have been.

As she entered the house again, her anger still seethed.

She took out one of her mother's china plates, placing it at the head of the table. She looked at her clothes next, seeing them covered in dirt. She pulled out her father's chair and sat in it.

Her eyes burned holes into the patio door as she waited. It'd be a long wait. There would be only one reason for Daddy being so late, and he would come home looking for a fight.

The station wagon threw gravel as it barreled up the driveway. Sam heard it, aware she'd been right.

He was furious and she could even feel it in the way he parked the car.

She readied herself. He slammed the car door and heavy footsteps loomed across the patio.

Her dad threw the glass door open, surprise filling his face when he saw her.

"What are you doing up? Where's your mother?" His voice slurred as he spoke, and he wobbled just a little as he stood in the doorway. Sam stood from the chair.

"She's in bed."

"Go get her. I got things to talk about."

"No." Sam could feel her fists curl.

"Don't you talk back to me, girl. I'm still in charge here."

"No, you're not. Not anymore."

"I told your momma she'd given you too much rope. I'm gonna reel you in a bit."

Her dad slid his belt off from around his waist. He curled it around one hand.

Swifter than Sam had imagined, he closed the space between them. Sam barely ducked the belt as she ran around the opposite side of the table.

He tripped over the back of the chair. Standing again, he scanned the room for Sam.

Now, she stood in the patio doorway, daring him to follow. Using one hand to grab the table and steady himself, he pushed, lurching quickly toward her.

Sam desperately wanted them outside. He couldn't wake the babies, and Momma had to sleep.

He was so loud as he reached the doorway. Sam had quickly ducked outside.

"Come here, girl. Get what's coming to you. You can't stand in a man's place and not get the results."

"I'm not running. Not anymore."

Sam felt the sting as the belt wrapped around her arm.

She pulled, shock filling his face as the belt buckle slid from his hand. Sam stood there, now the one who was holding the belt, winding it around her own arm over and over.

Seconds passed. She'd had no idea she could do that.

She didn't know what she'd thought would happen, but it wasn't that.

He lurched forward again, blind fury filling him.

Sam closed her eyes, waiting for him to close the gap between them.

A growling sound came from beside her.

Sam felt fur slide just underneath her knuckles, just under the belt that was still wrapped tightly in her hand. She immediately opened her eyes. The largest, dirtiest, curly-haired dog she'd ever seen stood at her side. Her dad was frozen just feet from her, eyes wide, staring directly at the dog. Sam dropped the belt, throwing both arms around her new friend.

"Don't hurt him!" She could feel the dog's fur rising beneath her fingers, his hackles up. A low but persistent growl rumbled deep in the dog's frame, palpable.

Her dad laughed sarcastically, violence dripping from his words. It was one way that he knew to get at her, the girl who was talking back at him. "I'm not gonna hurt that dog," he threatened.

Sam tilted her head, staring directly at her father. "I wasn't talking to you."

Silence, thick and piercing filled the space between them. The dog's burgeoning growl was the only sound now as they stood with their eyes locked.

A voice came from the darkness by the fence line. "Stop! Both of you!"

The farmer slid underneath the wire, almost breathless as he approached the patio.

"I am not gonna let this happen. I don't want to see a father beat his girl."

That was, of course, what he assumed must have been about to happen. Never would he have imagined a father could be momentarily less powerful than his own kid, barely eight years old.

And her humongous stray dog, of course.

Sam's dad eyed the farmer, a puzzled look beginning to form.

As for Sam, she wasn't sure about anything, especially what had just happened.

She felt the dog take a step forward, the huge canine's meaty shoulders coming to just below her armpit. Her eyes widened. This really was a massive animal, huge and majestic.

The farmer slowed as he approached.

Her dad stood with his shoulders squared, facing the farmer.

"Sam, if you know what's good for you, you'll go inside, right now."

Her dad didn't even glance at her, simply issuing the order as if she was still one of the minions. She was not. He no longer had the right to make her do anything.

Only she wasn't altogether sure that he realized when things had changed.

Sam stood, resting her hand on the dog. Sam felt the hair still raised but the growl was gone. She felt the outline of her matchbook in her pocket.

Quietly she said, "Happy face, sad face." Sam breathed with the words, calming herself. Suddenly, one hand curled around as much fur as she could grip. The other held tight to a belt.

She wasn't sure when she'd picked it up again. She could hear the buckle swinging, tinkling metal sounding each time it swung side to side.

The farmer, the dog, her dad and Sam just stood staring at each other.

The rooster crowed. The farmer cleared his throat.

"You don't have to do this."

"Oh, I just might." Her father glared at her, hatred and anger spilling from between his teeth. Sam felt his fury, absorbed it. It no longer had any power to frighten her.

Violence had just become a language she spoke fluently.

The farmer stepped in front of her. "You've been drinking. We've all been there. Just settle down and go to bed."

Anger slipped from her father's lips as he quietly said, "You should go home."

"Well, I'm not going home. Not until you cool down."

"This isn't your business."

Her dad's anger had clearly shifted from her to the farmer.

Sam was sure this wouldn't end well. Both men stepped forward. Sam noticed a shovel in the farmer's hand, and that he shifted it into a more useful position.

Suddenly, the glass door swung open. Sarah came running out, throwing both arms around the dog. She squealed with delight. "A dog, oh Daddy, it's a dog."

Her father shifted his weight, his eyes tearing, taking in the sight of his sweet Sarah. "Yeah, Sarah, it is. And it's the dirtiest, scruffiest dog I've ever seen."

"Oh, I can fix it," Sarah said as she bolted back inside, quickly returning with dish soap.

Sam wasn't sure how it had happened, but no one was going to fight anymore. The farmer had put the shovel down and her dad was wiping his face on his sleeve.

Sarah, oblivious to everything, was trying desperately to get the hose untangled to start washing the dog.

"I can't say thanks for coming. This still isn't your business," Dad said quietly to the farmer.

The farmer replied, "Get some rest, the sun's coming up; makes things look different."

He turned and walked up to the fence, glancing over his shoulder.

He cried out, "Sam, don't forget the eggs, and ol' Willie's waiting here for you."

Sure enough, ol' Willie was standing at the fence line, furiously stomping his hooves.

Sam grabbed her basket from the house. When she left, her dad was sitting at the kitchen table, slouched across the top, sleeping.

She heard her momma rustling in the bedroom.

Sam slid the patio door open, slipping outside.

As she passed Sarah, the dog gave a 'please help' look toward Sam. He was covered in soap and Sarah was furiously rubbing his coat.

Sam smiled. "Sarah, I'll be back to help you rinse him off in five minutes, okay?"

Sam reached the fence in record time. As she patted ol' Willie, she could feel him calming. The big bull leaned his giant head against her shoulder.

Wire from his pen hung from his horn. Sam was puzzled. She backed up, astonished.

Looking at ol' Willie again, she said, "Did you go get the farmer?"

The answer came clearly as she reached the round pen, and the farmer was repairing the wire. Ol' Willie walked back into his pen as if nothing had happened.

"Dunno what you did to ol' Willie, but I think he might be in love."

The farmer winked at Sam as she ran to the chicken boxes.

The farmer's wife said they had enough eggs for the week, and Sam could keep them all. A dozen eggs nestled in her basket, which swung in her hand as she walked through the field.

A rustle came from next to the hay bales. Sam smelled smoke.

There stood Thomas, smoking a cigarette.

"Where you going, all skippy?"

"Aren't you ever leaving?"

"I will when I'm ready." He smiled, showing his yellow teeth.

Sam wondered, *what is he up to?*

"Well, you should get ready. No one wants you here."

Thomas laughed loudly.

Sam blinked and he was gone. Mom said the hobos never stayed long, but Thomas didn't seem like he was leaving anytime soon. The lingering smell of smoke made her quicken her steps just in case hobos were not as harmless as Mom said they were.

At the back of the house, she saw her sister still furiously trying to wash soap out of the fur of a very tolerant, but unhappy hound. How could she have forgotten so soon?

Thomas creeped her out, but now, she had a dog.

Her very own dog. Sam walked closer and Sarah tipped the hose, wetting Sam and her basket.

Sarah gasped, but all Sam could do was laugh. She put her basket down and let the water cascade over her, happily washing the dirt from the night away.

Her arms were wrapped around the most wonderful dog in the entire world, and she wasn't going to let anything happen to change that.

"It's so good to hear you laugh." Mom was standing in the doorway, the patio door all the way open. Sam looked at her. She was smiling too.

How quickly things could change.

"Did you see the dog?" Sam ran her fingers through the soapy fur.

She dropped to her knees to rub the dog's belly.

"Stop it, you're in my way." Sarah was wiggling the hose, continuing to rinse the dog, getting most of the water on Sam who didn't care. This was the most wonderful morning of all.

Sam begged to her mom, "Can we keep him? Please? Will you talk to Daddy?"

"Don't look like it's up to me. I don't think you could chase that dog away. Besides, that's a royal dog."

Sam's eyes grew wide.

"A *royal* dog?" She released the fur and fell backward to get a better look at the dog.

"Your dad's asleep but he won't make that dog go away. We're Irish, remember? Well, your dad's grandfather was black Irish, but Irish nonetheless."

"What do you mean, Momma? You're not making any sense."

Her mother spoke in an Irish brogue, "I will give thee a dog I got in Ireland. He is huge of limb and for a follower equal to an able man. Moreover, he hath a man's wit and will bark at thine enemies but never at thee friends. And he will see by each man's face whether he be ill or well-disposed to thee. And he will lay down his life for thee."

Sam huffed, now more confused than ever.

Sarah giggled, finally getting the soap cleaned off the dog.

Their momma sighed, sitting down on the patio.

Sam asked her, "What's black Irish? And why is the dog royal?"

The dog shook off most of the water and soap everywhere, then rubbed up against Sam, settling next to her on the ground as if sucking up all her body heat.

Her momma was deep in thought, looking at the dog.

"Sam, this is an Irish Wolfhound. Dog of the Irish, and I have never seen one here. What I know about them, I only know from myths and books. Come here, boy. He sure is a big dog!"

The dog rose, walked over and gently nuzzled into Sam's mother's outstretched hand.

"The quote is from The Icelandic Saga."

"What's a saga?" Sarah was joining them, seated on the patio.

"Sarah, it's an old story. One that has usually been written down about a journey. Sam go get the encyclopedia, alphabet 'I.' Let's see if I'm right."

Sam ran inside, grabbed the book labeled 'I' and ran back to hand it to her mom.

Mom flipped through the pages of the book. "Here it is, girls, look."

There was a picture of the same dog that was lying on their patio. Sam fixated on the words and the image, then gasped. "So, it's true! It's an ancient breed."

Her mom laughed. "Yes. It is. An ancient Irish breed. Being here for a little Irish girl, it must think you're royalty!"

"Maybe we are royal!"

Sarah bounced on the spot, saying it with the widest of eyes as if believing it. It was the kind of cute gaze she got when she wore a princess dress or put Momma's best shoes on.

Sam smiled, rolling over on the patio.

"Sarah, don't be silly. Of course we're not royalty."

Mom cleared her throat. "This dog is a royal dog. It will take care of you. Both of you. All he needs is a name."

"I want to name him," Sarah squealed. "He's called Beautiful!"

Mom patted her daughter's shoulders. "You want to name the dog, Beautiful?"

Sarah nodded, crossing her arms determinedly.

"Well, 'beautiful' begins with B-E-A-U. Pronounced 'Beau.' So, how about *Beauregard?* Means beautiful gaze, something about the way this dog looks at your sister. Sam, have you seen this dog before?"

Sam said, "Just from a distance."

Momma asked Sarah, "What do you think? Beautiful or Beauregard?"

Sam smiled. "How about just Beau? Beautiful and Beauregard, all in one?"

Sarah nodded and threw her arms around the dog again, nuzzling into the wet fur. "I love that name!" she shouted, excited. "Beau, Beau, Beau!"

"That's a brilliant name!" enthused Mom. "Beau it is, then. Sam, the dog's not the only one who needed a bath; you're covered in dirt. Let's get some breakfast, some for you and some for the dog, then off to the tub with you. What do you girls say?"

"Momma, can we feed the dog first?" Sam looked desperately at her mother.

"Sure we can, Sam. Are those your eggs in that basket?"

"Yes," Sam said, proudly picking up her basket. "A full dozen."

"There's about three pieces of leftover ham in the kitchen and some rice. Sam, go get it and feed your dog. Then promise me you'll be getting in the tub."

Sam saw her momma pick up the shovel by the door and head out into the front yard. Even though the morning had been pleasant, Sam could feel tiredness radiate from her mother.

Sam ran and closed the front door before her mom could step outside.

"Please don't dig anymore." Sam looked pleadingly at her mom.

"I still have to fill that hole." Her mother's face was so intent that Sam just stepped aside.

Her mother stepped onto the front porch.

Sam said, "No. You don't." Her voice was trembling.

"Sam, you didn't? Have you even been to sleep? Is that why you're so dirty?" Sam's mother looked astounded at Sam, then back out at a completely filled hole. "I'm so sorry."

Sam could barely look up. This was so unbelievably painful.

Her mother hugged her, then they walked back inside, silent and pondering, clutching tightly to one another's hands. Nothing more was said about the hole. Sam was—just this one time—grateful for their never-ending silence.

Together, they quietly fixed ham and rice for the dog.

Beau showed his gratitude by eating every single bite, his massive tail wagging.

Her father sat at the table, head resting on his arms, his breathing rhythmic. An occasional snore reminded them all that he was there. No one dared to wake him.

Momma said, "Sometimes, the world's too big for us all. Even your dad."

Momma ran the tub in her bathroom. Sam lowered herself in, and feeling her muscles relax, she realized she was more tired than she'd ever been in her life.

When she finished washing, she dried off.

Her mother handed her an old t-shirt. It was so soft. Sitting on the bed was Sarah, who was busy eating scrambled eggs and buttered bread. Her mom handed her a plate.

Sam sat on the bed, eating and talking to Sarah about crayons.

Their mother brought in paper for her girls to draw on.

Sarah was so happy to share her crayons, and Sam thought nothing could be sweeter than breakfast in bed with Sarah, coloring crayons, and their mom.

She didn't even realize that sleep had overtaken her.

Chapter 15

When Sam woke up, it was dark outside. Her sister was sleeping soundly, and she thought maybe everyone was right and Sarah was filled with nothing but sweetness.

She slipped out of the bed. Her mother slept on the other side of Sarah, with the little baby.

It didn't seem so tiny anymore. Finally, that little thing was growing, putting on some weight. Gone were the skinny little legs and the bloated stomach from under-nourishment.

Sam thought maybe it was big enough to be all right without any more formula.

She glanced back one more time, thinking again how sweet they all were, just resting together as though the big world didn't exist.

She just had to find Beau, had to know the dog wasn't just another one of her dreams.

She slipped quietly past her father, still sleeping slumped over the table.

As she opened the patio door, a rustling sound came from the side of the house.

"Beau?"

A big shaggy dog appeared, sliding right up against Sam's side. The dog leaned into Sam, and Sam leaned into the dog. Tears began to stream like a river down Sam's face.

As Sam slid to the ground, the dog held her weight, easing them both onto the patio concrete.

The dog wrapped completely around Sam, resting its heavy head on her stomach.

Sam buried her head into dense gray fur. She felt the up and down of the dog's breathing, stroked the fur and glanced up into the night sky. When she cried until there were no more tears, she said, "You don't think I'm too much, do you?"

The dog responded by nuzzling into her face.

The cold concrete and early morning air were brisk, refreshing, calming.

The dog's face was just inches from hers.

She knew somehow, it would all be all right—that Beau would make it all okay. He tilted his big head, resting it again on her stomach. Sam felt safe for the first time since the 'event,' the thing no one would explain to her. The big secret seemed small at that moment. They both rested there until the rooster crowed. Sam stood. "I gotta get my basket. We've got work to do."

Dad slept late into the morning. No one woke him, and no one spoke about what had happened. Sam wasn't sure anyone knew but her, the farmer, and her dad.

She was sure that the relationship with her dad had somehow changed.

It was Saturday morning and her dad made french toast, and sausage. He had fed all the babies by the time Sam returned with her treasure, this time a whole jar of orange marmalade.

"I cannot believe you like that junk. It's nothing but sugar."

Her dad tried to sound irritated, but his smile betrayed him.

"I don't like it. *I love it!* Best thing is, I earned it myself."

"Yes. You did."

Sam asked her dad, "How big is the world?"

"My God, girl, what kind of question is that for asking over breakfast? Do you mean how big the world is? It is very big. Why?"

"Momma says sometimes, it's too big for people. I just wanted to know how big that is."

"Well. It's not all that big. I guess it depends on where you decide to live."

"That doesn't make any sense, Dad. The world is either too big or it's not. If it's this big from one place, it's the same size from all the other places."

She eyed her father as if he was clueless about the world, and she already knew more.

Perhaps she did.

Sam put her hands on her hips. "How will I know if it's too big for me?'

"The world will never be too big for you. You're kinda made for it. I think maybe God's just letting us borrow you, you know, because you're too head-strong to stay in this little town. I doubt it will hold you here."

"Is there a bigger place?"

"There are lots of bigger places, Sam. What's this all about?" She could tell her dad was getting irritated.

"Can I give some of that to the dog?" Sam pointed to the dripping from the sausage.

"No. You can't. Your mom's got some dog food. I don't know why because we aren't keeping that dog."

"Yes. We are. Mom said so."

"I don't care what she said. He can't stay."

Sam squared her shoulders, taking in a deep breath. "Yes, he can stay. You couldn't make him leave anyway." Sam looked her dad directly in the eye. "He's my dog and he has a name. His name is Beau, and he's beautiful. And he's mine."

"You keep putting yourself in a place that's not yours," her dad said, annoyed but also growing resigned. "It's a man's world, girl. You'll learn it soon enough, and this isn't your decision to make. It's mine." Her dad was gripping the spatula just a bit tighter than he should.

Sarah came running into the kitchen, sliding sideways in her sock feet on the linoleum floor.

"Mom says there's dog food." Sarah slid all the way across the kitchen floor, gliding right into the door of the cabinet below the sink, laughing as she went.

Momma was right behind her. "It's right there under the sink." Sarah opened the cabinet, and as she was pulling out the dog food, a can of formula fell and rolled across the kitchen floor.

"What's that?" Her momma picked up the can. Tossing it in the air and catching it twice, she looked at Sam. There was a note attached that said, 'Feed little one a scoop at a time.'

Her dad eyed the big almost empty can of powdered formula. "Where'd that come from?"

He was so annoyed, hating to see any kind of formula!

Sam scuffed at the ground. She grabbed the bag of dog food and started quickly toward the door.

Her father said, "You forgot your sausage dripping." He eyed her suspiciously, then added, "And don't get too comfortable with that old hound."

Sarah insisted, quick as a flash, "It's a royal hound. Momma says so."

Sarah saved Sam from coming any closer by grabbing the dripping bowl and heading toward the patio. Together, the girls headed outside through the glass door.

Sam poured the dog food out on the patio, then dribbled the sausage dripping on the food. The girls could both tell Beau was hungry by the way he eyed it. He waited so patiently.

Sam patted his head.

Sarah presented the food with a bow, and Beau ate.

"He's so *beau*-tiful!" Sarah threw both arms around the dog's neck.

"Sarah, at least let him eat."

"He doesn't mind!" Sarah still wouldn't let go of the dog's neck.

Mom called out, "Time to come eat, girls." Both girls left the dog and scampered up onto the chairs at the table. They ate, and Sam slathered orange marmalade on her toast.

"Can I have some?" Sarah's eyes pleaded with Sam. Begrudgingly, she handed the jar to her little sister. Sam's eyes widened, astounded as she watched her sister.

"You're not supposed to mix it with syrup," advised Sam.

Sarah answered her sister by putting a syrup and orange marmalade-soaked piece of toast into her mouth.

"Sam, not everyone is gonna do what you say," Dad said with an only halfway joking tone.

"Sarah can do what she wants; she's my sister."

Sam straightened her back. She wasn't gonna be made fun of this morning. "Besides, maybe it's good." Sarah nodded, mouth still full of breakfast.

Her lips and cheeks were smeared with sticky sweet stuff.

Momma looked at Sarah, then back at Sam.

She chuckled, then started feeding a baby seated to her right. "Sarah is your sister, and you are right to defend her. But Sam, we're your family, not the enemy."

"Let's talk more about this dog, why don't we?" Her dad eyed her thoughtfully.

"Nothing to talk about. He's staying."

"Such a big dog might hurt you girls. I don't want you getting bitten. We don't know anything about this animal."

"He's Beau, not *this animal*. And I know this dog." Sam said it a little more forcefully than she meant, but she wasn't backing down now.

"Sam, I just never know what you're going to do next. You know you aren't in charge here."

"When it comes to that dog, that's what I am: in charge. You aren't going to do anything."

Momma took in a deep breath.

"Sam, we are your parents. Your dad decides if the dog is gonna stay or not. And that's going to be the final word on the matter. I don't want to hear you answering back."

"No, he doesn't have the final word," Sam protested, not willing to give up Beau for anything or anyone. "That's my dog." Sam stood. She was supposed to ask to be excused from the table, but she said nothing. Sam stomped out toward the patio, leaving her half-eaten breakfast.

"Don't open that door. You can't leave this table without permission."

Her dad was starting to sound furious.

She didn't care. She opened the sliding glass door anyway, in defiance of him.

She heard her father's chair creak as he went to stand.

"Good God, someone's gotta teach that girl a lesson."

She heard her mother answer, "Just let her go. It's been a tough few days."

Just as her father reached the door, Sam turned and faced her father. The dog was at her side again. This time, there was no growl. They both just stared reluctantly at him.

"I'm not coming back inside."

Her father seemed to settle something inside his head. "You're too much, Sam. Really, it's gonna cause you trouble. Go work your attitude out. Just be home by lunch, that's all I'll say."

"I'm taking the dog."

"You said he's yours anyway."

He slammed shut the patio door.

Then they ran, Sam and her dog. They ran straight into the woods, down the trails, running past the big oak, past their special hiding place, sliding and pushing past the foliage.

She ran until she'd lost all her air, until the world wasn't so big anymore, and until Sam was so tired and breathless she just ground to a gasping halt, keeping Beau in her line of sight.

Beau wasn't even tired! As a matter of fact, he had just been trotting along as if they'd been out on some casual stroll. She smiled brightly, beaming.

Then there was a splash in the water.

Sam put her finger to her lips, telling Beau to be quiet. They eased up toward the creek bed. She saw Theresa first, then Matt standing next to her. Matt was pulling up a rope with six big catfish strung on one, then he hauled in the other, pulling it proudly out of the water.

"That should be it. You can feed 'em all wi' these." Matt was holding the fish up, looking at them swinging on the rope. He smiled, tapping Theresa fondly on the shoulder.

Theresa sighed, saying, "Nope. Not enough yet. My brothers eat first and I won't get any. I need more."

Matt said, "Well then, looks like we're eatin' 'ere."

He turned. Sam was almost sure he'd spotted her, but he just kept picking up sticks.

"Matt, there's no time. I got chores. Just help me get a few more."

Sam noticed there were several jugs in the water. She was curious, but not enough to let herself be seen just yet. She wiggled, questions brimming in her head.

"You know you don't have to help me."

"I know." Matt kicked at the ground, tossing a baseball in the air and he caught it. One of the jugs started bobbing in the water. Matt put his baseball back in his pocket. He used a stick to pull the jug near the shore. Grabbing it, he pulled a line out of the creek. A catfish was attached to the end of it. "I wish you'd just let me cook one. It wouldn't take a minute."

"That's a little one." The fish flopped and splashed Theresa with water. She laughed as Matt took it off the hook. "Should I toss it into the water?"

"Hmm …" Theresa looked at the little fish.

Sam watched in fascination as Matt adjusted the jug and sent it sailing back into the water. She had so many questions about the jugs. Sam was pondering if they'd talk to her.

Just then, Beau trotted out and sat right next to Matt.

"Crap," Sam said as she bolted after the dog.

"That's a huge dog." Theresa took a step back. "Kevin had a big dog; it was so mean."

Matt swung the fish in front of the dog. The dog watched it swing side to side but didn't move.

"His name is Beau. I promise he won't hurt you." Sam patted Beau on the head.

She watched as Matt knelt, handing the little fish to the dog who took the fish gingerly. As they watched, the dog eased into the creek bed.

Matt laughed, asking, "Wha', your dog's gonna wash its dinner?"

Beau held the fish just under the water.

Astonished, Theresa knelt at the edge of the water. "He's letting it get its strength."

Matt looked surprised too, exclaiming, "Never seen nothin' like that before."

He leaned into the water, reaching for the fish. "Gimme that fish back. We caught it."

The giant dog waded just out of Matt's reach.

Theresa put her hand on his back, and in a hushed voice, she said, "No, wait."

Sam waded into the creek, standing right next to Beau, who was still holding the fish. She started to take it back to Matt, but something about the tenderness in Beau's eyes made her pause. Beau's nose was just above the water.

He held the fish just below the surface.

Sam put her face just next to Beau's. In the water, she saw the fish moving its body side to side, Beau barely holding the fish in his teeth. Then without any fanfare, Beau opened his mouth.

The fish paused, almost suspended for an instant, then calmly swam away.

Sam smiled and hugged Beau.

Sam thought it might have been the most beautiful thing she'd ever seen.

Then Matt huffed, "Dammit. Fish are for eatin'. Dumb hound."

"Don't know how you can say that; you gave it to him!" Sam was wading out of the creek, the dog loping right behind her.

"Where'd you get that big 'ol dog, anyhow?" Matt held out his hand. Theresa was behind him. Sam was puzzled because she looked scared, as in really, really scared.

"He found me. That's what the farmer says, anyway." Sam stroked the dog, rubbing her face in his shaggy wet fur, smiling proudly.

Theresa gasped, backing up into the tree line.

Beau stopped. He angled his head, his eyes fixated on her.

Matt stepped in quickly between the dog and Theresa. "She don't like dogs."

"Who doesn't like dogs? Theresa? Why not? *Everyone* should like dogs."

A jug began bobbing up and down in the water. "That's got to be a big one." Theresa moved slowly toward the water, keeping one eye on the dog suspiciously.

Sam huffed, "He won't hurt you."

"Just make the dog keep away from 'er." Matt sounded overly serious to Sam, but she stepped in between the dog and Theresa. "Come on, Beau, let's go over here."

Sam was just glad they were talking to her, and it wasn't super odd. Sam didn't know what to expect; it just seemed that people didn't talk to her the way they used to.

The dog walked behind Sam, who then squatted on a root.

She watched as Matt used a stick to pull the jug toward the bank, then tugged out a huge catfish. Theresa smiled. "That'll do. Just a few more and we're done."

Beau shuffled, taking two steps toward Theresa. She jumped, looking absolutely terrified, and fell back into the creek. Sam was there in a flash. "I'm so sorry!"

Sam said it as she helped Theresa out of the water, feeling her shaking.

Matt swung at the dog, creating space for Theresa.

"Stop it." Sam stood between Matt and Beau.

Matt said seriously, "Then ya keep 'im back. I told you!"

Theresa started to cry.

Sam kept repeating, "I am so, so sorry," over and over.

Matt added the fish to the others on the rope, then took three steps to join the girls.

"It ain't your fault. Why you always gotta make everything your fault? Stuff just happens; ain't no reason, just does." Matt sounded irritated. So irritated, it made Sam shut her mouth.

He helped Theresa up onto the bank. The dog settled by the edge of the woods, watching.

Matt looked at Theresa. "She's right though. That dog ain't got a mean bone in him."

"But what if it decides to be mean?"

Theresa looked lost. Matt eased her down on a rock by the creek.

"Ya gonna be okay."

Another jug bounced. Sam couldn't help herself.

"What are the jugs for? How are you doing that? Do the fish just attach themselves? What's at the end of the string?" Sam wanted to know how it worked. She just had to know.

Matt cocked his head to the side. "Ain't you ever been jug fishin' before?"

"No." Sam looked wide eyed at Matt and then Theresa. Both kids laughed. Sam crossed her arms. "Don't laugh at me."

"We ain't really laughin'. Just ponderin'." Matt smiled.

"Pon-der-in? What's that?"

Theresa interjected, laughing, "It's when ya thinkin'. Kinda like what you do *all* the time. You bein' so *intellectual* an' all."

Sam stiffened her back and stood to leave. She wasn't gonna stay and get made fun of. Just as she reached the tree line, Matt called out, "Ya sure ya don't wanna pull this one in?"

Sam turned and ran over.

Matt had the stick wrapped around the line. He handed it to Sam.

"Now pull."

He helped Sam pull in the fish, a line attached to the jug. As Sam pulled the line out, she saw the hook and wiggling on the end was a big ol' catfish. Sam smiled wide, beaming ear to ear.

Matt took the fish out of the water and Sam grabbed it. It slipped to the ground, wiggling. Sam laughed. Matt and Theresa did too.

Sam was thinking, *this is what it used to be like to have friends.*

Matt straightened, looking very serious. He tugged both the jug and line out of the water.

Finally, he spoke. "The jug floats on top of the water. Ya put whatever ya got on the hook for bait. These cats will eat anythin', but ol' food works better, food that smells. When the jug bounces, you got a fish."

Sam held the line. The jug's cap was on tight, and the line wrapped around the handle.

And there, right at the end of the line, was a sharp hook.

"Here." Matt handed her the nastiest thing she'd ever seen, something that stank to high heaven. She gingerly accepted it, holding it at arms' length.

"It's a liver. Chicken liver. Put it on the hook," he insisted.

Sam did, marveling at how easy it slid on. But then again, it was foul and slimy. She leant forward, rinsing her hand at the water's edge, getting rid of the feeling and the stink.

"Now throw it," Matt said as he gestured to the stream.

Sam threw it as hard as she could, sending the chicken liver flying off the hook. The jug flipped and landed on a rock. Theresa laughed so hard she had to sit down.

Matt stepped forward, reaching for the jug and in one motion, he loaded the hook and threw the jug perfectly. The hook followed the jug, settling down below the water.

Sam was standing with her hands on both hips. She stared at Theresa who was pointing now, laughing so much she could barely breathe. Sam couldn't believe she was laughing!

"Girl, we ain't gonna fight. I'm a full three years older than your little ass."

"I'm not little, and I may not be able to throw a jug, but at least I'm not dirty and smelly *all* the time!" Sam regretted saying the words as soon as they'd flown from her mouth.

She wouldn't back down, just like the hook couldn't stop once it hit the water.

Matt stepped in between the girls.

"You know, not everyone's got a ma living at home or a pop who works an' all!"

Sam couldn't hold eye contact with the boy, thoroughly ashamed of herself.

Theresa wasn't smiling anymore either.

Sam walked up to the trees.

"Why you always leavin', always overdoin' things, then runnin' off like you ain't done nothin'?"

Matt shook his head, then was preoccupied by another bouncing jug in the water.

Sam glanced back one more time. She didn't really want to leave. She hadn't visited anyone her own age in so long that she was aching for it. She hung her head, then turned.

"You know you ain't gotta leave," Theresa said. She was looking at the ground, drawing circles with a stick. "I'll pet the dog if you stay."

"I didn't mean it." Sam still hadn't turned around. She knelt next to Beau, brushing her fingers across the dog's fur. Beau stretched.

"You could say sorry." Theresa was looking at Sam's back and she could feel it.

"Aren't you mad at me?"

"It was the truth. Can't get mad about that. You think you're the only kid who's ever said that to me?"

"I'm so sorry Kevin got fired." Sam made a huffing noise and took a step forward to leave.

It was Matt who broke the silence this time.

"He deserved it."

Sam turned. "What did you say?"

"He said he deserved it." Theresa said it with force, putting her hand gingerly on Matt's shoulder. "His words don't always come out right."

"I can always understand him. I just … Well. Isn't Kevin your brother?"

"*And* Bobo's my dad. Don't mean I like either of 'em."

Beau stepped forward and Theresa gingerly put a finger on his haunch.

Matt was pulling all the jugs in, wrapping up the lines, storing them in a hole at the bottom of a big tree. "My momma says family always sticks together. Said I can never forget that."

Sam walked back toward Theresa. She had questions now.

"Why are you older than me? We're in the same grade," she wanted to know.

"You sure are full of yersel', askin' all kinds of questions. Can't you just be normal?"

Matt sounded very upset and seemed agitated.

Theresa tossed a small rock at him, missing and hitting the water.

Matt said, looking at Theresa from the corner of his eye, "Ain't none of her business."

He took out his baseball, tossed it up in the air, then caught it again.

He repeated the process, preoccupying himself. Sam could tell he was irritated, but she wanted to know stuff. *Needed* to know stuff.

Theresa answered her question. "I failed first grade twice and started late, too. Hey, why don't we swap questions?"

Sam froze. No one but Sarah ever asked her questions about anything that really mattered.

"What do you mean?"

"I'll answer your questions, but I get to ask you some."

Sam made a clicking sound with her tongue, calling the dog. Beau stretched, stood, and walked over to her.

Theresa was settling on a big rock on the ground.

Sam sat too, and as she did, Beau sat behind her, and she leaned into the dog.

"Okay." Sam said it, but she didn't look as if it was at all okay. She was actually terrified that she might say the wrong thing.

"Here's a question for you. Why does your mom call you like you're a hog?"

Normally, this would make Sam so defensive, but Theresa asked it as if it wasn't a big deal. As if maybe lots of people did weird stuff like that.

Sam thought about it. "'Cause Momma can't whistle, but I can hear her call almost all the way to the country store." She stood tall, waiting for Theresa to make fun of her.

But Theresa didn't.

Matt lit a cigarette and leaned into Theresa, wrapping his arm around her.

She smiled at him, leaning back into his arms.

"My girl's somethin', ain't she?" Matt kissed Theresa gently, on the cheek.

Sam gasped. "Your girl? Are you dating?"

Theresa smiled sweetly, answering for him, "Not really, 'cause you can't exactly date if you ain't got money for nothing. We're 'going' together." She winked at Matt.

"We gonna marry when she turns fourteen," he said, his eyes not leaving Theresa.

Sam had no doubt he was serious.

"Matt, my daddy ain't gonna give you no note."

Matt smiled. "Then I'll drive ya 'cross state lines. We gits married an' starts livin' for real."

"You can get married at fourteen? Where? Momma says you shouldn't marry till you get outta college."

"And your momma spends actual money on those big books, *and* you be blessin' everybody. *And* she pulls out her boobs in public for yo' brothers to hang off of, *and* you carry a squid matchbox every place you go." Matt sounded so mad.

Sam didn't understand what she'd done to make him this mad at her.

Theresa interrupted, saying, "Stop it. She ain't got no meanness. She's just don't know about mindin' her business is all." She looked curiously at Sam. "Why do you be blessing everyone?"

Sam swallowed hard.

"Momma said you have to say 'God bless' to people to chase away the evil eye."

"I ain't been givin' you no evil eye!" Matt stood, throwing his cigarette out over the water.

"Please don't be mad." Sam's lip quivered. "Anyway, I quit saying it to people with the evil eye because it doesn't work." Sam scuffed at the ground, swinging her left leg. "So, no matter. Now, I say it instead of thank you to people that deserve it."

Theresa was very interested. "What's the evil eye?"

"Momma says it's when people look at you all jealous, but that's not true either. Mostly, men have it. I know when I see it because it makes my stomach hurt."

Sam adjusted herself, readying to educate Theresa.

"Yeah. Kevin has it. He makes my belly hurt when he looks at me."

Theresa was so serious that Sam was at a loss for words.

Sam had thought all this time she was the only one who noticed it.

"He better not even look at you."

Matt threw his baseball hard into a nearby tree. It hit and dropped to the ground, and he huffed, obviously irritated. He walked over and picked up his ball.

Theresa scolded him. "Hey. That tree didn't do anything to you."

Sam was determined not to let this moment pass.

Theresa needed to talk more, and Sam needed to be sure Theresa knew what *she* knew.

"Yes. He does, and so does the man who lives at Matt's house. You know, the one who's—" Sam leaned in and whispered to Theresa—"not his dad."

Matt commented, "Uh oh, ain't no secrets here."

Theresa looked knowingly at Sam.

"Matt, is your stepdad okay to live with?" She didn't take her eyes off Sam when she said it.

"Heck, no. It's why I talk funny. It's from the first beltin' I took off him."

Sam gasped out, "I'm so sorry." She'd never heard something like that; something so terrible would have never occurred to her!

"An' you, Sam, quit actin' all high and mighty. You ain't perfect, neither. Tell us, what's with that matchbook you always carryin'?"

"It's kinda magic." Sam wasn't sure she could explain what she didn't even understand.

She paused, thinking.

"Can I see it?" Matt said, genuinely interested.

"Sure." Sam pulled a torn and tattered match-book from her pocket.

Watching Matt turn it over in his hand, Sam was suddenly terrified. What was she going to do when it was completely unusable? What if he wrecked what was left of it?

Matt looked puzzled. "How's it work?" He opened and closed it. "Ain't no matches in it."

"No matches, no but it helps you make better choices. Not sure how it works but it does. Here, let me show you." Sam took the matchbox. Sliding it open on one side, she said, "Happy face." Then sliding it to the other side, she said, "Sad face."

"Girl, you ain't makin' no sense. How does that help you do anythin'?"

Theresa reached out and took the box. "Wait a minute."

She also slid the box open and closed, open and closed.

"It's great." She started smiling. "Smiley face, sad face! It slows everything down. It's perfect."

Sam was looking wholly confused.

Theresa continued, "You can't stay mad, Matt. Look at this. Try to be mad now!"

Matt looked as confused as Sam was feeling.

Sam smiled. "Is that why it's magic?"

"My mama used to say before she died, God rest her ..." Theresa looked up at the sky. "... that if you slow the world down, the devil can't catch you."

Sams shook her head. "Why would the world be trying to 'catch you'?"

Theresa handed the matchbox back to Sam. "The devil's best friend is anger. That matchbox chases it away."

Sam huffed, now she was wholly mixed up inside. She didn't understand any of it, but all that really mattered was that it worked. She could think clearly as long as she had her matchbox.

Matt reached out and Sam handed the matchbox to him again.

"You girls, never make any good sense." He walked out, sliding it from side to side, a puzzled look on his face. "Ain't no devil in this little box."

The dog shifted its weight behind Sam. She voiced loudly, "You promised to pet Beau."

Sam moved to make room for Theresa.

At first, Theresa stood stock still, then in one sweeping motion, she shifted across to the rocks next to the dog. Beau looked over Sam's shoulder at the girl who now sat by his haunches.

Theresa looked terrified. "You sure he don't bite?"

"Positive." Sam smiled and laid her arm along the back of the dog.

Smiling, she ran her hand along his side.

Theresa was trembling, and Sam leaned over. "Like this. Go ahead, it's nice." Sam petted the haunches of Beau, careful to follow the contours of the fur. Then she pulled back.

Beau looked at her with puzzled eyes.

"What the ... dang it!" Matt dropped the matchbox into the water with a gasp. "I swear, I didn't mean to drop it."

Sam darted into the water, making a grab for the tiny box. She found it, grabbing it, then she squeezed; the worn cardboard was wet and falling apart.

She looked at it with dismay, shoving it into her pocket. Disbelief crowned in the corners of her eyes, and a tear fell. She wiped it. *I can't let them see me cry. That would be awful.*

As if on cue to save Sam from another embarrassment, a sound erupted from the distance. "Soweeeeee!"

Matt walked toward Sam. "I didn't mean nothin'."

"I gotta get home."

Sam turned, running toward the sound of the hog call.

She didn't look up at Matt, didn't say goodbye to Theresa either.

No, she just ran and ran, the wind in her hair. There was something that cleaned her insides when she ran. She looked down, Beau loping beside her, keeping pace with her.

Sam stopped by the big oak, catching her breath.

She looked down, seeing footprints, big boot-prints pushed into the clay, just above the tree roots on the hill. Sam stood in the prints, able to see through the trees from just here. Theresa had packed up and was carrying her fish, while Matt was following behind with the fishing jugs.

Beau looked up at her, blowing a concerned huff out of his nose.

Sam squatted, feet still in the prints, and he patted Beau on the head.

"Boy, he's gonna come for us. I just know it." She saw the shadow of a man in her mind, just standing there, looking in through her window. She could almost see him.

Almost.

"SOOOWWWWEEEEEE!"

Sam reached in her pocket. "Dang it!"

The matchbox fell apart as she tried to pull it out. She didn't know how she ever got by without it, and she had lots of questions for her momma.

Chapter 16

Summer days came and went, and these days, Sam no longer went very often to get eggs. The farmer's wife had said that because it was summer, she could just come on the mornings she was awake. Summer was a confusing time for Sam.

The days were so long, but they passed so swiftly she couldn't keep track. This particular morning, she was *way* busy. It had rained and the creek bed was full of treasure.

"Sarah, look, I found one!" Sam pointed into the water. "It's just here under this rock. You hold the jar. I'm gonna move it."

Sarah dutifully squatted by the rock in the water.

Sam could see her concentrating as she positioned the glass.

To Sam, she whispered, "Ready."

Sam pulled on the large flat rock. As she did, several fish scattered. Looking into the water, she saw the mudbug flick its tail, propelling itself backwards. "There it is, Sarah, get it!"

Sarah swiftly moved the jar through the water, narrowly missing the crawdad.

Sam watched it zoom under a nearby rock.

Sarah slumped, saying mournfully, "I'm just not fast enough."

"You're plenty fast enough; they're just faster, that's all! That was a big one."

"Where do they come from?'

"I don't know for sure. I think they're baby lobsters."

Sarah giggled, falling backwards into the shallow water. She giggled so hard she dropped the glass. "Lobsters grow in the ocean."

"And where do you think water comes from?"

"The sky! I know it comes from the sky when the clouds cry, and God moves his furniture."

Sarah stopped giggling. Sam could almost feel her thinking.

She couldn't help but smile at her sister. Sam pushed a splash of water at Sarah and said, "Let's go ask Momma. She'll tell you it comes from the ocean."

Sam helped her sister up. Sarah grabbed another jar with two crawdads in it off the creek bed while Sam retrieved the jar from the water.

The girls walked up the trail. When they reached their spot, Sarah slid under the brush. Summer had made the spot almost invisible with greenery by now, but both girls knew exactly where it was. Sam joined her sister underneath the privet. The branches hung low, heavy with leaves. Inside the opening, Sam grabbed an orange from a paper bag in the corner. She peeled it, offering half to Sarah. The girls both leaned against the tree trunk in the center.

Sarah was the only kid Sam knew who could eat an orange loudly.

She slurped the juice, munching so happily that it made Sam smile wide, enough that she could feel the happiness reaching her brain. Happiness was like that. It could reach all the way inside her, making her believe for just a minute that the world was wonderful.

A squirrel ran through the branches, chittering loudly when it saw the girls.

It was so noisy that two birds flew out of the brush to safety.

Sarah gasped, almost choking on her orange.

Sam giggled, saying, "It's just a tree rat."

"Why do you call them that?"

"Because that's what they are. People eat them but we shouldn't because they're just rats that live in the trees."

"They sure are noisy."

"He's just letting everyone know we're here. If you listen in the woods, you can hear almost everything."

"Is that what you do when you go out at night?"

"How do you know I go outside?"

"You're not there anymore in your room when I look for you."

Sam felt guilt pulse through her veins. Sarah had looked for her and she hadn't been there.

Quiet replaced the laughter. How could she tell her sister what she'd been doing?

Shame shrouded her mind as she thought of the many nights curled up with Beau on the patio when she was afraid she couldn't ever scream again.

Nights of wandering in the woods, sure she could find the man, armed with a kitchen knife. Sam couldn't tell her sister that she would always wake up if the crickets stopped.

Summer had chased away the man from her window. Summer had given her time, but she wasn't sure how much. She hadn't found any more footprints since that day she'd last seen Matt.

She was sure he would be back, but she couldn't tell Sarah any of it. She just couldn't.

"You're too big to be still looking for me. You should stay in your own room with the babies." Sam said it a bit more harshly than she meant it, and Sam was sure Sarah had felt it.

"But I'm not a baby anymore. I'm five!" Sarah was now standing, looking down at Sam.

"Then you shouldn't be looking for me when you're scared if you're *so* big."

Quite right, Sarah retorted, "I didn't go looking for you because I was scared, though, did I? I never said that." She scuffed at the ground with one foot. "Anyway, I'm gonna tell Momma you go outside by yourself at night." Sarah crossed her arms and huffed, sulking.

"These are my woods, and it's my business."

Sam stood looking fierce and sounding even stricter. She didn't want Sarah venturing anywhere near those trees; for goodness sakes, she wasn't sure what was out there.

Sarah carried on, still not willing to let go of the topic, "I knew you went into the woods. I just knew it. I looked all around the house and couldn't find you."

Fear shot through Sam. She grabbed her sister's arm and shook her hard.

"You can *never* go outside at night. Never. You hear me? Never!"

She shouted so loud, her sister trembled. Sam had lost all control.

Tears filled her sister's eyes, spilling down her cheeks. Sarah pulled away, wiping her eyes. Looking down, she said, "I just wanted to be where you were."

Sam could feel her sister's anguish, and she couldn't be angry. The thought of her sister outside, alone, in the dark, petrified Sam.

"Sarah, it's my job to keep you safe. I can't do that if you won't stay in. Sometimes, things happen that little girls don't need to know about."

Sarah squared her shoulders. "I'm not that little."

"You so are," insisted Sam in their usual playful way, trying to get a smile back on Sarah's sad face. "Did you tell Momma?"

Sarah sniffed, wiping her nose on her sleeve. "No." Sarah was still looking down, pushing leaves around with her foot.

"Good. Don't." Sam wasn't at all sure her sister would keep the secret. "Promise me you'll stay inside at night."

"It was scary though."

"What was?"

"Walking around the house, looking for you in the dark."

Sam hugged her sister. "I promise to only go out onto the patio if *you'll* promise to not go out at all."

"I promise, but I need you sometimes," said Sarah in a very small voice.

"And I always need you."

Sam could smell the sweetness in the air around her sister. She thought that there wasn't anything she wouldn't do for her, now hugging her tight.

They both sat under the canopy and finished their oranges. They chatted about squirrels and crawdads just a little, neither girl saying much else.

Sam slid out first and reached back in to help her sister out from under the canopy. A sudden rustling sound came from beside them, and Beau emerged from under the brush somewhere.

He stretched. Sarah hugged him, and he took his place right next to Sam.

The girls lazily headed toward the house, Sam marveling at everything in her woods. She knew all the trees, knew all the burrows where she imagined little animals lived. She'd poke a stick in them periodically to see if something would come out, but much to her dismay, nothing ever did. She imagined huge groundhogs or foxes living in the holes.

Just then, a small deer ran across the path in front of them.

"Do you think that's the one?" Sarah gasped.

"Maybe. It's small enough to have been new this year."

Sarah grabbed her sister's hand and squeezed. "I hope it is."

Sam smiled, looking down at her sister.

Sarah said, "I just hope it's okay."

"That fawn is fine. Mommas take good care of their babies." Sam pulled away from her sister. "Race you home."

Sam ran, sliding around the curves of the trails. She felt the wind, and could hear her sister coming behind her. Sam slowed just a little, waiting for Sarah to almost catch up, then she'd shoot forward again. The two girls burst out of the woods into the yard, heading toward the patio.

Sam pushed stretching out in front, leaving her sister behind.

She curved to the right around the corner of the house, where she saw her momma filling something

with water from the hose. Sam slid right into the corner of the patio.

"Whoa, girl." Momma's smile broadened the
second she saw Sam. "I thought I heard you two
coming. I could hardly miss it, could I?"

Sarah made it to the patio still carrying the jar.
"Look, Momma! Crawdaddies!"

"Oh my, look at those." Momma put down the
hose and turned off the water. She wiped her hands
on a towel hanging at her waist. The not-so-little-
anymore baby was sleeping swaddled next to Mama's
breast. She took the jar from Sarah. "Wow they're big
ones, aren't they."

Sarah smiled. "Yes. Are they baby lobsters? Does
the water come from the sea or the sky? I said that
the sky cries the water but Sam said it comes from
the sea. I have never seen the sea. Is it big? Are there
more crawdaddies in the sea? Oh! And we saw a little
deer. Could it be a baby from this spring? How fast
do baby deer grow?"

Mama interrupted Sarah with happy laughter and a look of big-eyed bewilderment. "Boy, oh
boy. You sure have a lot of questions for a summer
afternoon."

Sam leaned on the side of the house just behind
them both. "Been going on all day. She's got questions about everything." Sam smiled as she playfully
rolled her eyes.

"Right now, you two clean up. I filled the cooler
so you could rinse the river off before you come

inside." The cooler was the most fun in the whole world.

"You two jump in and I'll get some towels. Your dad's bringing home a surprise. You'll both wanna be in pajamas for this one. Sam, where's my other jar?"

Sam thought for a second, but she couldn't remember.

"Momma, I lost it." Sam looked down at her toes, all her excitement draining from her.

"Easy, Sam. It isn't the end of the world. It's just a jar." Sam met her gaze, hopeful. Momma added, "Pick it up next time you're at the stream and see it."

Momma smiled down at Sam. In the center of the patio, a large green Coleman cooler was filled to the brim with cold water. Momma made a motion, indicating the cooler was now open.

Sam and her sister squealed with delight. They jumped in and out of the cooler on the patio. They splashed each other and dunked their heads inside.

Momma came out with a freshly dried towel for each girl. "Now strip off those dirty clothes, wrap up and go get your pajamas on. Dinner's almost ready. Your dad will be home soon."

As Sarah took off her clothes, she said, "What's the surprise?"

Sam couldn't hold it in either. "Yeah, Momma, what is it?"

"Well, it wouldn't be a surprise if I told you, would it?" Momma smiled brightly at them both, shrugging her shoulders.

Both girls squealed with anticipation.

Wrapped in their towels, they headed quickly to find their pajamas.

By the time the station wagon pulled up the driveway, they were pink from the bath and dressed in fresh pajamas while Momma was putting the finishing touches to dinner. Sam opened the patio door and ran toward the station wagon. She reached it just as her dad was getting out.

"What's the surprise? What did you bring us?" Sam was looking in the windows of the station wagon. The biggest box she'd ever seen was wedged into the back.

Her dad opened the back hatch and smiled. "Check it out, Sam!"

Sam excitedly asked again, unable to wait, "What is it?"

Sarah joined them. "Daddy, what is it?" He picked Sarah up.

"It is the newest thing! A 1978 Zenith System 3-Color console television set." Daddy made motions as though he was advertising when he said it. Sam couldn't wait to see it for real, marveling at the big box. "How are we gonna get that inside? It's so big?"

"Your mom and I will get it. Don't you worry. Look up at the roof! See it?"

Sam couldn't see anything. She backed away from the house to try and view the whole roof.

A metal thing protruded from the corner. "Sam, do you see it? It's a big new antenna for the new television. Biggest and best there is."

Sarah looked too, putting her hand to her eyes to shield them from the sun.

"How did anyone get that thing up there?"

Their dad smiled and answered, "I did it while you girls were out playing."

Sarah's eyes were wide with wonder.

"Well, I still don't see it." Sam was shielding her eyes with one hand, squinting up. "I'm trying to."

Her dad came up behind her, placed Sarah on the ground, and lifted her up to his shoulders. "You see it now?"

There it was! Huge metal rods protruded from a center post in a grid-like fashion.

"I see it! It's huge!"

Dad gently set her down, and once she knew where it was, she couldn't *un*see it. Her mind began brewing all her questions, forgetting about anything else.

"Daddy, why does it look like that? Will lightning get it? Is that thing really safe? How come you had to put it up so high? How does it connect to the TV? Is the box heavy? Was the antenna heavy? Can I go up there? How are you gonna hook it up to the TV? Will we be able to move it? It looks heavy. *Is* it heavy, Dad?"

"Whoa, girl." Her dad interrupted her with a huge smile and his hand up. He loved answering her questions. "Yes. Lightning might get it, but it's been made special. Yes, it is safe. I put it as high as I could to get the best signal. It's not heavy. You *cannot* go up there. There's wires that hook up to the TV. As for moving it, well, watch this. Just keep watching it."

Her dad disappeared inside the patio doorway.

Sam walked back. She could see the antenna now that she knew where it was, by standing on her tippy toes. She blinked. Did it move? Yes, the antenna moved!

No more climbing up high to adjust it; it moved all by itself. "Oh, Daddy, it moves, it moves!" Sam squealed and started jumping up and down.

Her dad came back outside, looking very accomplished.

"Oh, Daddy, did I really see it move?"

"Sure did. It moves side to side; we'll still have to adjust it occasionally but looks like we won't be getting up on the roof that much anymore."

Sam ran up and grabbed her dad.

He swallowed her in a huge hug.

"Oh Daddy, that's so wonderful. I can't believe it."

Sarah was still looking at the box in the back of the station wagon, running her hand across the pictures. "Is it really a television in a cab-i-net?" Sarah was so amazed that she just stared at the picture. Daddy grabbed her by the shoulders. "That thing is bigger than you are!"

Momma walked to the station wagon, the baby gone from the swaddle around her shoulders.

"Let's get that monster of a TV inside." She was smiling. "You girls go in. Dinner's on the table. Sam, remember to feed the babies."

Sam and Sarah scrambled inside. Putting one baby at a time up at the table, Sam dutifully fed them mashed carrots, potatoes, and stew. Sarah sat and devoured her food. They stopped briefly as the TV was gently maneuvered into the living room.

Sam thought her mother might be the strongest woman in the world; she carried just as much weight as Daddy and never once faltered. Inside a few minutes, Momma joined them at the table.

"Did you say grace?" Both girls looked at their momma.

Sarah smiled. "Sorry momma, we forgot?" She smiled, talking through a mouthful of food.

Mom put a hand on Sam's shoulder. "Well, it's not every day that we get a new TV." She smiled too. "Get yourself a plate; I got the last baby."

Sam piled a plate as full as she could. Playing all day at the creek made a girl terribly hungry. Sam tasted the food as if it was the first time she had ever had stew.

"Oh, Momma, this is the best dinner, and this is the best day."

Sam stuffed another full fork into her mouth.

Mom said, "You were both right."

Sarah's head tilted, listening intently, whereas Sam thought and thought, but had no idea what

Momma meant. "Right about what?" Sam asked thoughtfully.

"About the rain. The clouds get water from the sea and other places. The clouds carry it until it's too heavy to bear. Once it's so full, it can't hold any more, so it lets it out. Then, it's rain."

She picked up the jar from the table, then explained, "Crawdaddies are crayfish. They aren't lobsters. Well, kinda. They're very different from lobsters, but kinda the same because they look alike, just one is smaller. Lobsters live in the sea, where everything is bigger. Crayfish are only in freshwater, like the creek. The sea is salt water, so that means you can't drink the water in the sea. Sarah, was there anything else?"

Sarah smiled, food still in her mouth, bouncing on her seat. "The deer. The baby deer."

"Oh yes, the deer. That one, I'm not really sure about."

Sam looked up from her food. "But Momma, you're supposed to know everything."

"No one knows everything, and anyone who pretends to is a fool."

There was a scratch at the patio door. Beau looked longingly at Sam. "Can he come in? Momma, can I please let him inside? I promise I'll clean up after him."

"Your Dad barely allows him to stay in the yard. I think coming in is absolutely out of the question. You can, however, give him this."

Momma wiped the face of the baby she had been feeding, getting up and using a ladle to scoop out a full bowl of stew. "I made extra just for him."

Sam smiled. Carefully balancing the bowl, she got up from the table, using her elbow to open the sliding glass door. Beau must have smelled the stew, dog drool dripping on the patio in anticipation. Sam laid the bowl on the patio. Beau rubbed up against her before he started eating.

"Sorry, you can't go inside."

Sam huffed, crossing her arms as she sat by the dog bowl, just grateful Daddy was letting Beau stay at all. She thought Momma must have had a lot to do with his decision.

"Would you still stay if my daddy chased you away?"

She rubbed under his chin as he finished the stew. He licked her face in gratitude for the meal, stretched and lay down right behind her. Sam relaxed into the dog, sliding down on the patio concrete, her back leaned squarely against the dog. "I wish we could stay like this forever."

Sam gazed at the sky as if drinking it all in, holding onto it.

Summer days stretched out wide, so the sun hadn't quite faded yet. The dog turned its head around, yawned and laid it in Sam's lap. Sam stroked the scruffy fur. She messed it up, then laid it back. Sam thought this was the best day in the whole world.

By the time Momma called for Sam, she had done the dishes and put all the babies to bed. Sarah was in the living room, hanging over Daddy's shoulder, holding a screwdriver.

"Sarah, just hold it for a second. I'll have the antenna hooked up just in time for the evening news. Won't that be great." Sarah smiled brightly at her dad.

Sam watched for a while from the entrance, always so envious of how well Sarah helped Daddy. They were made of the same stuff. Sam was sure that if she'd been the one helping, he would be yelling by now. The thought made her just a little melancholy. She never wanted to switch places with Sarah, though. Sarah was too sweet, too little, and needed far too much. Sam straightened her shoulders. She didn't need much. Truthfully, now that she had Beau, she was sure she could do anything, even hook up a TV she'd never seen before.

Sam entered the room completely. Neither of them noticed her.

She watched as Sarah and her dad finished attaching the wires to the TV, her dad handing the cord to Sarah. She plugged it in.

Momma had bought lemonade for the girls and a beer for Dad.

She laid it on the coffee table, then left. Sam thought she heard popcorn being made on the stove, certain of what it was as soon as the smell hit her nostrils.

Sarah giggled with delight as Daddy pushed the TV against the wall, preparing to turn it on.

"Everyone gather around. This is the moment of truth."

He made motions with his hands several times as if he was switching it on. Sarah giggled each time he faked and winked at her, while Sam was sitting cross-legged on the carpet.

"Sarah." She shoved her sister, whispering, "You be still so he'll turn it on."

Momma came in with bowls of popcorn for everyone, as if they'd gone to see a movie.

This was exciting, the whole family gathered around, waiting and eager!

Momma sat down on the couch in the back of the room, and yet again, Dad winked at Sam with one eye, then the other. Then he gave up.

Finally, he said, "It would do you some good to smile. Not everything's a fight."

Sam couldn't help it.

Her dad was truly charming. She smiled and blushed. "Just turn it on! Please! Daddy!"

He turned the knob.

In a flash, a color picture appeared on what was the biggest TV screen Sam had ever seen. Not that she had ever seen more than a handful, and almost all of them in store windows.

Sarah sat right next to Sam on the floor, and now, they both leaned forward.

Momma said, "You girls move back a bit; the TV will make you go blind if you sit too close."

Both girls scooted back, just a little.

Dad changed the channels.

Sam gasped. "There are *four* channels! Wow!"

"Yup. It's the antenna!" Daddy smiled, stretching out both arms and taking a bow.

Sarah clapped.

Sam watched as the weather lady said there would be days of bright summer sun with 'only scattered showers occasionally.' Sam marveled at the color of the lady's dress and how yellow the sun looked as she pointed at it. Momma always said that the weather ladies weren't hired for their brains, but Sam thought she was beautiful.

Sarah pointed at the screen, squealing with delight as they talked about the first big story.

Jimmy Carter had said or done something or other.

Sam yawned, just as the anchor said, "President Carter met with them to decide."

It droned as if going on forever. Sam thought she heard Daddy say, "He's gonna ruin this country with all that women's rights garbage."

Sam wiped her eyes, trying to stay awake. Sarah laid her head in Sam's lap, closing her eyes and drifting off quickly to sleep.

The anchor appeared again, saying this time, "Now, in local less happy news, the community continues to look for three young girls who are still missing. The first, seven-year-old Molly, disappeared in January off Route 3. Sandra, aged ten, was last seen on Oak Street in March. And Amy, six, went missing from her parents' camping tent ..." He closed that story, then finished the report with, "Finally, the ladies' bake sale at the YMCA made $38.50 for the quilting guild."

The day faded from Sam as she closed her eyes, only briefly waking as her daddy lifted her and tucked her into bed.

Chapter 17

Sam tried to fix her matchbox, opening her bedroom window just a smidge to let the air flow over it. She left the matchbox in the window to dry. Then, she used tape to make the corners match. She tried and tried, but the box wouldn't slide.

The ink was so faded you could see neither the smile nor the frown, but Sam wasn't giving up. She turned the crumpled mess over and over, examining every single part.

Perplexed, but sure she could fix it, she sat in the middle of her bed.

Frowning, she huffed loudly, turning the matchbox.

She laid it on the bed, turning it again just as Momma walked by her room.

Momma stopped.

"What in the world are you doing?"

"Fixing my matchbox." Sam said it with great force. "I just know I can fix it."

"Why don't I just make you another?"

"But it won't be magic. This one is magic. It gives me choices." Sam held it up, looking through the cracks she'd taped up. She was thinking that maybe she could sand it.

Daddy had sanding paper in the garage.

"Oh, my fiery Irish girl." Momma looked at Sam. She put her hand over the matchbox, sitting next to her on the bed. "Sam. The magic isn't in the matchbox. The matchbox is just a game."

"But Momma, it makes me so strong. I can make any choice I want. I can choose to be happy or sad. I can choose!"

"But you can choose anyway, Sam. The choice has always been yours. The matchbox just slows you down, like a rhythm." Momma saw Sam balling her fists.

"Yes, but I need to fix it!"

"Not everything is a fight. Not everything can be fixed." Momma stood.

"But this one is special. It's mine. There won't ever be another."

"Yes there will." Momma left the room.

Sam was filled with distress. Determined, Sam tried again. She just had to fix it. She needed it. She turned the box over and over. It just wouldn't slide. Sam frowned.

She tried again, then frustrated beyond her own comprehension, she crushed the box inside a fisted hand. When she opened her hand, there was only crumpled tape and cardboard.

The magic box was truly broken now. It would never work again, and she so wanted to cry. Sam threw it at her door, the crumpled mess bouncing off her mom's shoulder.

Momma had returned with a new matchbox.

She showed it to Sam, saying, "Look, this one slides easily. Sometimes, you just need something new…it doesn't mean the old one is gone. It's just replaced by something better."

"But that one's not the same."

"Sam, I am going to say it again. Listen, not everything is a fight. And not everything can be fixed."

Sam burst into tears.

"But that one was mine. Special. You made it just for me. *And* it was magic."

Sam spoke between gasps as tears streamed down her face.

She didn't wipe them away, just letting them fall. "Everything I have gets destroyed. I try to fix it. Momma, I do. But it *always* falls apart."

Sam was hysterical now.

Momma tried to draw her into a hug, but Sam pulled away.

"Sam. Oh, Sam." Her momma sat on the bed.

Sam stood. She squared her shoulders, tried to take a deep breath. No air passed. She gasped and sobbed again. Her momma reached for her. Sam pulled away again.

Momma drew a smiley face on the inner part of one side of the new matchbox, and a frown on the other. She slid it side to side, then held it out to Sam.

Sam turned away, facing the wall.

"Sam, you cannot fight your way out of everything. You cannot. Some things just are what they are."

Sam crossed her arms across her chest. She drew in all the air she could. She was so embarrassed. Sam didn't know why she was crying, and also didn't know why the matchbox was sooo important; but it was.

Sam turned and faced her mom, feeling as if she was being such a stupid baby.

"Momma, it's just a stupid matchbox, anyway. I don't care."

But she so clearly did.

"Obviously, it's not 'just' anything."

Sam screamed at her mom, "Yes, it is!!" She stomped across the room, looking out the window at the road.

"Sam, it's okay to be sad about something you lost. It's okay to want something to be fixed, but equally, you have to understand it's also okay to not be able to fix something. And not everything is your fault. Sometimes, stuff just happens."

"I try, Momma. I really, really try."

"Oh, child. Sometimes, we do the best we can and it's still not enough. That's just how the world works. Do you know the Irish blessing? I taught it to you. You remember?"

Sam turned, wiping her eyes. "May the road always rise to meet you, and may the wind always be at your back."

Momma finished, "May the sun shine warm upon your face, the rain fall softly upon your fields."

Sam said, "And until we meet again, may God hold you in the palm of His hand."

They both smiled at each other, grateful and happier, just a little.

"Sam, some things are just ours for a minute, then they're gone. Very few things are with us our whole lives. So, you see, fighting isn't the answer. Sometimes, God just holds you till it's better."

Momma's eyes momentarily filled with tears, and Sam's did too.

Momma just had a way of explaining things that made sense. She was the best mother anyone could possibly have.

Sam ran into her mother's arms, crying again, so much that salty tears dripped from her chin.

She still didn't know why she was crying; it was just a matchbox. But her pain was deep, and she secretly knew it was because of everything, all mixed up together.

The matchbox, momma being sick, the strangers in the woods, and Daddy getting angry sometimes. All these things were all tangled together.

"Now, Sam, there's work to be done. Your wash is way behind. Our babies will be up soon. And ...

Wait for this …" Her mother winked at her. *"Sarah has been doing Beau's hair."*

They chuckled, then with a glint in her eye, Sam leapt to her feet.

"Oh, crap!" Sam started to run out the door, then stopped.

She turned. Looking around, she saw the new matchbox on the bed.

She grabbed it and shoved it down into her not-so-new-anymore pants. "Sarah, no!"

When she reached the patio, Sarah was holding onto Beau's tail.

He kept wagging it and then sitting down. Sarah was following the dog's movements, trying desperately to braid the short length of hair.

"Sarah, stop it."

"But I'm almost done. He is *beau-t-i-ful.*"

She bowed when she said it.

Sam had to laugh, Beau's eyes meeting hers as he blew air through both his nostrils. The dog then promptly lay flat on the ground.

"Sarah, I don't think he likes that." Sam examined the dog closer. Making eye contact with Beau, she could have sworn she saw him roll his eyes.

Momma poked her head out. "Sam, can you walk up to the store? We're out of milk."

Sarah jumped up, pleading, "Can I go too? Pleeeaase?" Sarah hung on Sam's shoulder, trying her best to look sweet.

"Of course you can go with your sister. Can't she?" Momma looked at Sam.

Sam looked at Beau and rolled both eyes. "Come on Sarah, let's go."

Sarah jumped up and down. Looking at the dog, she said, "I get to go too!!"

"Only if you don't bounce up and down the whole way."

"Easy, Sam. She's your sister; take care of her. Here's an extra nickel for those candy cigarettes you like so much."

Momma was smiling when she said it, but Sam knew Momma hated candy cigarettes. Sam always got stuck with Sarah when the fun stuff happened … but Momma always made it worth her while. Sam grabbed the dollar and stuffed the nickel down with her matchbox. She headed toward the dirt road in front of their house, Sarah just behind her, matching … every … step.

As Sam cleared the view of the house, she started running, Beau at her side.

Sarah called out something behind them, so Sam said, "All right, boy, we gotta slow down for the little one." Beau looked over, unconcerned, barely moving anyway.

Sam just wanted to get to the store. It was a marvelous place. Daddy said it was just an old country store but to Sam, it was full of everything that she shouldn't have. A magical place.

Momma didn't like anything that had artificial flavors or colors. Candy, soda, potato chips, chewing gum, all bad for you, and Sam loved it all. Sam especially loved the old men who sat outside and the old ladies quilting in the back. She could hardly wait to get there.

"Saaaamm, waaaiitt." Little Sarah was breathless by the time she caught up. They stopped. Sarah leaned over with her hands on her knees, catching her breath. "Don't leave me."

"We aren't leaving you. I just like to run."

"Can we run through the corn fields?"

"It's too high. I'll get lost."

"But it would be a fun adventure!"

"Sarah, when the rows are high, you can't see over. When I can't see, I get lost, and we might never get out. You know all about this."

Sarah sighed, letting her shoulder slump with her exhale. "But it's a shortcut."

"Are you rested?" Sam shot off again, Sarah trailing just a tad behind.

Sam was sure she could hear her sister trying to complain, but she stayed just far enough ahead to be sure she couldn't really hear.

"Sam, Sam." Sarah was catching up. "What's on the list?"

Sam flicked her sister on the ear. "List? It's just milk."

"Milk and candy. Can I buy it? Please?"

The dirt road ended just ahead. Sam looked ahead; just one turn to the right on the paved road and they'd be there. She bounced just a little with anticipation.

"Sam. Did you hear me?" Sarah was running around Sam in a circle.

"Stop it. Calm down, and don't embarrass me." Sam had to look good when she approached the store. She made the right turn. A car drove by her left arm, almost hitting it. "Sarah, come get by my right. Beau?" Where was Beau?

Sam turned in a panic. Nothing. No smooshed dog in the road where the car had just passed. Sam sighed in relief. There was no sign of anything but she held Sarah's hand just in case.

Off ahead to the right, she saw Beau already at the store, begging for scraps.

The old guys lined the storefront, each sitting in rocking chairs and one of them was whittling away on a piece of wood. Sam strained her eyes to see what he was making but they weren't close enough. A lone gas pump stood in the parking lot in front of the store.

A red Plymouth pulled past Sam and eased up to it.

Sam leaned in and whispered to Sarah, "I think that's a brand-new car. Like a real new one."

"Really, are you sure?"

"No, but I think so. See how shiny it is. And its wheels, they look like chrome."

Sarah scrunched up her small face. "What's chrome?"

But her elder sister didn't answer, Sam's eyes already fixing on the next thing.

They walked past the car, toward the row of men as Sam thought back to what Momma had said. She'd told her that men like this solved all the world's problems, sitting in those rockers.

Beau joined the girls and Sam patted the dog's huge head. The first man looked at Sam.

"Is that huge guy yours?"

Sarah ran ahead. "Beau. His name is Beau!"

Sam sighed; so much for not getting embarrassed.

"Well, ain't that a fine name for a dog!"

"He's beau-t-i-ful!" Sarah was bouncing and talking. Sam lost track of all she said. As usual, the men were enraptured by every word her sister spoke.

Sam just tried to look cool. She wasn't exactly sure what 'cool' looked like, but it wasn't spurting out a million questions like Sarah.

She walked up to the man whittling. "Whatya making?"

"I'm making what the wood tells me it is."

"Does it talk to you?"

The man smiled. "Don't the woods talk to you?"

Sam nodded. The woods really did talk. She was always shocked by how much these old men actually knew.

He turned the piece of wood in his hands. "We all know those are your woods." He winked at Sam when he said it.

Sam thought, *there really are no secrets around here.*

"Here, hold it a second to see what it says to you." Sam turned the wood, smelling it. Her nose wrinkled. The aroma filled her airways. Yes, she knew this tree!

"It's cedar. I do know this tree."

He let out a big belly laugh. Not a mean laugh, more the kind that carries love with it, across time. Sam smiled back, returning the stick.

"You just might. The trees give me enough branches to work with. I have never had to cut one down to whittle. I think this one just might be the spirit of that big ol' dog you got."

Sam's eyes got wide. "But Beau's still alive."

"That doesn't mean the tree hasn't absorbed some of his being. Trees are like that. They live so long and see so much that they only absorb and remember things that are important. And well, that dog's special. Never seen one before in these parts."

Sarah was right behind her now. She piped up, "Momma says it could be a *royal* dog!"

"Could be. I've only seen them on TV." He leaned forward. "Y'all know what kind of dog this is?"

The man at the end spoke up. "Wolfhound, and a mighty big one."

Sam had noticed this man always had a big piece of straw in his mouth but never dropped it. She couldn't figure out how he did it.

Sarah asked, "Is it really royal?"

All five men burst out into laughter.

"Your momma sure has stories." The straw bounced in his mouth as he spoke.

Sarah had both hands on her hips now, about to speak. Sam knew it would be something entirely silly. She took her sister's hand before she could embarrass them both.

"Come on, we got shoppin' to do."

The man whittling spoke up. "Sam, royal or not, that sure is a good-looking dog." He winked at the girls as they entered the store. Sarah pulled away from Sam and ran straight to the back.

Down the only hallway, Sam could just see the edge of the quilting rack.

The men sat outside while the ladies quilted in the back. Sarah loved the ladies.

They loved her right back, and from where she sat, Sam could hear her sister's excited giggles. They always had peppermint candies. Not the hard ones, the soft ones that melted in your mouth. Sam wandered the rows of stuff in the store. There, again, was lots of candy, all kinds lined up on the shelves. Bottled soda sat in the corner inside a big machine.

Sam peeked around the shelves at the counter, where the candy cigarettes sat. She was getting excited when she heard her sister.

"*Sam*, come look!"

Sam rolled her eyes, her shoulders dropping. "Be there in a minute."

The lady behind the counter leaned forward.

She asked, "Sam, what does your mom want? I'll go ahead and get it, so you needn't rush."

"Milk. And I have money for candy cigarettes. Will you put them in the bag? Sarah wants to pay."

"Okay. You run along; the ladies want to see you too."

Sam sighed. The ladies were nice, but they didn't know about guns, wood, boots, or wild animals. The ladies also definitely didn't like her mom. Sam walked toward the doorway where she saw the corner of the quilting rack poking out. She also heard Sarah giggling as she entered the back room, large and rectangular with a quilting rack lowered in the middle. This quilt was so large the ladies barely had room for their chairs along the edges.

"Sam! Welcome. Your sister was just telling us all about your adventures. How are you?"

"Fine, ma'am." Sam was immediately aware of how dirty she was. She had worn her bellbottoms almost every day of summer. She looked down. They were ratted at the ends, and her shirt was the same one from yesterday. She looked at Sarah, seeing she was clean, with fresh clothes and a bright smile. Sam shook her head, but grinned at her sister.

The lady on her right reached out with a piece of peppermint. "Thanks ma'am, but Momma already gave me money for candy."

"Oh, go on. One more piece won't hurt you."

Sam reached out and took the candy, finding that the peppermint melted in her mouth.

Sarah was sitting in the lap of one of the ladies at the end, one who was dutifully stitching in the quilt. Truly, it was beautiful.

Sam was always amazed at how these ladies could take the tiniest scraps of material and make them into something so beautiful. Sam was afraid to touch it, afraid she'd mess it up.

"Sam, the quilt won't bite you."

"It's so beautiful. Who is this one for?"

The woman said tenderly across the quilt, "It's for your mom. She's had a hard year, and we thought she'd love this. What do you think?"

Sam was speechless. When she realized her mouth was open, she closed it, hoping they wouldn't notice. The ladies here worked sometimes for months on their quilts, yet always gave them away and to get one was quite an honor. Sam stood confused. It was all perplexing because until now, these ladies had never acted as if her momma was anyone but an outsider.

"Sam, what do you think?"

"I think, well, it's beautiful." Sam hesitated. She didn't know if her momma would take it.

Momma was proud.

"We give it to someone we know has been struggling."

"We aren't struggling, though. We're just fine." Sam backed away into the wall.

"Easy, girl. It's not charity. It's a gift. Much different." The lady wrinkled her nose. "I know your mom's proud. Thinks she's better than us all." She was looking right into Sam's eyes now. "But we want her to know we're all here if she needs anything. You're much bigger than you were so I know you can keep this a secret, can't you? We want it to be a surprise."

Sam didn't see any malice in her eyes, only a kind old lady who wanted to do a nice thing.

Sam relaxed just a little. "It's beautiful." She almost wanted to cry.

"Sam, come here."

Sam walked away from the wall just a little nearer to the quilting rack.

The woman motioned her even closer.

"See this." She pointed at the piece of scrap sewn into the quilt.

"Yes, ma'am."

"That's my husband's church shirt." She pointed to another spot on it. "See that?"

Sam nodded.

"You know your neighbor, the farmer?" Sam nodded again. "That's her baby's quilt."

Sam gasped. "She doesn't have any babies?"

"She did. Frankly, she had several. They just never lived long. She saved just one blanket, and she gave it to us when she found out about this quilt for your mom. The whole county puts in scraps for the one quilt we make for someone special."

Sam's eyes were big—and her heart even bigger. She thought it might burst. "You didn't tell Sarah, did you?" Sam wanted to know, aware that her little sister would just blurt it right out.

"Oh no. She's too young for a secret like this one but we'll mark where she sews so your mom will always know she helped. Why don't you go over into the bathroom and wash your hands? When you come back, you can help. Just a few stitches? Maybe?"

Sam didn't know what to say. She just turned and walked into the bathroom.

She washed her hands and dried them on the towel that was hanging. It just didn't make sense. They hated her mom? Why would they?

Sam dutifully returned with clean hands.

"Here."

One of the ladies pointed to a piece of material pinned into the quilt, a beautiful piece with spring flowers. Sam paused, then gasped, putting her hand over her mouth.

It was her dress. Sam let a tear fall as she reached and stroked the material.

"What's the matter, Sam? You think your mom doesn't always send fabric for these quilts, don't you? Well, she does, every year."

"She made me a dress this year ... those flowers are beautiful."

"That's why these are special. More people donated to this quilt than we ever had donate before. Your dad sells everyone an appliance of one kind or another. Your mom helps all over town whenever anyone is sick. Don't you pay attention?"

Sam was trying to absorb everything. "What do you mean 'helps'?"

She smiled at Sam. "You never wondered why your mom is on the phone at night? She talks to the sick folk around here. Ain't no sickness she can't at least help with. Doctors are way too high for most of us. Girl, close your mouth. Here's your thread. Stitch the part your mom sent."

Sam's hand shook as she took the needle and thread. "I can't sew well enough."

"Yes, you can. Our stitches are tight enough to make room for a tiny bit of slack if yours are wide. Besides, you're stitching the quilt, not sewing the pieces together. We already did that."

Sam stood by the chair she had been given, sticking her tongue out between her teeth because it helped her concentrate. The needle was bigger than she expected.

It made threading the needle easier.

Sam tied a knot at the end, then pushed the needle up through the fabric, and down through the quilted mat. The woman next to her clipped the end of her knot, and Sam watched it disappear into the material. Sam held the thread firmly, went under the rack, pulled the needle through, and sent it up again.

Her arms weren't quite long enough so she had to keep getting out of the chair and going underneath the quilt. She watched the thread as it pulled through the quilting, concentrating so intently she didn't hear anything anymore.

There was only her and each stitch. Up and down, through the material.

When the thread ended, the lady next to her cut and tied it, and Sam pushed more thread through her needle and started again. When she finished the piece, she drew a deep breath.

She stepped up into her chair and looked at it.

"Sam, that looks amazing. Who taught you to sew like that?"

"My momma."

"But I thought she had a machine."

"She does, but I get to sew patches with her."

"Well, she did a fine job teaching you. And how old are you now?"

"I am eight." Sam stood proudly. She liked giving her age, especially when she had done something that made them praise her.

"Eight! My word. That's quite something! Look how tight and straight those stitches are."

Sam looked closer. All she saw was the stitches that wavered, the uneven ones, or the few that were too wide. She looked at the woman.

Her eyes were warm, looking at Sam with kindness. Sam smiled at her.

"I guess, it's all right. Not nearly as good as yours but it's all right."

"You're a tough one. You should be easier on yourself. Second graders can't usually do that."

"Well, I'm in third grade now. It's summer."

"Oh, sorry. Still true."

Sarah squealed from across the room, "I did it. I did it. Sam, I did it." Happy, she bounced down out of the woman's lap, coming over to grab Sam's hand. "Come look, I did a whole row!"

Sarah pulled Sam around the quilt, just to the spot she'd been working on.

She pointed. "Look right there!"

Sam looked, grinning at Sarah. The stitches were wide, sideways and crooked, right, and then left. "Sarah, those are the best stitches in the whole quilt." She had just learned something precious from the old lady, and now, she was passing it along to Sarah too.

Sarah ran her little hand across her stitches. "You really think so?"

"Yeah. I really know so."

Sam heard Beau bark, then growl. She immediately ran through the store out of the now propped-open front door. There was 'not his dad.' Beau was growling, backing away.

The man who had been whittling was standing. "Looks like the dog don't like you."

'Not his dad' spit a black dot on the ground. "I will kill that damn dog."

"I doubt you'll do that here." Another one of the men in overalls was standing.

Sam ran past 'not their dad' and both men to wrap her arm around Beau. She squatted just next to the dog. "He's my dog and you'll do that over my dead body."

"Girl, you've got no idea how easy that can be arranged." He spit again. Juice from the chewing tobacco slid down the side of his mouth.

A woman's voice called out through the doorway. "You won't be doing none of that today. Trouble just seems to follow you around. How about you take it with you down that road there."

The lady from behind the counter was standing in the doorway now. A shot gun rested firmly in her hand.

"I still gotta pay for my gas."

"Not today. I'll pay your tab to just get your sorry self off my property. Next time, stop somewhere else."

'Not his dad' looked as if he might be in the mood for a fight.

Sam stood and readied herself. She wouldn't let him hurt Beau. The remaining men in rocking chairs were standing now, between Sam and 'Not his dad.'

Handing Sam the wood, the whittling man stepped forward.

"Don't want no trouble here, do we?"

'Not his dad' smiled at Sam. "I didn't mean no harm there, Sam. After all, we're neighbors."

Sam replied, "Yeah, we are but I'm still not going to let you hurt my dog."

"I wouldn't dare." He smirked when he said it, so Sam didn't believe him at all.

Sarah came running out, stopping right in front of Sam. As usual, she had no idea what was happening. "I need the money. I wanna pay."

Sam dug out the dollar and nickel from her pants pocket, handing it to her sister. She patted Sarah on the head. "You be sure to get the right change."

"Oh, I will. I'll count it twice." Sarah smiled so cheerfully at Sam that she almost forgot about everything around her. Sarah ran back into the store.

A black spitball hit the ground right by Sam's feet.

'Not his dad' gave a twisted grin at Sam. "See ya around."

He made Sam's stomach hurt every time he looked at her.

Chapter 18

'Not his dad' had gotten into his beat-up old Ford truck and headed down the road. Sarah had insisted on saying goodbye to absolutely everyone. While her sister was saying goodbye a hundred times, Sam stayed outside the store.

She just wanted to get home.

She tried to reach in her pocket to stroke her matchbox.

The piece of cedar was still in her hand. She walked over to return it, holding it out.

"Nope, it's yours now." He smiled and spit his tobacco into a coke bottle. "You need a good memory to end this day."

She looked at it. About four inches long, it was untouched on one end. On the other, a form had started, a crude chest and head of a dog carved out ... but it resembled a dog enough that Sam just knew it must be Beau. Sam smiled and put the wood in her pocket.

Sarah came running out with a lollipop hanging out of her mouth, her pockets bulging.

Sam took her sister's hand. "You filled those pockets up with peppermints again."

"They're so good." She handed one to Sam, and she popped it into her mouth.

Sarah was right. They were 'so' good.

Beau disappeared again as the girls skipped and jumped down the road. Sam was careful to keep her sister on her side away from the traffic till they reached their long dirt road. She sighed.

Going home always seemed so much farther than going *to* the store. They turned left.

Sam kicked a rock or two, while Sarah chatted on and on about the ladies and their families. She wanted lots of babies just like Momma when she grew up.

Sarah droned on and on as she walked. She wanted a little house and a handsome man like Daddy. She wanted flowers in the front and a quilting rack in the garage instead of a car.

She said cars didn't belong in the house anyway. Sarah said Daddy was smart to not own a house with a garage because it was wasted space. She skipped as she talked and gathered wildflowers along the side of the dirt road. Sam listened so long that in fact, she stopped listening, lost in her thoughts of her and Beau running through the woods.

Wind flying through her hair, the dog was just at her fingertips, the trees growing around them. She was so lost in her thoughts that she barely noticed the truck pulling up beside them.

When Beau came out of the cornfield, Sam was jolted back into the present reality.

The dog let out a low growl.

Sarah was standing by the edge of the dirt road to Sam's left, Beau between the girls.

"Not his dad' had opened his truck door and was standing in the road.

Sarah held Sam's hand over the top of Beau, with her flowers for Momma in the other hand. Beau's fur stood tall on his back.

"You girls don't need to walk all the way down to ya house. I'll give you a ride." He smiled. Sam could tell he was trying to look like a nice man. She was still sure he was not.

"C'mon on now. Tell the dog I'm all right. It's not like I'm a stranger."

"Thank you. We can walk."

Sam started walking away, pulling Sarah just a tad too hard by the hand.

"Sam, you're hurting me." Fear crept up through Sam's back into her shoulders.

Quietly, through her gritted teeth, Sam said, "Come on Sarah, now, just come on."

'Not his dad' stepped forward to take Sarah's hand, barely missing.

"I just wanna give you girls a ride. Sam, you can ride in the back. I'll even take the dog. He can ride up back with you, Sam. It'll be fun." Sam began to walk faster, pulling Sarah in tow.

Beau was walking backwards, both eyes on 'not his dad.'

'Not his dad' said, "Sarah, those sure are nice flowers."

Sarah called back, "They're wildflowers. Momma says so."

"Don't talk to him," Sam was whispering to her sister.

"But Sam, he just wants to give us a ride."

"He's not your friend, Sarah; not everyone is your friend."

It was sometimes difficult to bring the world's dangers to the mind of a little, innocent girl who saw no bad in anyone yet. So, Sam just kept hurrying her sister along.

Sam was beginning to relax as she left the man standing by his truck, beginning to put some yardage between them. 'Not his dad' got into his truck. Sam heard him start it up behind them.

He sped past the girls, the truck pulling sideways in the road.

It parked at an angle, taking up most of the road in front of them.

'Not his dad' got out again.

Sam had hold of Sarah's hand on the right and a milk jug on the left. She lifted the jug.

"Leave us be."

Sam squared off with 'not his dad,' trying to make herself as big as she could.

He sneered, "What you gonna do with that?" He spit tobacco on the ground. "I ain't gonna do nothin' to you girls." He reached for Sarah, but Beau eased forward, a deep growl permeating the air.

Beau's hair stood as a warning of what was to come.

"I'll beat that dog to death."

Sam called out, unable to hide the desperation in her voice, "Beau, no! Stop!"

The cornfield was just behind 'not his dad.' Sam had a thought. She pulled Sarah and tried to get around the man. Beau held him off. Sam thought he must have been more afraid of Beau than he was letting on. He stepped to the left, just stopping Sam from getting by the truck.

Sam heard a loud popping sound, and she looked at 'not his dad.'

Stunned, she realized a baseball had hit him squarely on the left cheek.

It had been thrown so hard it must have bounced off his face and dented the truck.

Sarah gasped. Sam dropped her hand for just a moment, then reached out. She grabbed her sister by the wrist, making her drop her flowers and run into the cornfield.

Beau was right behind them. She pulled Sarah, running until she was sure they were safely hidden in the field's long stalks. Sarah was crying, and Sam put down the milk on the earth.

She looked at her sister. Whispering, she asked, "You okay?"

"My flowers. I don't have flowers for Momma." Sarah sounded so miserable, it was heartbreaking.

Sam hugged her sister, offering the only solace she could in the moment. She tried to sound upbeat, removing the fear from her subdued voice, but her words were shaky.

"We'll get more. They're wildflowers, so they're everywhere."

Little Sarah was rubbing her wrist.

From somewhere near the road, Sam could hear cursing.

She imagined the unpleasant, creepy man's face wasn't the best. 'Not his dad' called out, "I was just wantin' to give you girls a ride! No need to run off."

Was he going to lurk around this place, searching for them, hunting them down?

Sam squatted, holding Sarah, and petting Beau in hopes of calming the big dog. She held a finger to her lips, indicating that Sarah should be quiet for a minute.

Her heart thumped deep inside her chest, sounding in her ears like a drum, racing, panicky. What would that man do if he were to catch up to them?

Sarah whispered, "Was that a baseball?"

Sam nodded. They heard 'not his dad' curse again.

Sure enough, he even entered the cornfield a few times. Sam could hear him pushing the stalks around. Beau's fur was flat, meaning 'not his dad' wasn't that close.

Somehow, the dog knew to do nothing but crouch and keep silent. Fear shrouded them, covering everything. Sam felt every second ticking by.

They heard the truck door open, close, then open again. 'Not his dad' called out, "Hey, I got your ball. Why don't we settle this at home, boy, since you ain't comin' out neither?"

Sam stayed squatting in the corn rows until long after the engine had droned off into the distance. Sarah spoke first.

"He just wanted to give us a ride, Sam. Why did we have to hide?"

Sarah was only asking a question, an innocent question, but it was not one that Sam desired to answer. In all honesty, she didn't really understand what had just happened, so she hoped Sarah wasn't going to ask more and more as she usually did.

Sarah couldn't take her eyes off Sam.

She was sitting between the cornrows, just underneath where Sam was squatting.

"That was scary." Sarah must have picked up on Sam's fear, and started weeping quietly.

"I don't even know how to tell Momma, but we have to," Sam softly said.

The girls both stood, Sam listening for anything that would indicate which way was which. The corn rows were taller than she was. Way taller.

"Sarah. You gotta stay close. We're lost in the rows." Sam knew how bad this could be because she'd spent all day the year before lost, wandering around before finally coming out behind the store. The corn rows went on for what seemed to Sam like miles.

Beau kept moving slowly in and out of the rows, weaving as if in an obedience class.

Sam kept thinking about what boy 'not his dad' had been talking about.

She just couldn't put together everything that had just happened. She wandered the rows, milk jug in one hand, Sarah holding the other hand. Sam tried to put it all together.

Was she just making a big deal out of nothing?

After all he'd just wanted to give them a ride, hadn't he, like Sarah had said?

He'd only hated the dog. But even if he didn't like the dog, it didn't mean he would hurt them, did it? And where had the baseball come from?

And why didn't Sam like the man? He hadn't really done anything to them, had he?

Plus, who was the boy?

Sam was hopelessly lost. She stopped and sighed.

Sitting down, Sam was sure she was in big trouble. If she ever did get out of this cornfield, she still had to deal with scaring Sarah for no good reason. Sam was sure she'd overreacted.

She looked at Sarah.

"You okay?"

"Yeah. But there aren't any flowers."

"We'll get some as soon as we get outta here."

Beau had been frolicking around in the corn-rows. Sam looked at him, then reached out. He rubbed under her hand as if by command, looking at her, then straight ahead.

Sarah popped up from beside Sam. "He knows the way!"

Sam looked deep into the dog's eyes. "You know the way out?" Beau looked off to the right, then back at Sam. "All right, Beau, it's up to you."

As Sam followed Beau, Sarah in tow, she tried unsuccessfully to work out why she had run into the corn rows in the first place, why she had been afraid. He was just their neighbor.

Just because he made her stomach hurt, it was no reason to run off into the cornfield and get lost. She lost Beau twice, then started holding the very tip of his tail.

It seemed like forever before Sam followed Beau out of the rows just up the dirt road from their house. When Sam placed a foot on the dirt, she was sure all of this was her fault. Somehow, she had created a mess. Sirens blared up the road, and a fire truck eased past Sarah and Sam.

Sam looked ahead. The truck had stopped just in front of 'not his dad's' house.

Sam reached the front yard, taking a left heading toward the house.

Sarah was wiping her nose, while Momma was standing on the front porch, looking upset. She ran into the yard to meet the girls. "You two all right? It took you long enough to get home."

"Momma, I dropped your *wild*flowers." Sarah was now sobbing. Sam thought she might just get killed for this one.

Momma picked up Sarah. "No reason to cry over lost flowers, is there?"

She carried Sarah to the edge of the woods. "Look there!" Momma pointed to the clumps of bright flowers along the edge of the woods. "Sarah, pick some of those."

Sarah wiped her nose again on her arm. "Momma, my wrist hurts."

Momma looked at Sarah's wrist. Sam winced, noticing that a bruise was forming. She backed away, almost falling into Beau standing behind her.

"What happened?" Momma was looking at Sarah, but Sam felt the words sting.

"I got peppermint and flowers, then the man came. He just wanted to give us a ride home. Beau was mad and a baseball hit the truck, and Sam was mad at me and pulled me into the corn."

Sarah started sobbing so hard she stopped talking.

Momma wrapped her up in her arms.

Sam could feel her mother looking at her, and she felt her whole body turn red, shame filling her. She'd scared *and* hurt her sister for no good reason.

'Not his dad' had just tried to give them a ride. She felt silly.

Momma carried Sarah to the house.

Sam didn't follow, staying behind, just petting Beau. She noticed that the fire truck was easing past the front of the house.

Maybe the man's face was hurt worse than she'd thought.

Momma had come up behind her.

"Sam, *what* was it that happened, exactly? You know your sister isn't making much sense."

Sam didn't look at her momma; she just couldn't, and didn't know what to say.

Her momma moved the dog, and it took its place right in front of her. Sam knew she was gonna have to answer for it all.

"Mr. Leiven tried to give us a ride home."

"The fire truck's been up there a while; it just left. You know anything about that?"

"He got hit in the face with a baseball."

"You hit him in the face with a baseball? How hard did you hit him?"

"No. I didn't hit him."

"Who hit him?"

"I don't know."

"What do you mean, you don't know?"

"I don't know." Sam could feel the heat of anger climbing up her spine.

"Sam, don't get an attitude. I am just trying to find out what happened."

Sam looked at her momma, seeing true worry and concern filling her mother's face. She wished she could just sob like Sarah and climb into her momma's arms. She just couldn't.

Right now, anger was Sam's only companion. She was sure this was all her fault.

"Well, it's all my fault. It's always my fault!"

"Wait a minute, girl. Don't yell at me."

Momma reached out to take Sam's arm, but she pulled away and ran into the woods. She had to run. She just had to. Her mother called out, "Sam! Come back here!"

Beau was beside her too, and they were running.

Past the big oak, they slid sideways between the privet hedges. Scaring squirrels and birds from their branches, they ran, hurtling right into the stream. Sam ran till the water was up to her shoulders. And there, she stopped and felt the water wash her guilt away.

Sarah's wrist was bruised for sure.

'Not his dad' must also have been hurt pretty badly for the fire truck to come.

"Oh boy," Sam thought out loud. She looked at Beau.

He was thoroughly enjoying the stream, splashing and barking, excited.

She wished she could enjoy life like dogs did. They moved onto the next thing without a thought. Sam, though, had to think.

"Sowwweeee!"

There was desperation in her momma's call. She knew she had to go home, so she gathered her thoughts. What would she say? How could she describe what had happened?

So, what *had* happened?

Nothing, really, other than Sam running from their neighbor who'd been trying to give her a ride. She stared at Beau. "What am I gonna do? What's wrong with me?"

Beau understood. He understood everything, his warm eyes settling her.

She patted his head. "We gotta go. Momma sounds so worried."

Sam gathered herself and headed home.

When she exited the woods, her momma looked frightened.

A baby was hanging on her hip.

"Sam. I was frantic. Where did you go? You've been gone forever. Your dad's on his way."

"I went to the stream."

"Well, you're soaking wet. You better dry off."

She went inside and came out with a towel. Sam wrapped herself up in it.

"Go change into something clean. We've got a lot to talk about. Don't wake up your sister."

Sam reached into her pocket, now realizing she'd just ruined another matchbox.

But this time, not upset about it, she just shook her head.

It didn't matter anymore if it was ruined; she could always make another now she knew how. The piece of cedar also fell out on the floor as she pulled the wet matchbox from her pocket.

She picked it up, and looking at the crude carving made her chest feel warm.

"I do need a good memory," she said aloud to herself.

She put the wood and her wet matchbox on the bedside table, changing into dry clothes.

She would refuse to bathe, telling herself the stream had washed away any real dirt. She would tell her momma the same thing too.

When she entered the kitchen, fresh bread sat on the counter. Her momma was mixing spaghetti noodles with sauce that smelled amazing. Sam still had no idea what to say or how to say it. She quietly tried to ease toward the sliding glass door. But only halfway to the patio—and to Beau, who was standing there waiting, outside—her momma cleared her throat.

"Umm, and where do you think you're going now?"

"Just outside to see Beau; he's waiting for me. Can't we let him in?"

"Hmm. Your daddy would have ten hissy fits."

"Just this once?"

"Why don't you sit down and drink this?"

Momma handed her a drink she'd never seen before.

Sam smelled it. "What is it?"

"It's Irish cream and instant coffee with milk. It will settle you. Whatever happened, I want to hear about it before your dad gets here."

Sam sat at the table and sipped the drink. It was cold but warmed her insides. She looked at the glass and took another sip. Her momma sat across from her.

"Sam, your sister was really scared. Whatever happened, I need to know."

"He just tried to give us a ride."

Her mom tilted her head just a bit, leaning on the table. She took Sam's hand.

"I know it wasn't just that, Sam. Whatever it is, you can tell me. We can work it out together."

"He makes my stomach hurt."

"Mine too; he isn't a nice man." Sam's eyes shot up.

Maybe Momma would understand, after all.

"Beau almost bit him."

Momma just squeezed her hand and nodded for her to continue.

"He wanted to take us in his truck, said he was just going to give us a ride home. He even said Beau could ride."

Sam could feel tears behind her eyes, holding them there. She would not cry. She wasn't a baby, and she didn't understand why she was so scared. Her momma nodded for her to continue.

"The way he looked at Sarah …" Sam stopped talking, sitting quietly emptying her glass. Her momma held her other hand and quietly waited. Sam felt as if her throat was closing.

"Beau was really upset. I should check on him."

Momma held her hand tightly. "The dog is fine. You gotta tell me. Your daddy will be here soon and I can't help if I don't know."

"I don't know what happened! He just wouldn't leave. I told him we didn't need a ride, and Beau was gonna bite him. He tried to grab Sarah, so I ran. That's all there is!"

She never mentioned the man's threat to beat the dog to death; it was too much to think about.

Now, she pulled her hand away from her momma and ran to the patio.

"Sam, stop."

But momma wasn't yelling this time, her voice dripping with concern. Sam didn't stop until she had opened the door and buried her head in the scruffy fur of a 'very happy to see her' dog.

Sam's momma followed her outside, then sat on the patio.

Sam was so upset with herself, frustration growing inside her as she tried again and again to make sense of her situation. What could she say? Nothing that would redeem her.

She should have just taken the ride and been done.

She grabbed Beau's fur and sat down heavily on the patio with a huff.

Her momma was still looking at her, but she just couldn't make eye contact. Beau licked her face and rubbed his head along her neck, then he rested his head on her shoulder.

Sam wrapped both arms around the dog.

"You know, Sam, if the dog was upset, you probably did the right thing."

Sam thought this might just be a trick to get her talking. She never completely did the right thing. She tried but there was always something *completely* wrong. Always.

Momma continued, "You know my mother raised big shepherd dogs. Champion Anatolian shepherd dogs to be exact." Momma moved closer.

Sam felt her momma reach out and pet Beau's head.

"The dogs always knew when someone was outside before any person put even one foot on the porch. They also knew if someone had bad intentions."

Sam huffed again. "What are intentions?"

"Intentions are what people are thinking about doing."

Sam turned to look at her mom, needing to know more about intentions. "Can dogs read minds?"

"I think it's more like they have a feeling about what some people are going to do. You can trust dogs more than people, sometimes. They can sense people, Sam, sense if they're bad."

Beau shifted as Sam turned and leaned against him, looking directly at her momma.

Maybe Momma did understand that 'not his dad' scared her. Sam thought he must have been going to do something really bad if Beau was that upset with him.

"Beau was really upset when he stopped the truck. He wouldn't let us by."

"I bet that was scary. Did he touch you or Sarah?"

"No. I wouldn't let him, and neither would Beau."

"Sam, it's okay if you were scared. Everyone gets scared."

The sound of screeching tires interrupted their discussion. The station wagon slid sideways around the house on the gravel drive. Momma looked concerned.

By the way the station wagon pulled into park, it seemed that her dad was really upset.

"Sam, take Beau and go play by the woods. I'll call you when dinner's ready."

"But Momma, dinner *is* ready."

"Sam, just go." Her mother sounded mad too. Sam stood, Beau following.

She never had to motion, the dog simply following wherever she went.

As they rounded the side of the house, Sam stopped. "Beau, I gotta listen. We shouldn't but we gotta." Sam slid into the bush just beside the property.

The station wagon door slammed, followed by heavy footsteps on the gravel.

"Dammit woman, what did you let the girls get into this time? Did you know the dog tried to bite our neighbor at the old store?"

"Calm down; there's more you need to know. We just needed milk."

"Don't tell me to calm down! And all I need to know is what I've been told, that you let Sam run wild, *again!* Where is she? She threatened a grown man. You gotta learn to keep her home."

Sam crouched down further into her bush, aware her dad would come around the corner any minute.

"She's off playing with the dog."

Her dad was so loud, he woke one of the babies. As if on cue, the screaming echoed, the other babies starting to cry in unison.

Momma sounded irritated. "Look, you actually don't know what happened. Sometimes, Sam is right. Sometimes, *you* don't know everything."

"I know you gotta get that girl under control and get rid of that dog. Someone is going to get hurt. I swear she loves to fight with everyone and everything."

Sam heard the patio door open, both her parents retreating inside.

She could hear them talking but not pick up what they were saying.

Beau was standing on alert, and Sam brushed his fur down.

"It's just Daddy. He's mad at me again."

Sam let a tear fall. Ashamed, she wiped her cheek.

The babies were quiet again, and Sam walked down to the tree line and rested on the dogwood. She picked a piece of tall grass and picked her teeth.

Beau was sniffing along the tree line, not particularly concerned about anything. Sam looked at the dog. "You know I won't let him take you, right? We could leave and find our way on the trains. Thomas said he rode the trains. I think you just wait for it to start and then jump on. It's a free ride. You know we could look at stuff we've only seen in National Geographic. I wonder if the train goes all the way to the frozen tundra?"

Sam chewed on the end of the stalk of grass. She had reread the edition of National Geographic because they had dogs pulling a sled on the cover.

She imagined living in a place where she could have ten dogs at once and no one would ever take them, as dogs were very important there. They worked just like people did.

Sam sighed. Of course, the train must not be able to go there; it made sense that they had to use dog sleds to get there. She wanted to know so much more about the world.

Beau barked softly. Sam paused her musing to see him, tail wagging and running around Sarah. She had just walked around the side of the house, now running toward Sam.

"Sam." Sam rolled her eyes. What did Sarah want now?

"Momma says dinner is ready in five minutes. Look!"

Sarah held out a pack of candy cigarettes to Sam, stretching her arm as far as it would reach. Breathless from running, she tried to talk. "Sam, I found them."

Sam smiled at her sister. She had forgotten about the candy.

"Yes," Sam said as she reached to take the pack from Sarah. The candy came in a box just like Momma's cigarettes. It even had a red tip like fire at the end.

Sam took the candy and held it.

"Sarah, this is very important. You have to eat your dinner if we eat these first."

Sarah nodded, excited to just be alive.

Sam thought she would never understand how Sarah could be excited about everything but she had to agree that candy cigarettes were one of the most exciting things around. They each took a cigarette. Sam thought she looked so cool as she held it just at the edge of her mouth.

Sarah had her head held back, trying to look as grown up as she could while puffing away.

Sam looked around on the ground. Hadn't she left a mason jar somewhere?

"Where's that mason jar?"

"I dunno."

Sarah licked the side of her candy, careful not to break it.

"If we can find one, I can put this up for later instead of having to throw it away. Help me look."

Sarah and Sam slowly looked along the tree line. There it was. Sam reached down. The mason jar rested at the base of the dogwood, and she picked it up.

Sarah crooked her head to one side and said, "Whatcha gonna do with that?"

"Hide candy cigarettes in our place!" She handed her cigarette to her sister. "Hold this. I'll be right back."

Sam slid the candy into the mason jar and tightened the lid. Then she ran.

Beau appeared at some point, so Sam laid her hand on his fur and pushed forward.

Just outside the privet, she stopped. Their place ... this was the one place that was always safe. Sam slid under the brush and into the opening, scooting all the way to the back. Testing the lid one more time to be sure it was tight, she laid the mason jar between the rocks on the ground.

She grinned at how clever she was. She patted the jar, saying, "We can eat you later."

Sam slid out from under the brush onto the trail, Beau rubbing across her legs. She buried her head in the dense, soft fur. "I love you more than anything."

She ran back, proudly sliding right next to Sarah with a huge smile. She took her candy cigarette from her sister and pretended to smoke again.

Sarah asked, "Where'd you leave them?"

"In the far back part of our place, right where the baby deer was. I made sure the lid was tight. We'll go tomorrow after Momma feeds the babies."

"We are almost grown-ups now." Sara giggled and bit down on the mint candy. She leaned in to her sister, who put her arm around Sarah, smiling.

"Sowwieeee!"

Sarah giggled," She doesn't know we're *right* here."

Sam ate her cigarette in one big bite, then tapped her sister on the shoulder.

"Race you to the patio."

The girls didn't stop till they were both bumping into each other, trying to wash their hands in the bathroom sink. Sam had so much fun she had almost forgotten the day's events.

Forgotten until she slid into her seat, ready to eat Momma's delicious spaghetti … She finally made unwanted eye contact with her father.

He said, "Let's say grace." Sam was glad she could close her eyes for the prayer. They all held hands. "Thank you, Lord for this meal, and our time together. Amen."

Sam looked down at her plate. She twirled her spaghetti, not sure what was going to happen. She was sure *something* was going to happen.

Daddy cleared his throat as he picked up a piece of freshly sliced bread, then asked, "What have you girls been up to today?"

Sarah perked up in her chair, mouth full of spaghetti. "We made a quilt. A whole quilt."

"You did?"

"Oh yes. I stitched it all by myself."

"I hear they're almost finished with this year's quilt. I wonder who they're gonna give it to?"

Sarah smiled. "I hope we get it. It's beautiful."

Her father laughed. Sam sighed loudly, and he gave her a sharp look, then smiled at Sarah when she responded, "The ladies were nice."

"Well, Sarah, wouldn't that be something? They give it to someone who means something to all of us. I don't think we've done anything special this year, have we, Sam?"

Sam swallowed a too-big bite of spaghetti, coughing a bit as she responded, "Oh, I don't know. Maybe?" She tried to smile. It was feeble but she pushed one out. She was also struggling not to tell about the quilt, not to spill out the secret she knew and was holding on to.

She would not ruin the surprise for her momma.

Momma never got good surprises, and she deserved one. All the same, Sam needed a diversion right about this very second. Her brain was thinking so hard that it hurt.

"Anything else happen at the store?"

Sarah had spaghetti all over her face. "Yes. We got candy! Peppermint candy, the kind the ladies make at home."

"You did."

"Oh yeah. Didn't we, Sam?"

Sam couldn't help herself. Sarah looked so excited and so silly at the same time. So, she laughed. "I think you got most of it."

Sarah reached into her pocket, pulling pieces of candy out and placing them on the table. "I got you some too."

Momma said, "Hold on. Dinner first."

Sarah wiggled in her chair, feet swinging, smiling and eating spaghetti as quickly as she could get it into her mouth.

Daddy twirled spaghetti with his fork, his eyes piercing the air.

Sam felt them and refused to look up from her plate, chewing slowly, knowing something was coming. Sam was not excited about finding out what that 'something' was.

Sarah piped up, "Can I be excused? All done." She held out both hands, giggled and swung her too short legs even faster under the table.

"Yes, you may. But no going outside. It's almost time for bed. How about a story tonight?" Daddy winked at Sarah.

"A story! Which one?"

"Any one you pick!"

With that announcement, Sarah leapt from her chair.

Sam knew it would be forever before she came back, when she heard the chest open.

Sarah would be rummaging through all the books, holding every single one, carefully trying to make a decision about which story she wanted to hear. There was no rescue for Sam anytime soon. She swallowed hard, no spaghetti left on her plate.

Momma got up from the table, moving with purpose into the kitchen. Her hands were full of dirty plates. No help there.

Sam knew her daddy was still looking at her. She raised her eyes, making a choice.

As their eyes met, rage seared through her. She was surprised; never before had she felt so much anger at once.

"What happened? Sam, you have to tell me."

Daddy's voice didn't meet her anger. He was genuinely concerned.

Sam couldn't help herself. She'd heard him. She knew what he really felt.

"You can't take the dog!" she squealed, panic and fear in her eyes.

Sam's chin raised just a notch. She wished she were stronger, bigger, more fearsome.

"Well, do I need to take the dog? Aren't you gonna tell me what happened? I shouldn't have to ask you again, Sam. Once should be enough."

Sam panicked inside her head. If she told the truth that they had just refused a ride and offended 'not his dad,' then it really was all her fault.

If she lied and said anything else, Sarah would contradict her later when Daddy talked to her.

Momma had already tried to tell him the truth.

Sam was stuck. "You don't really want to know what happened. You just wanna take my dog. And that's not fair. He didn't even bite anyone. Didn't even *nearly* bite someone!"

"We cannot have a dog that might bite you girls. We just cannot. You have to understand."

Sam grabbed both sides of her chair so hard her fingers went numb.

He continued, "I just want you girls to be safe. You can't keep wandering around. I have talked to your mother; we agreed that the dog must go. Tomorrow, I'll take him into town."

Sam felt all the air leave her body and her face grow pale. When she spoke, it was in the very slightest whisper. "You can't."

"I can, or I'll eventually have to shoot him for biting someone. Sam, you have to understand. A dog that big cannot be in the least aggressive."

"But he was protecting us; he didn't actually bite anyone."

Sam had released the chair, completely defeated. If Momma agreed with him, there was no hope.

"Protecting you from what?"

"He isn't a nice man."

"Everyone isn't nice sometimes, but he's a man just like all of us. He's just trying to keep his family fed. It's tough working every day for not enough. He won't hurt you."

Sam's insides were turning. She *had* to do or say something.

All at once, so no one could stop her, she jumped from the table, reaching the sliding door just as her father's hand grasped her wrist. She struggled against it and was able to barely open the door, just a little more than an inch.

"Run, Beau, run away."

Beau did not. Sam was struggling against her father's grasp, so the dog stood in the middle of the patio, hackles raised, teeth just barely showing, looking at her dad.

"Beau, noooo! Run! they're gonna take you to town tomorrow!"

Sam leaned into the opening of the patio door, pushing her arm out, making shooing motions. "Go away! We don't need you here anymore."

Beau motioned his head to one side as Sam looked into his eyes.

She had to get him to leave. "We don't want you anymore! *Go away!*"

Sam saw hurt pushing forward inside Beau. She couldn't let him see her eyes, her sadness. She stared into him, pushing forth all the anger she could muster.

"Go on! *Git! Git outta here!*"

Her father pulled her off her feet, her arm sliding inside. He shut the patio door, hard.

Sam saw Beau turn and run as fast as he could toward the tree line. She hoped he understood.

Sam wiggled, pushing her attention directly at her father.

When she raised her head, she was furious. "Let me go!"

"Sam, stop fighting! We need to talk."

She could feel him trying not to be angry.

Momma was right there. "Let her go! She won't calm down until you let go of her."

"Shut up. This is your fault anyway. The damn dog was gonna bite me."

Anger seethed in his voice.

She couldn't have her momma take the punishment that was all her own. She couldn't see the dog anywhere on the patio and all the fight had left her body. Sam hoped Beau would run free and that they would see each other again. She knew he had heard her. Sam just dropped to the ground. Her dad huffed, dropping her wrist. Tears began to leak down Sam's cheek.

"You didn't listen to her, did you?" her mother quipped.

"Listen to what? That the dog was gonna bite me … again?"

Her momma was kneeling at her side.

Sam eyed her father. He rolled his eyes and left the room.

Sam pulled away from her mother; this was her fault too. Her momma just slid down, back against the patio door, and she waited. Waited till Sam couldn't hold it anymore.

Tears streaming down her face, she laid her head in her momma's lap and cried.

Cried like someone does when their heart is broken, because hers was.

Her momma just sat with her hand on Sam's shoulder, letting her cry.

Chapter 19

Weeks passed. Sarah looked for the dog every day, leaving scraps of food every night on the patio. Every morning, she was thrilled that it was gone. Sarah was absolutely certain Beau had eaten his fill

Sam didn't cry anymore after that one night. She wouldn't. It was for the best. When she grew up, no one would tell her she couldn't have a dog. No one would tell her she wasn't telling the truth. Sam would be free of people and their mistaken judgments.

For now though, nightmares plagued her sleep. Every night, she would wake, wet with sweat.

Looking at her window, she found it always devoid of the man who had visited. Still, she would get up, put her hand on the red phone to be sure it was there, wander down the hallway through the dining room ... and sit on the floor, looking out the glass patio door.

Sam would wish for Beau, staring out, remembering how he'd curled around her.

The raccoons would be there on the patio too, devouring their fill of the food that Sarah left.

Sam liked them. There were five in total, one of them huge.

Sam was sure that was the momma, the rest looking so much smaller.

Sam had decided they must be her babies.

The first night she'd sat there staring, hoping Beau would be there. The raccoons had stayed just outside the light. Sam had known they were there and eased herself just inside the house.

She had quietly slid the patio door shut, enamored by how beautiful they were.

Tonight was no different. She sat, pleased just to be watching the raccoons eat. She stuck her feet out, resting them on the glass, her bell-bottom pant legs hanging off her ankles.

She muttered to herself, "It must be so hard keeping babies alive out there; you're doing a great job, Momma Racoon. My momma tried hard too, but not all her babies survived."

"No, they didn't. And even though she's doing a great job, she may already have lost one. Chances are only one will live to be older than two years old. Life isn't always kind."

"Momma, I didn't—" Sam let her voice trail off.

She hadn't heard her momma get up or enter the dining room.

"It's okay, Sam, I hear you all the time. I'm used to it. Your father sleeps harder than I do."

"Sorry about the noise, Momma. I try to be quiet."

Her mother put her hand on her shoulder.

"We have already established that your idea of quiet doesn't necessarily correspond to everyone else's." Sam could see her mother's smile in the moonlight. "Look at those raccoons in the light. I see her and her kits leaving in the mornings, but they're stunning in this light."

"They're beautiful, Momma. See their hands; they *do* have hands."

Her momma sat beside her, pulling up both knees and wrapping her arms around them. Momma then placed her head on her knees, watching the raccoons with Sam for quite a while.

"You know your father and I are doing our best. Just like that momma raccoon."

"I know. I just want Beau to come home." Sam let out a deep sigh.

"Sam, you told him to leave. No one made you do that. Your father would have taken him to town and he'd have been home by sunrise the next day. Dogs are like that."

"I didn't know what to do; Daddy said he'd shoot him."

Sam drew a circle on the carpet with her finger. She hadn't been this mad in a long time now. She let her sadness flow through her fingers as she drew another circle.

"There's no way I'd let that happen. Anyway, your dad's been out there looking for any sight of that dog every day. He's sure we're going to be responsible if it bites someone."

"Beau isn't gonna bite anyone who doesn't deserve it." Sam tapped her finger on the floor, beginning to fidget uncomfortably. She knew it was her fault the dog was gone, but she wasn't the least bit sorry. At least he was safe from men and their plans.

"Truth be told, he wants the dog home almost as much as you girls do. He loves you and wants you to be happy. He won't hurt that dog."

"Daddy doesn't always act like he wants us to be happy. He just wants us to behave. I don't think I am ever gonna be a 'good girl.'"

Sam made a strange face when she said it, as though she'd eaten too many lemons.

The raccoons started chittering to each other, then two of the smaller ones started fighting and tumbled off the patio.

"None of the 'good girls' ever make great women. This town is just too small for you, Sam. Didn't I say that earlier to you? I seem to remember it. Anyway, you'll see when you grow up. Obeying the rules isn't always the right thing to do."

Sam huffed and settled leaning backwards on her hands.

"Momma, sometimes, you don't make any sense at all."

Her momma laughed. "Well, that's awesome, because sometimes, you don't either. Maybe we're more alike than we're different."

"Where do you think he went? Do you think he's okay?"

"Sam, I think that dog was doing great before he came here and he's doing just fine doing whatever he was doing before he stopped by to spend time with us! Don't you think? If you remember, he wasn't the least bit skinny."

"I miss him."

"Oh, I know you do. But this is life. Sometimes, we don't get what we want. Sometimes, we even get what we ask for, only to find out it's not what we wanted. And that's why there is a saying about it: *be careful what you wish for!*"

Her momma leaned over and tried to pull her into a hug.

Sam slid away, not wanting to be comforted. She deserved to be sad.

Her momma settled for stroking her hair, then stood. "I'm headed back to bed. You stay inside, okay?"

"Yes, ma'am." Sam had no desire to go out.

Without Beau, the outside just didn't look the same anymore.

All the color was gone. She felt nothing but a heavy aloneness, and when she ran through the woods, she felt that eyes were watching.

She told herself it was just the squirrels giving her palpitations, but knew inside that it wasn't.

Sam watched the raccoons until she drifted into sleep.

***

When she awoke again sometime later, the moon was high in the sky.

She could still see the little shadows that were raccoons playing on the patio, chittering to each other. Now and then, they would run in front of the door.

Sam yawned and headed back to bed, pulling up her covers. Sliding her hands under her pillows, she turned to her window, the moon lighting the glass and the sill.

As usual, nothing at all was there. Yawning, she closed her eyes.

A branch from the bush outside scraped the glass, rendering Sam suddenly wide awake. She looked at the window. Squinting, she still saw nothing. Inside her head, she told herself, "Stop it, he's not there. He was never there. It's just your imagination."

Shortly afterwards, the silhouette of a man appeared. Sam blinked, trying to wipe the image from her eyes but she could almost swear he remained, and that she saw him smile.

His hat threw a shadow over his eyes, but Sam was still convinced he was grinning.

Why though? Why would he be smiling? She wiped her eyes again; she had to be dreaming.

Sam heard her window creak. *No!* His right hand was on the glass.

She slid out of bed, terror gripping her throat.

She opened her mouth to scream. Nothing came out. No sound. No breath, panic ensuing as Sam tried to calm herself enough to breathe. She pushed her back against the wall by her bed.

The glass slid open quietly. Her eyes grew wide. *When did I leave the window open?*

His right hand slowly guided the glass upward. He stared, not letting her escape from his sight again. "Sam, you didn't think I would forget you? Did you?"

Sam slid away from him along the wall.

She drew in a haggard breath. In a whisper, she pushed out, "Daddy, Daddy."

But it was nowhere near loud enough for Daddy to hear.

Nor even for Momma, the self-confessed light sleeper.

The man quickly reached inside with his right hand, pushing himself into the house.

Sam glanced to her left, seeing in the darkness the silhouette of the red phone, picking it up.

As she did so, she held onto her breath, also fixated on the man—unable to *not* look at him. She had backed herself into the corner. How had she done that? Why couldn't she think? He was coming fast. One leg inside the house. She held the receiver and heard the phone ring.

The bush outside her window suddenly shook like crazy.

Sam heard a deep guttural growl and a snap, Beau clambering up, wild-eyed, tongue lolling out with the effort. He pushed his head through the window and closed his mouth, clamping down on the man's left arm.

The dog violently pulled backwards, shaking his head, his jaw firmly attached to the man's forearm. The man turned his right shoulder to square off with the dog.

Now, one leg was inside the house, and one was hanging out the window.

Beau snarled, never letting go of the man's arm.

The dog pulled.

The man tumbled back outside with an almighty yell, full of pain as he hit the ground.

"Damn dog. I'll show you."

Sam had dropped the phone to her neck, eyes wide.

She heard a struggle outside the window, the wretched man yelling again.

Beau growled and Sam heard his jaws snap closed, hard. Beau must have missed because that was the sound of his sharp teeth clacking together.

"Sam, Sam!" her dad yelled through the receiver. Sam put the phone to her ear, breathing into it, unable to speak. She *couldn't* talk. Her dad let out a strangled yell via the phone pushed against her ear. "Sam, I'm coming."

A loud pop sounded, then another!

Sam cried out, "Noooo!" That couldn't be a gun. Beau was out there!

She dropped the phone and ran to her window, in time to see the man running across the front yard. She looked down, looked across. Where was Beau?

A flash of light came to the left of her window, followed quickly by a loud *boom.*

Sam leapt. She had to get outside. She looked out the window, too scared to jump. Then she ran to her door just as her father opened it. She ducked under his arm and ran into the hallway, toward the front door. Shocked, Sam saw it open.

Standing at the edge of the porch was her momma.

Her mother chambered another round, the stock of the Remington pushed back against her shoulder. The moon lit her mother's red hair just a tiny bit.

Sam had never seen her momma look so fierce.

She could see her concentrate. Momma squinted, then squeezed the trigger.

Sam covered her ears as another shot rang out.

Her father was now standing behind her, but little Sarah came scurrying, somehow managing to push past all of them. "Beau, Beau is back!"

"Sarah!" Sam's mother called out briefly, then stopped when she saw Sarah wrap her arms around the dog.

Sam looked at her mother, blinked and looked again.

She had never seen her momma look so big before. Momma tilted her head to look at Daddy.

"You will keep my girls safe. You *will.*" Daddy's face turned red but something in her momma's eyes stopped him short. He looked down.

Momma stood tall. "I think I might have grazed him. Maybe. We won't know for sure till first light." Momma let the rifle slide onto her back, its strap hanging over her shoulder.

Sam couldn't get over how in control, how in charge her mother had become.

Sarah started screaming, a deep and visceral scream that meant something terrible was happening. Momma ran toward Sarah. Scooping her up in both arms, Momma looked down at Beau, heaped on the ground. Blood covered Sarah's hands, arms, chest, and face.

Sarah's eyes were wide, and her thumb was stuck in her mouth.

"Sam, get my sewing kit from beside the bed."

Daddy was furious. "Damn dog." He stepped up. "Give me that gun before you shoot your goddamn foot off."

In a flash, her mother had Sarah in one arm. The Remington was on her shoulder again, then she was pointing it at Dad. "I won't shoot my foot. I shoot what I aim at."

Momma snapped her head up.

"You will go get that 'damn' dog and lay it gently on *my* dining room table. Right now!"

She let the rifle slide onto her back again.

Turning from him, Momma said, "Sam, go get my box. The one I use when people are sick."

Daddy took a deep breath but decided against anything he might have been fixing to say.

Sam ran into her momma's room and grabbed the kit.

The basket was about as big as the bread box. It was heavy, too. Sam used both hands to carry it into the dining room. When she entered, Sarah was still sucking her thumb, staring wide-eyed at Beau. Blood was dripping from the table, and Beau was lying on it.

Blood had also sprayed all over her daddy's neck and face.

Sam gasped, dropping the sewing basket.

"Not you too ... Sam, I need you."

Fixated on her mother, Sam lifted the basket.

"Put it on the chair right here." Her mother pointed at a seat to her right. Sam deposited the basket right there.

"No promises, Sam, but I'll do the best I can to save this dog."

Momma looked at her daddy with such disdain that it made Sam even more uncomfortable.

Beau's eyes opened slowly, then closed. Her momma was holding his shoulder with her left hand and digging in her basket with her right. She tilted her chin at Daddy, her eyes landing on him with a sharpness that chilled Sam to the bone.

When Momma spoke to him, however, it was quiet and controlled.

"Take Sarah to the back bathroom," she ordered him. "Clean her up. Feed and change the babies. And for goodness' sake, wash yourself too. Then, for all that is holy in this world, do something to keep us safe in the place you want us to call home."

Chapter 20

S am wasn't sure at all how much time had passed, but the sun was high in the sky when she and Momma finally finished. The first bullet had passed straight through Beau's shoulder.

The second had entered his chest, but Momma said it hadn't done much damage because the dog was breathing well, and his stomach was soft, not full of blood.

She'd said they'd done all that could be done. There was nothing to do now but wait.

Daddy had called the police, but Momma and Sam were so busy with Beau that Sam had hardly noticed the blue and red lights flashing, or the police as they moved in and out of the house. Daddy had done as he was told all night, thankfully.

Sam was busy helping her momma, but it didn't escape her that somehow, her daddy had become so small. He had always been the biggest and strongest man she'd ever known.

Somehow, right now, he'd been dwarfed by the fierce woman with whom Sam had worked all night.

She looked at Beau; Momma had cleaned as much blood as she could out of his fur.

Sam stroked his head. "You're gonna be all right, boy. You have to be."

She buried her head in his fur, his breathing rhythmic and easy.

Momma put her hand on Sam's shoulder.

"They want to talk to you. Just tell them what happened. Everything, the best way you can." Momma guided her away from Beau to the patio door where the police were waiting for Sam.

Sam stepped onto the patio.

The bright sun was hard on her eyes, so she shielded them with her hand.

Her father, the farmer and 'not his dad' stood on the patio, talking. A police officer, clipboard in hand walked up to Sam. She was too tired to be afraid, too worried about Beau to be anything to be irritated by this interruption. What could they do?

The man was gone. Momma's shot had missed.

"Are you Sam?"

"Yes. My name is Samantha. They call me Sam." Sam stared at the police officer.

She wished he'd had a kind face but he didn't.

He looked like the characters on TV, overly serious and not genuinely interested.

In all honesty, he looked as if he'd rather just go home and put his feet up.

"Are you all right?"

"Yes, sir."

"Can you tell me what happened?"

"A man tried to come into my room."

"Do you remember what he looked like?"

"I remember he was smiling."

"Smiling?"

"He said something. I don't remember what. His smile was not a real smile. It was strange."

"Did you recognize him?"

"No. I mean I didn't see his face. It happened fast. Beau bit him. You can't be mad at Beau for biting him though. He deserved it."

"Sam, no one will ever take that dog from you after last night."

"I can't have a dog that bites. Daddy says so."

"Sam, do you understand what happened?"

"Beau bit a man." The questions seemed repetitive, and she really didn't care.

"The dog bit a man who was trying to get into your bedroom. Is that correct?"

Sam was overwhelmed with how tired she was. She blinked and looked at the police officer. She leaned on the patio door. "Yes, sir. Can I go to my room?"

"As soon as we're done, you can do whatever you want. It's important to write down what happened, so later, we'll know, and have a record of it all. You understand that, right, Sam?"

Sam stood tall, once again, anger pushing her spine straight.

"We didn't do anything wrong. Beau didn't do anything wrong!"

Her fists clenched at each side. The police officer took a step back.

"Write whatever you want," she spat. "If I knew who that man was, I would tell you."

The police officer squatted down, looking up at Sam.

"Easy. I know you've been through a lot."

Sam looked at him, blinking several times, trying to think. Why couldn't she think?

They were trying to take Beau and she couldn't let them. He was still hurt, so she had to go to him. Sam turned to slide the patio door open.

Her father's hand stopped the door from shifting. "Sam, the officer just needs your statement and then they can go. He's waited a hour already. Can you just talk to him for a second?"

Disdain—so loud she could taste it—filled her body.

Her eyes fixed on her father, when she spoke, it was controlled, cold, calculated.

"Where were you? You said you'd be right there if I called!"

He looked at Sam. She stared deep into his eyes, no longer afraid of anything she might see there. This time, it was her father whose eyes dropped downward.

He let his hand fall from the patio door too, turning toward the police officer.

The officer said, "Sir, I just need her statement."

Her father responded, "You'll have to come back. It's been a long night. She can't do it now."

Sam pushed the door open and stepped in. Momma had a toddler swaddled on her side while she was cleaning the dining room table.

"Where's Beau?" Sam sounded more panicked than she meant to.

"I put him where I thought you'd want him. Sarah's there too."

Sam looked at her mother.

"He's in my room? Really? Can he stay in the house?"

"Sam, as far as I'm concerned, that dog can stay anywhere he wants to be. I'm just so grateful you're okay."

Sam wasn't so sure she was okay.

Tiredness was enveloping her whole body and she picked up her feet slowly, exhausted.

Moving slowly forward down the hallway, she paused at her door.

In her mind, she could still see his sneering face and hear his voice. "Sam." Had he really called her by name? What else had he said? She shook her head.

It was all so fuzzy.

Sam thought maybe it had been just a dream.

She turned the knob. As she opened the door and peered inside, the idea that she had been dreaming was wiped from her mind. Beau was lying on her bed.

And there, curled underneath his paws, Sam could see her sister Sarah staring out from underneath the withers of the dog. She sucked her thumb and stared too, obviously scared.

Sam approached her bed.

"Sarah?"

No answer. Sarah just sucked her thumb faster in response.

Sam looked at her, really looked. Sarah was clean, but far from unhurt.

So, she stepped away, pulling off her shirt—then she realized she hadn't cleaned up at all.

She pulled her shirt back on and grabbed a nightshirt. "Sarah, I'll be right back. It's gonna be okay. I promise."

Sam patted Beau on the head. "You're gonna be okay too."

But why had she promised? She wasn't at all sure it would be okay.

She was only sure she couldn't sleep covered in Beau's dried blood. Tiredness was one thing, but she had to wash this away. In the bathroom, she looked in the mirror, seeing the dried dirt and blood covering her face and chest. She peeled off her clothes, turning on the faucet before stepping into the shower. Sam let the cool water run over her until it ran clear.

She used the washcloth and the soap. She thought, *maybe this is why grown-ups like showers.* She let her anger and her fear slide down the drain. Then came a knock on the door.

Her momma asked, "Sam, are you taking a shower?"

Momma sounded very alarmed. "Are you all right? You've been in there a while."

"Yes, Momma. I'm getting out. I'm fine."

Sam wasn't sure she'd ever be fine, either. She stepped out of the shower. Looking at the pile of clothes, she saw her bell bottoms, blood splattered across the fabric.

She picked them up, sighing.

She'd never cared for fancy clothes anyway. Beau was back, which was all that mattered. Sam put on her nightshirt, then carried her clothes into the kitchen and threw them away. Her momma just watched her, and when Sam made eye contact, her mother nodded in understanding.

When Sam reached her room again, Sarah's eyes were closed, Beau looking up at her. Sam looked deeply into the kind eyes of her fierce friend, quietly saying, "Thank you."

She patted his head. Beau sighed, laid his head all the way across Sarah, and closed his eyes.

There was almost no room on the bed. After several tries at lying down with the dog and her sister, she sighed, then settled on the floor, her back against the wall and her bedpost.

She sat between the bed and her window, willing herself not to be scared.

If I could just look up. Finally, taking a breath, she slowly looked up at the window.

And she almost leapt out of her own skin. What on earth were those?

Huge iron nails were sticking out of each side of the windowsill. She tilted her head to get a better look, then got up, running her fingers along the edge of the windowsill. Tears welled.

After everything that had happened, having the window nailed permanently shut should make her feel better but it was just another thing she had lost, wasn't it?

Now, she could never open her window again, even if she wanted to.

Daddy had made sure of it.

Beau huffed. She turned and looked at him. At least she had her dog.

She settled back against the bedpost, leaning halfway against the wall, a new sensation filling her. Sam knew that her life was forever altered.

What had changed, she wasn't entirely sure, but something had. She slid to the floor, then reached up and felt the fur, felt his chest rise and fall.

She closed her eyes.

"Sam, you didn't think I would forget you. Did you?"

His smile. Yes, he was smiling. Sam reached up. The dog was gone, and with the man's Dakota hat just shielding his eyes from view, he pushed at the outside of the windowsill.

One at a time the nails pushed out of the woodwork, landing on the floor.

Sam gasped but didn't get up, just couldn't move. She just looked at the man, trying to see his face. *Who even is he? How does he know my name?*

"Sam, Sam!" She opened her eyes with a gasp, seeing her mother squatting in front of her. The sun had gone down, and little Sarah was standing wide-eyed beside her momma. "You were breathing super-fast. Sarah came and got me. You were dreaming. It's okay now, Sam."

Her heart raced. She sucked in air, had to have air. Then she tried to stand.

Beau was immediately sliding between her and the wall, pushing her up. Her breath was ragged. She looked at her window, her arm resting on top of Beau.

Her mother reached out. Sam turned sharply away from her, burying her face in fur.

Beau held her up as she leaned into him. She reached around his haunches and stopped when she felt the sudden shaved patch and its rough stitches.

She remembered it all. Sam buried her head into the fur a second time and sobbed.

Beau wrapped his head around her. Exhausted, they both slid to the floor.

She heard her momma. "Sarah, let's go get a snack. I think there are some cookies in the kitchen." Her bedroom door closed softly. After that, Sam felt as though she cried forever.

Sitting there wrapped in fur, she felt safe.

Safe from the perils of the world. Safe from all the creepy smirking men with no faces.

She finally gained the strength to stand on her own, leaning back from the dog.

Holding his face in her hands, she said, "I didn't really want you to leave. I didn't mean it."

Beau pushed forward through her hands, licking her face. He nuzzled into her neck, his tail wagging frantically, and she hugged him. *He's here. Beau is alive.*

Sam thought that was all that should matter, but it just wasn't. The man was still out there.

He knew her name. He knew *her.*

She would never be safe.

Beau would never be safe.

Chapter 21

"When can we move?" Momma had both hands on her hips. Her words weren't really a question.

"It's gonna take a minute, but I'm working on it. I have to have a job first. I *am* looking."

Shame filled her father's words. Shame that he had not seen what was happening. Shame that his family had almost come to harm. Shame that he hadn't been vigilant, had not protected them.

"You're not looking fast enough." Momma's words were sharp.

Daddy slammed his fist on the table. "Woman, I told you it takes time!"

Everyone at the table heard the low growl from Beau, but it was Sarah staring with those wide eyes that stopped everything. Her father cleared his throat, saying softly as he could, "Sarah, I'm sorry. I didn't mean it. Daddy's just having a hard time."

Sarah just stared through him as if he just didn't matter right now.

Momma brought biscuits and scrambled eggs, placing the food on the table. They said grace over it, then Daddy filled everyone's plate. A knock sounded at the patio door, and there stood the farmer, looking in. Daddy got up, sliding open the door just a little.

The farmer spoke first. "You guys okay in there?"

"Yeah, just having breakfast. What brings you by so early?"

The farmer chuckled. "*Early?* This isn't early."

When he saw no humor in Daddy, the farmer cleared his throat and continued, "I brought you … this." He handed Daddy a newspaper. "At least they waited a few days, and the article isn't very long."

Daddy looked down at the paper, opened the front page, then closed it again.

"Thanks for coming by with it," he said in a gruff tone, almost dismissive.

Daddy sat at the table, coffee in one hand and the local paper in the other.

The headline read, 'Girl Attacked Inside Home, Beloved Dog Shot.'

Sam looked at the words in horror. Everyone now knew that her daddy couldn't keep them safe, that he had failed in his one real job. Sam was furious with him, and herself. She should have stopped this way before anything happened. She could have nailed that windowsill herself.

She sat at the table, pushing her eggs around with her fork.

Sarah ate slowly, across from her. Sarah didn't giggle anymore; she just stared out at the world, not speaking much either. Sam was very worried about her sister.

She had to do something to fix it. Something, anything to fix this.

"Sarah, the eggs are delicious, aren't they?" Sam smiled as brightly as she could at her sister. "Maybe we could play in the cooler today?"

Sam looked down when she failed miserably at trying to get her sister's smile to radiate from her eyes like Sarah's always had. But Sarah just looked back down and ate more of her eggs.

Her father reached over, putting his hand on Sam's shoulder. "She'll talk when she's ready. The doctor says she's fine, physically. She's just upset."

Beau sat right beside Sam's chair on the floor. Now, no one said a word about the dog being in the house. He came and went as he pleased, but he was never far from Sam.

"She's sick, Daddy. You have to help her."

Sam felt sadness seeping into her words, sadness and the sharp edge of anger. She wanted her sister to be annoyingly happy again. If she'd just swing her legs under the table, make endless noise, kick her tiny feet and smile once, Sam would believe it would be okay again.

When her father didn't say anything at all either, Sam shrugged, moving away from his hand.

He was the one person who no longer mattered. He clearly couldn't help anyone.

Silence overtook the breakfast table.

Her momma laid a plate of food down on the floor beside Sam for the dog.

She cleared her throat.

"Sam, healing takes time. It always does."

"But Beau is better and he's the one who was shot."

"Yes, and that's a strong dog. I'm still not sure how he's up and about so fast," Momma said.

"He limps."

"He might limp for good. I don't know how bad that shoulder is and we can't afford a vet. We'll have to wait and see."

Momma was squatting by Beau. "I sure am glad he came back. Thank you, Beau. Thank you for living. Thank you for being with us." Momma stroked Beau's head.

Sam's father cleared his throat. "Sam. I owe you an apology."

Her momma put her hand on Sam's, still squatting beside her. Sam straightened her back against the chair. This was weird! Daddy never apologized for anything. She looked at her dad.

He cleared his throat again. "I should have believed you. I should have listened."

Sam just looked back at her eggs. She had nothing to say.

She had no time for small men and their games. She needed solutions.

When Sam did look up again, it was Sarah she looked at—Sarah who was somehow hurt but not hurt, all at the same time. Sarah, who didn't swing her legs or giggle.

If her daddy wanted to do something to make this right, he could fix her sister.

They all ate the rest of breakfast in silence.

Sam wasn't really sure how much time had passed since the man had tried to get into her window. One minute, it seemed like forever ago. The next minute, Sam was sure it had just happened. When she'd finished her breakfast, Sam just slid down onto the floor.

She stroked Beau's fur. Laying her head on his chest, Sam listened to him breathe as she faded in and out of sleep. She heard her mother clear the table, babies crying, off in the distance.

In the midst of everything, Sam's world was centered around each breath Beau took.

Sarah sat next to Sam, so Sam reached up. Her sister lay back, curling into Sam's arms.

Contentment filled Sam's world now; everything that truly mattered was close by, in her arms or touching her skin.

"Sarah."

Her sister looked up at Sam, sucking her thumb, saying nothing.

Sam wrapped both arms around her. "It's gonna be all right, Sarah. It will be. You'll see."

Days passed, like summer days do, long, hot, and easy.

Beau healed quickly. Sarah, not so much. She slowly started talking again. Short sentences.

Momma said she still needed time, and to be patient.

Sam taught Sarah all about the matchbox, about choosing a smile over a frown. Sam would push the box open and yell, "Smiley face." Sarah would smile briefly, always fading quickly back into her mind and sucking her thumb.

Sam learned how to bake bread and talked incessantly to her sister about yeast, little growing yeast creatures that made the bread rise. Sam was so worried about her sister that she had stopped doing anything but following her around.

Sam tried everything, even walking Sarah into the field with ol' Willie.

With all her might, she pushed Sarah up, onto the broad, muscular back of the old bull.

Sarah just sat and stared, sucking her thumb as they walked around.

Sam was always careful not to wander far, always staying where she could see the house.

They lay in the grass just in front of it, Sarah looking up at the sky, making quiet sucking noises with her thumb in her mouth.

Sam watched the clouds move, shapes forming before they'd disappear.

"Sarah look! It's a dragon, I think? What do you think?"

Sarah just stared.

"Maybe it's a bunny." Sam patted her sister's shoulder.

Beau had been rolling in the grass just a few feet from them when he suddenly stood. Sam sat up, leaning on her elbows. Beau wasn't growly, and his hackles were down.

She followed his gaze.

Matt and Theresa walked slowly across the front of the yard, along the edge of the road. Theresa had a string of fish, while Matt was carrying fishing poles and had his arm wrapped around Theresa. Excitement filled Sam. *This is what Sarah needs. Company!*

"Come on, Sarah." Sam jumped to her feet, pulling her sister up. Sarah easily complied and Theresa waved when she saw Sam.

Sam ran to the yard's edge, pulling Sarah in tow.

"Whatcha doing?" Sam smiled brightly.

"Fishing. Matt's so good at it." Theresa looked at Matt adoringly, giggling. Sam felt a tug at her heart. It had been so long since anyone had giggled around this place.

Matt looked at Sarah. "She okay?"

Theresa shoved him. "No, she ain't okay, not at all. It ain't been long." Theresa trailed off and didn't finish her sentence.

By now, Sarah was looking wide-eyed at the fish.

"Sarah, it's fish." Sam reached out toward the line and Theresa gave the small fish to her.

Sarah reached out and touched one, running small fingers along the spine of one, then she dropped her hand. She looked at Sam as if her sister had all the answers, even about fish.

"Sarah, it's a fish." Sarah's look changed, eyeing Sam as though she didn't quite understand.

Theresa took the line, kneeling in front of Sarah, holding one of the fish in both hands.

Sam was surprised when Sarah looked right at Theresa.

Theresa turned the fish in her hands. She didn't speak either, just turned the fish slowly over and over. Sarah reached out again, touching the silver-hued little fish with its glassy eyes.

She looked at Theresa again and said shyly, hesitantly, "Fish."

Theresa smiled slightly. "Yes, Sarah, it's a fish."

It wasn't much, but it was some sort of breakthrough, at least.

The two girls stood there a long while, turning the fish over and over. Sarah held it, looking at all its scales. Theresa held Sarah's hand, letting the fish fall on the string.

When Theresa finally spoke, it was rich with kindness and understanding.

"It must have been very scary. Sarah, you're safe. You really are."

To Sam's surprise, Sarah nodded in understanding. Then in a flash, it was over.

Sarah stuck her thumb in her mouth, and was gone again, staring off into the distance at whatever it was she saw.

Theresa stood, brushing off her pants.

"I can't believe someone climbed into her window. That's so scary."

Sam was too worried about her sister to correct Theresa. She didn't care what people thought about what had happened. It wasn't important anyway; Sarah was all that mattered.

"Kevin beat my brother once so badly that he didn't talk for over a month," Theresa said, snuggling into Matt's chest.

Matt cleared his throat. "Well, he won't ever do that to you." Matt looked at Sam, who was so confused. Somehow, she knew that Theresa had spoken to Sarah without speaking.

"How'd she do that?" Sam sounded so distraught that Theresa patted her on the shoulder.

Matt said, "Theresa's good like that. She's good with horses too. Can draw them outta their stalls even when they're really spooked."

Sam looked at her sister, then at Theresa. "How'd you know to do that? How do I do that?"

Theresa looked puzzled. "I don't know. I guess I've spent my whole life scared, so I understand it. I don't *understand* alot but scared, I know *all* about that. She's stuck, that's all."

"Stuck?" Sam didn't understand at all. She needed to understand.

"Yea. Stuck. Like when the creek runs low and it's hard to walk in the mud. I can't explain it, you just feel it. Feel it when something's stuck."

"How do I fix it?"

Theresa looked at Sam as though she might have been an alien.

"I don't know. They just kinda fix themselves."

Sam looked down and brushed the ground with her feet.

The thought that Sarah could fix anything—least of all, herself—was beyond comprehension. Sarah wasn't a fixer. Sarah was gentle, kind, and happy; she was *supposed* to be happy.

She was a kid. Sam was a kid too, and she knew it, but somehow, she didn't feel like one.

Sam could feel the anger growing again inside her. She should be the one 'stuck.'

If she had just stopped Sarah on the porch … if she had thought more deeply about her little sister, not about her dog … She hadn't thought about anything but Beau and her momma. Sam saw her momma in her mind, standing fierce and proud on the porch, the wind just barely moving. Momma looked across the rifle, concentrating, slowly, purposefully pulling the trigger.

Theresa tapped her shoulder.

Sam jumped; she hadn't realized how angry she'd become, her fists tight at her sides.

Theresa stepped back.

"You can't fix this Sam, it fixes itself. Being angry will just make it worse."

"I am not angry." Sam stood tall, shoulders back. She was angry, every fiber of her body almost seething, trembling with it, but admitting to that state of mind was something else.

Matt lit a cigarette. Taking a deep draw, he blew out the smoke. "Well, you sure look pissed off to me." He smiled, looking sheepishly at Sam, and the three of them burst out laughing.

Theresa patted Matt. "You made a joke."

Sam could see how proud Theresa was of Matt, standing there wrapping her arms around him.

For a moment, Sam was envious of the warmth they shared.

Her momma didn't speak much to her daddy anymore; he had become so very small inside their home. When her parents did speak, it was as if a cold breeze entered the house, passing through but touching everyone. Sam shuddered.

Theresa patted Sarah on the shoulder, smiling. Sarah's thumb was still in her mouth, but Sam thought she might have seen the very beginning of a smile. Just a tiny one. Maybe.

Matt tugged on Theresa, saying, "We gotta go or dinner will be late."

Theresa promised Sarah to come visit soon.

Sam held her sister's hand as they watched the happy couple trot up the road toward home and she couldn't help herself from watching them until they disappeared.

It had been nice to have company, even if only for a few minutes.

She looked down at her sister, reminded of her predicament.

Sam could not simply wait for Sarah's problem to fix itself, just the way Theresa had said. No, she had to do something, to act, making it happen.

Wasn't that what elder sisters were supposed to do?

Chapter 22

am had made darkness her friend when she'd worked for the farmer's wife. People shied away from the blackness of the night, intimidated and spooked by it, but this was not Sam's way.

No, she loved the dark, the peacefulness and calmness of it.

Well, that was unless 'he' was lurking again in the window of her room.

But now that Beau was back, so was most of her courage.

She slipped into the kitchen, needing to make sure everything was safe. She had to fix Sarah.

The first item of business was making sure the man was really, really gone.

Sam opened the kitchen drawer, pulling out a kitchen steak knife, holding it up in the darkness. It felt right, and Beau was standing beside her, looking up. Sam felt his concern. "It's all right. We're just checking the trails. We gotta make sure he's really gone."

Sam slipped out the patio door.

She shut it as quietly as she could, then reached down beside her, feeling fur and breathing in the night air. Sam quickly reached the tree line where shadows loomed everywhere. She touched the dog, finding his fur was flat, just as it should be. No hackles, not tonight.

The moon was high and bright. Sam was glad she'd chosen a night with enough light to see just a bit. Her eyes adjusted quickly as she slipped away, into the wood line.

Sam was too apprehensive to run, but she ached for it. She hadn't run in so long. She checked the first trail, then the second, peering around the big oak.

When the ground bustled with activity, Sam froze in place, unable to quite see what it was. Something jumped on the tree beside her, and she stood motionless, her breath ragged. She tried to breathe in and out, telling herself, "Slow … easy." She heard chittering, realizing the raccoons were just doing raccoon stuff. Sam let all the air out of her lungs.

"Gosh, y'all are loud!"

She continued down the path, Beau no longer beside her. She heard him pushing some leaves around in the underbrush, and just knowing he was nearby helped her push onward.

When the trail opened, the moon was glittering off the water.

Sam squatted on the shoreline, spotting a snake slithering through the water, gliding along as if guided by the moonlight. There were always snakes, always.

Momma said they were there, even if you didn't see them. So, Sam just watched, quietly. There was nothing else. Maybe everyone was right; there was nothing in these woods to scare anyone. She stood. These were her woods, and Sam was finished being scared.

When she turned, Beau was there at her side. He licked her hand.

She patted his head but said nothing.

The pace back was quicker, Sam glancing around, surveying everything she could. She paused at the oak. Looking back through the woods, she saw the moonlight flicker off the water.

Moving forward, she headed to their place, then veered off to the right.

Reaching the spot, she stood as still as she could, looking at the privet, waiting for the woods to come alive. The sounds began with a bullfrog in the distance.

Once the crickets started, Sam was satisfied. There was no one here but her, her and Beau. Sam turned up the trail and trotted quickly toward home, easing around the front of the house.

She had one more thing to check: her window. Easing past the bushes, she peered up at her windowsill, so inconspicuous, just a regular sill. She stood there for a long while, just looking at it, taking it in. By now, she had almost convinced herself she had imagined it all.

The wind blew through the bushes next to her.

Sam shivered, but there wasn't any chill to the air. Taking a step backwards, she started edging back into the yard. A twinkle caught her eye.

Sam knelt. Reaching her hand underneath the bush, she pulled out a hat. The moonlight glistened off the small brass buckle that held a strap around the leather fedora's brim.

Breath filled her lungs quickly. She'd seen this hat before. She heard him say, "Sam."

She stood stock still, having learned by watching the animals that if you stood motionless, you would almost disappear. She looked around, not moving, hardly daring a breath, waiting on the crickets to tell her it was okay.

She heard nothing of interest. Nothing but Beau pushing his way through the bushes to check on her once more. When she felt safe moving, Sam stepped back, dropping the hat. Her steps quickened. She moved around the house, looking over her shoulder every few seconds.

When Sam reached the patio door, Momma pulled it open for her.

Sam drew in a breath, hard. It wasn't a gasp, more like a gurgled cry.

Momma looked down at Sam, both hands on her hips.

"Your father would have a fit if he knew you were outside, running around in the middle of the night."

Sam huffed. "I don't care."

She pushed past her momma and strode into the kitchen, reaching into her back pocket for the knife, to replace it where it belonged. She felt around. Nothing.

It was gone. She checked all her pockets. She must have dropped it.

"Sam, what are you looking for?"

Sam looked around.

Beau! He must have abandoned her. Sam wished she could bail from this conversation too. From the look on her momma's face, it was gonna be a long night.

"Nothing."

"It's not nothing. You checked your pocket about eight times. You better work harder at lying if you're gonna try doing it much."

"I am not lying." Sam was facing her momma.

She stuck her hands forcefully in her pockets and immediately regretted throwing away her bell-bottoms. Worn as they were, the pockets didn't have holes. Her index finger slid right out of a hole in her right front pocket. Sam instantly knew her finger was stuck.

She pulled back. *Stuck.*

Sam's face twisted as she tried to sort out her predicament.

Her momma smiled.

When Sam still couldn't free her finger, Momma burst quietly into laughter, putting her hand over her mouth, visibly trying to control herself.

"I guess, I can't be mad when you fail so miserably at being tough. Let me help you."

Sam pulled back. "I'm tough. *And* strong."

Momma smiled all the way into her eyes. "And your finger is still stuck in your pants pocket."

Sam wasn't the least bit amused. She pulled and released, pulled, and released. Sam sighed deeply; her finger was hopelessly stuck.

Sam conceded defeat by pushing her right hip forward.

Her momma reached out, pulling the fabric from below. Sam pulled and tugged, her finger magically releasing. She rubbed it.

Momma pulled out two cups. "Sit down. Let's have some milk and chat a bit about why you were outside in the middle of the night."

Sam plopped into the nearest chair at the table. She huffed and crossed both her arms.

Momma placed two cups of milk in front of them. "Do I need to turn on another light?"

"No," Sam answered quickly. "I can see fine."

Light spilled into the room from the kitchen light above the stove.

Sam didn't want to give her mother any more advantages in this discussion. Getting her finger stuck was enough embarrassment for the rest of her life.

"Now tell me, why *were* you outside in the middle of the night?"

Sam gripped her chair. She couldn't answer that. Momma would be furious. Sam was glad she'd lost the knife; at least she didn't have to explain that.

"Why are *you* up in the middle of the night?"

"Well, if you must know, I heard someone rather loudly close the patio door. So, I got up to see who it was. When I reached the door, I opened it and looked outside. And believe it or not, I saw my eldest child slipping into the shadows, closely followed by a rather large dog."

Momma tilted her head in a way that still demanded an answer. Sam wasn't off the hook.

Sam huffed.

"Huff if you will but we are still gonna talk."

"Why? Talking doesn't ever help anything."

"This is why you need to talk, because you refuse to."

"Sarah isn't talking, and you aren't chasing her around all night."

"Sarah has been sleeping with us. And we *are* chasing her around. We are all very worried."

"Well, I'm talking, and I don't suck my thumb. Enough?" When she said it, it dripped with disrespect that was not lost on her momma. Sam instantly regretted saying it.

"Sam." Her momma sat at the table, placing her hand over Sam's. Even in the darkness, Sam could see the tears shimmering on her mother's eyelashes. Her momma cleared her throat.

"No, you're right. You *are* talking. *And* you're not sucking your thumb. Sam, I just don't want you to be so angry. We love you. Your sister just needs time. I do keep telling you that."

Sam huffed again, this time crossing her arms.

"Time. How much time? When, when does it get better? She wasn't even hurt! Nothing happened to her! And it was *my* window!"

Sam sucked in a deep breath, shaking.

Why? She wasn't scared, was she?

Nothing made any sense.

"Sam, breathe."

"Don't tell me to breathe." Sam turned away from her mother in her chair.

"Sam." Defeat thickened her momma's words. "I wish you'd let us help you. Please tell me why you were outside."

"Help me?" Sam started to push her anger toward her mother, gazing up, preparing for the attack. Then she stopped. Her mother's tears rolled down her face, controlled and slow, tumbling rather than cascading. Tears that were leaking past all her mother's strength.

Sam reached up, astonished, and touched one.

Her momma held her daughter's hand to her face. "We all feel this, Sam. We all do."

Sam had never seen tears like these. With all her mother's strength, something was so terribly wrong that it pushed sadness past it all, leaking it out onto her cheeks.

Sam knew she had caused this too. Somehow, she had to stop it all, all of it.

"I'm sorry, Momma. I won't go back out at night."

"Why did you go out tonight?"

"I had to make sure the man was really gone."

"Was he gone?"

"Yes. But he left his hat. Do you think he'll come back for it?"

"No. I think Beau made an impression. All that blood didn't just belong to the dog. Where did you find the hat? The police checked for anything he might have dropped."

"In the bushes, under my window."

"I'll get it in the morning. You go on to bed and get some sleep."

Sam stood, then she hugged her momma. "I'm all right, Momma. I really am."

Sam lay down in her bed. The nails in her windowsill were all she ever saw anymore when she even glanced at it. Nailed shut. How did she get to be the prisoner?

Nothing added up. Her bedroom door was pushed open.

Sam glanced across as Beau slipped through the doorway, clambering up into the bed. Sam lifted up her covers, allowing him to slip under, curling his form around her, giving her the perfect place to lay her head. Sam thought about her mother.

She hadn't realized it until tonight, until she'd seen the tears leak past all that strength.

"Beau, we gotta watch out for Momma too. She's hurt. I dunno how, but she just is. How come everybody's hurt but not hurt? Beau, we gotta fix this, and we have to start with Sarah."

Sam pushed the fur up and smoothed it down. The dog studied Sam, curling tighter and laying his head right by her chest, nestling as close as a dog could possibly get.

Chapter 23

Sam jumped out of bed. She had the best idea. Candy cigarettes!

If anything could make Sarah feel better, it would be the forbidden cigarette candies.

Sam knew just where they were, hidden away from the ants in a mason jar in their place in the woods. *Today* would be the day Sam would make this better!

Stretching and smiling with her newfound answer, Sam jumped out of bed and ran into the kitchen. When she saw her momma, she ran up and hugged her.

Smiling, Sam let go and started setting the table for breakfast.

She felt her momma's eyes following her.

"Sam, what's gotten into you? Not that I mind; I'm just checking that you're okay."

"It's all gonna be all right now, Momma. You'll see."

"Why? What you got planned in that little head of yours?"

Sam turned her back on her momma, but she couldn't tell her the plan because she was sure Momma wouldn't approve of candy cigarettes. She never had.

"Nothing, Momma. It's just a beautiful new day, isn't it?"

Sarah came into the dining room. Sam hugged her sister.

She didn't care that Sarah didn't hug her back. She had the greatest plan … ever.

"Good morning, Sarah. Sit here. Breakfast's almost ready."

Sam pulled out her sister's chair. "Has Daddy gone to work?" Sam was sure he had. "Momma, I'll help with the babies."

"I've already fed them all. You've slept in, my little overachiever. Seems some rest might have been all you really needed."

Momma put a plate of biscuits and jam in front of each of the girls.

Sarah stared through her plate, then seemed to focus. She started eating.

Raindrops slid down the glass patio door. Sam looked out and saw Beau lying outside. She smiled wider. Beau would help her with her plan; he might even eat a cigarette too.

Momma sat at the table, coffee in her hand.

"Sam, what's your plan for the day? School starts again in about a week."

Sam smiled, her mouth full of food. She tried to answer but decided chewing was mandatory.

As her momma patiently waited, a smile just peeked out from behind her coffee cup.

"We're going to the creek today. Beau will be with us, so we'll be super safe. Sarah, you'd like that, wouldn't you?"

Sarah didn't answer but she seemed to understand. She looked right at Sam.

"Sarah, it will be super fun," Sam ventured. "We'll catch a crawdaddy."

Momma laughed. "Not today, you won't. It's been raining all morning. That creek will be too muddy."

"Oh, Momma, maybe not. But today is the day to do something spectacular."

"That's a mighty big word for a little girl. Where'd you find that one?"

"I'm a mighty smart girl." Sam smiled ear to ear, sure she'd found a solution.

Sarah was gonna talk to her all about candy cigarettes. Sarah was gonna be *soooo* happy.

It was gonna be the best day ever!

"Well, my mighty smart girl, be sure you stay close enough to hear me when I call."

Sam smiled. Momma still didn't know that everyone could hear her call, so there was no worry they'd miss her shouting for them. "I will, Momma. We won't go far."

"Just keep Beau with you. Okay?"

"Always. He doesn't ever leave us. Sarah, hurry up." She smiled at her sister. "We gotta get dressed."

Sam helped her momma with the dishes while Sarah dressed methodically in the clothes Momma had laid out for her.

Sam whispered to Sarah, "I got a surprise for you."

Sarah just sucked her thumb harder in response, her eyes as bewildered as ever.

Sam took her sister's hand. "Come on."

In Sam's room, she sat Sarah on the bed, quickly dressing too. As she put on her shoes, she peered up at her sister. "Sarah, you just wait. I got the perfect thing for today."

Sarah tilted her head, looking at her big sister.

Sam enthused, "There you are. Yes, you just wait! It's going to be amazing."

Sarah looked down just as quickly as she'd looked up, but it was all the encouragement Sam needed to know her plan was definitely going to work.

Momma handed Sam a sack with sandwiches inside. Smiling at her two girls, she said, "Sam, take good care of your sister. She won't talk if she wanders off, so keep her right next to you."

"Momma, you worry too much. Those are my woods, and Beau will find her right away if anything happens."

"Sam, don't go too far. I mean it."

"I won't, Momma. I told you, there's nothing there to be afraid of."

Sam took Sarah's hand. Sandwiches in one hand and Sarah's small fingers in the other, she pushed the patio door open with her foot, then stepped out onto the patio.

Peeking her head out the door, Momma looked at Beau.

"This is against my better judgment, but I trust you to look after my girls. I won't stop my girl venturing out; I love Sam's smile too much to do anything to make it fade."

The dog was standing. As if in response to Momma, he took his place right beside Sam.

Hand in hand, the two girls and a very big dog entered the woods right next to the dogwood. Sam whispered to Sarah, "Candy cigarettes."

Sarah pulled her thumb out of her mouth as if a magic code had been revealed!

Stopping on the trail, Sam said, "Yes, I have candy cigarettes, remember! My stash!"

She thought she saw the beginning of a smile on Sarah's face.

Sam beamed with delight.

"Sarah, they're just this way." Sarah smiled; Sam was sure of it! You feel like running?"

Sarah looked at Sam, nodding.

They took off so fast that Sam dropped her sandwiches.

She didn't care enough to look back, glancing at her sister.

Sarah was running, running without her thumb in her mouth. She was holding her sister's hand, and they were running! Sam was careful not to run too fast.

Beau was on one side and Sarah on the other, and this small thing made Sam happier than she could ever remember being before. This was gonna work. Sarah was gonna get unstuck!

A deer scurried across the trail in front of them, Beau giving chase. Sam smiled, having no worry at all that Beau would hurt it. He loved the woods as much as she did.

They reached their secret place. Sam let go of Sarah, sliding underneath the brush.

She could hear Sarah doing the same behind her.

In the opening toward the back, Sam saw it. The mason jar. She picked it up. Inside, the candy cigarettes were safe and sound. She turned.

Horror gripped her as she heard Sarah cry out. Not in words, but a whimper, a plaintive mew.

Something was pulling Sarah backwards out of the opening. Sarah's desperate hands and her short fingernails clawed at the ground, her tiny voice crying out again, a desperate plea as she dug into the earth over and over, trying to stay this side of the opening.

In a flash, it was over, done, and Sarah was gone.

Sam pushed through into the woods, following Sarah as fast as she could. She looked away from the ground and horror overtook her.

Kevin was standing there, holding Sarah up by one foot. She wasn't struggling; it was as if she was prey, prey that had given up.

Her thumb was firmly in her mouth and her eyes were dull.

Sam stepped forward, trying to make herself big. She tried to scream but was strangled, her body remembering being unable to breathe.

Kevin shook her sister. He laughed. "It won't be a lick of fun if she just hangs here."

Sam looked on in increasing terror as he shook her again.

She looked around, needing something to hurt him with. Anything. There on the ground was her kitchen knife. She reached for it.

Grabbing it in her right hand, she stared rigidly at Kevin, rage filling her veins.

She pushed off with her right foot, intent on lunging through Kevin, cleaving right through him with her blade. A gurgling cry left her throat as she felt a huge hand grip her hair.

Something pulled her up. She tried to turn her head but couldn't.

Her feet were on the ground, yet she couldn't get her footing. Beau growled. The hand turned, and Sam was looking up, directly into the eyes of her elementary school principal.

His snarl was predatory, and he looked all twisted but she knew him.

"Sam. You're going to be quiet, or we'll finish off your dog and your sister. Now, be a good girl. Tell the dog you're okay."

He said it with so quietly, and with so much control. Sam knew she had to comply.

"Beau, no." It was a whisper, but Sam got it out. Her throat was closing.

She started to struggle but he shook her, hard.

"Oh no, you won't be doing any more of that. Kevin, show her." Kevin shook Sarah so hard that her thumb came out of her mouth with a gasp. "Do you understand now, Sam?"

Sam shook her head. Beau was still growling, hair on end, slowly edging forward.

Sam reached inside herself, gripping her knife.

She told herself to think, saying forcefully this time, "No, Beau, stop."

The dog stopped moving, his growl still permeating the air around them.

"Good girl. Now I'm going to put you down and you're going to stand still." The principal looked at her calmly.

Sam had no intention of standing still but she forced herself to relax in compliance. If she could just get an opportunity, just one …

On the other side of the clearing, by the big oak, a shadow of a huge man appeared.

"Wait a minute, guys." His voice was matter of fact, even, and—Sam thought—terrifyingly calm.

Sam struggled to look up, but her principal had tightened his grip on her hair, lifting her higher.

"This is none of your business. Kevin, shoot that damn dog. This time, shoot him three times instead of twice."

The third voice was stronger now, closer. "No, you won't do that, Kevin."

She could see Kevin having trouble holding Sarah and reaching for his gun. He dropped Sarah. She crumpled on the ground, drawing up into a ball, thumb still in her mouth.

Sam could feel Beau getting closer. She had to do something.

When she saw Thomas's face, she gasped. He grabbed Kevin by the arm, wrenched him up off his feet. The gun fell to the ground, toppling near Sarah.

Thomas looked at her principal.

"Glad to finally meet you face to face. You've been hard to find." He waved his hand at Beau and the dog sat. "My boy and I have been hunting you for months."

Sam looked at Beau. Had he called him his boy? Beau's hackles stayed raised; the dog stood. And Beau eased across to stand beside Thomas.

Kevin swung a fist. Thomas dodged it easily. "Easy, boy." Kevin was so frustrated, he ushered forth a string of words Sam had never heard before. She was too focused on Sarah to care. Sam drew in a huge breath, then hollered, "Sarah, run!"

Sarah just lay there.

Her principal laughed. "Sam, neither of you are going anywhere."

He pulled her up again but Sam held her breath. "Let me go."

She thrust herself forward, trying to get free.

Kevin swung his fist again and when he couldn't hit Thomas, he kicked Sarah, all his anger and wrath coming out in the onslaught against her little, defenseless sister.

Beau immediately moved to put his body on top of Sarah, a guttural growl emanating.

Kevin sneered. "Damn dog. Told you we should have killed that damn thing before we came back."

Thomas grabbed Kevin, then threw him to the ground in front of the principal.

"*There's* your dog."

He spit chewing tobacco right next to Kevin, who was doing his best to stand.

"You shouldn't have let him go. We're gonna enjoy killing you, then we'll enjoy both these girls at our leisure."

He smiled brightly, then shook Sam again as if it was a period to his awful sentence.

Thomas wasn't fazed by it.

Sam briefly made eye contact with Thomas. For a split second, she thought she saw fear, then it was gone, replaced by cool water flowing toward her.

Who was this hobo, this stranger?

"Samatha, my girl, easy. We're gonna work this out like the hunters we are." Her principal sneered when he said it. Sam let her body slump, trying to make herself heavy.

Heavy like the babies did when they were pitching a temper tantrum.

Thomas squatted, leisurely tossing a stick he'd been chewing onto the ground.

Beau wasn't growling, but he wasn't leaving Sarah either.

He just stood over her, hackles still raised.

"Easy boy." Thomas reached out and patted Beau on the head. He looked at the principal, saying, "Best dog I've ever had. Samantha, girl, be sure to tell your momma thanks so much for patching him up so well. She's really got a gift." Thomas smiled genuinely at Sam, then turned his attention to the two other men in the clearing. "Now, boys, we got something to discuss."

Kevin was standing now, but the gun lay right next to Beau and Sam knew they wouldn't get it without a fight. She gripped her knife.

Thomas made eye contact with her again, lifting his finger toward her, warning her to be still. Sam gripped the knife harder but didn't move.

Her principal sneered again. "We got nothing to discuss. This ain't none of your business."

Thomas smiled easily, his face quiet. "But it is, it really is. You see, my wife died a few days after we found my little girl. The police couldn't find a trace because the water washed you all away but I knew we'd find you. Took us almost six months." He patted the dog again. "Beau found you first, but we had to wait for you to come back. We saw your hat and we knew you'd be around. I had to be sure it was really you. You are really the one."

Sam gasped, "His hat!"

"Shut up, stupid girl," the principal sneered. He looked at Sam, and she swung her knife as hard as she could. Her principal answered her swing with his fist.

Sam's world went black.

Chapter 24

O ne eye fluttered open to see Thomas standing over her. The other eye stayed shut.

Sam thought she was dreaming. Thomas was holding up a paper sack.

"Thanks for dropping these. Tell your momma she makes great sandwiches."

Beau licked the side of her face. Sam tried to sit up, touching her face, her left eye swollen shut. Beau nuzzled into her chest and she stroked the fur.

Thomas said softly, easing her back to the ground, "Easy, little butterfly, you took a hard hit."

Sam tried to push the darkness back, feeling herself being lifted off the ground.

The world went black again.

"Sooowwiiieee!" Her mother's hog call. Sam sat up. *We gotta get home. Sarah, it's late.* She was thinking it, not speaking it. No voice, like Sarah. She looked around, completely disoriented.

Sarah lay in a heap next to her. Sam couldn't see her face.

They were lying under the big oak. She panicked, when, all of a sudden, the events of the day came crashing into her mind. "Sarah." Her voice sounded foreign, raspy. Sarah didn't move.

Sam grabbed her sister, rolling her over. Looking at her, more panic filled Sam's lungs.

She watched as Sarah screamed, no sound permeating the air, only an anguished stare.

Sam touched her face, and Sarah wrapped both arms around her, weeping.

A hissing sound came from around the bend. Sam turned her head.

It came from their place. Looking up, Sam saw the vultures; they were circling.

She pried herself from her sister. They weren't dead. Sam touched the matchbox in her pocket. Yes, definitely 'not dead.' Vultures came for dead things; she knew that.

Sam touched her face, felt her eye. She tried to open it; she couldn't. She looked at Sarah, beginning to slowly check her sister. Legs first, arms, face …

Besides being dirty, and having a few bruises, Sarah looked fine, sitting there sucking her thumb, looking out into the nothingness that was her world.

Sam tried to speak as softly and reassuringly as she could. "Sarah, I gotta go check on Beau. I'll be right back." Sarah sucked her thumb faster in response, same as usual.

"Sooowwiieee!"

Sam knew she had to hurry. She stood and quickly, her body aching everywhere. She walked around the bend of the trail behind the old oak. A vulture hissed and hopped away from her.

"Beau?" Nothing. "Beau." She said it louder. "Beau!"

Dark pools covered places on the ground; she thought it might be blood, and it smelled terrible. She could see dog prints everywhere, also big bootprints.

She saw where Kevin had been thrown to the ground, a black spot marked by a single spatter of his familiar chewing tobacco.

Rain started falling gently. Sam ran the perimeter while she checked under the privet.

Nothing else. No Beau. No Thomas. No principal. No Kevin.

Nothing else. Her mind wandered.

"Sowwwiieee."

The sound snapped into Sam. Her mother.

Sarah!

Sam ran back to the oak, relieved to see Sarah still sitting where she had left her, still silent, still stunned. In Sarah's eyes, the gentle innocence was gone, replaced by fear and emptiness.

"Sarah, we have to go home. Can you stand?"

She took her sister's hand, and Sarah stood. Sam immediately noticed Sarah couldn't walk. Her ankle. Sam pulled the sock down. Purple bruises.

"Sarah, I'm gonna try to carry you, okay?"

No response.

Sam took her sister's hand, leaving the other one in her mouth. Sam bent over, then squatted, her sister heavier than she imagined. She tried carrying her under her arm. *Nope. Too heavy.*

Taking a deep breath, Sam squatted again, pulling Sarah across her shoulders.

Sam pushed up, standing, able to adjust to Sarah's weight.

She walked out of the woods, falling to her knees several times.

Each time, she would reassure Sarah that everything was fine, then push up again, regain her footing and keep moving forward.

At the edge of the trail, Sam leaned on the dogwood. She heard her mother gasp, and felt Sarah lifted from her shoulders. Rain started falling harder. Thunder clapped in the distance.

She thought she heard her mother say, "Sam, follow me inside."

Sam didn't move from the tree until she felt a hand take hers.

She looked big eyed at her momma—and silently followed.

The rain wet them down completely before they reached the patio door. When they stepped inside, Sam gazed at her mother.

Momma appeared enraged as she let go of Sam's hand, laying Sarah on the dining room table.

Sam said, "Momma, I tried. I really tried to keep her safe. I'm so sorry."

Her voice sounded funny inside her head, quiet, raspy, tired. Sam fainted.

***

When she woke up again, she was in her bed. Gazing toward the windowsill, she spotted that the shade was up. Rain was falling hard, pelting the glass and the sill, washing the grime from the windowpanes. There was thunder, this time close, and there came great flashes of blue and red lights in the darkness outside. Hounds were baying in the distance, eerie.

Sam sat straight up in her bed. *They are looking for—hunting—Beau. They smell him!*

They would kill him if they found him. And Thomas, they would also kill Thomas without a thought. Sam immediately regretted sitting up so fast. Her head swam.

She swung her legs over the side of the bed, slowly this time.

She had to get up, had to stop them. She touched her face, finding it clean. Her night shirt …

When had she gotten herself dressed for bed?

Dishes were clanking, a terrible cacophony.

Sam steadied herself, walking into the kitchen where her mother was packing dishes. Not with her usual care, either. She was cramming items quickly into boxes, crying.

No, her mother was not just crying; she was sobbing and enraged.

She was breaking the rest of her china as she crammed the pieces in, grabbing a trash bag before she started emptying the dry cupboard too, throwing everything inside into the bag.

Her mother glanced her way, then stopped, taking in the sight of Sam.

She dropped her bag. Her mother reached out her arms and fell to her knees.

Sam ran and wrapped her arms around her momma, feeling her mother's sobbing.

When her mother pulled back, she held Sam's narrow shoulders, looking at her. Momma wiped her own face with her apron, then cupped Sam's face with just one hand.

"We're moving, as soon as we're packed. Your daddy got a job four hours away in town, so we'll have to stay in a hotel. That'll be fun, won't it? I think they have a pool." Her mother's voice was strained with anger and sadness but her eyes were gentle.

Sam absorbed it all.

She stood straight, squared her shoulders, and prepared to answer her mother's questions.

None came. Her mother stood, grabbed the bag up from the floor and, as if nothing had disturbed her, continued cramming items inside.

The patio door flew open, Daddy stepping inside followed by two police officers … and the farmer's wife who patted Sam affectionately on the shoulder as she walked past to help Momma.

"Easy, we'll get all this. Easy." The farmer's wife spoke with tenderness to her momma.

Momma wiped her face again, then dropped the bag. Leaning her arms against the countertops, she stared out of the kitchen window.

Sam couldn't see her momma's face but was sure that whatever she saw, it was full of fury.

Daddy was standing in front of Sam. His stare—plus the baying of the hounds—pulled Sam into reality again. Sam's gaze took in the sight of her daddy, the strongest man she'd ever known, now dwarfed by her mother's anger. He looked at her momma, then back at Sam.

"Can you talk?"

Sam tried once, then cleared her throat. It was sore, very sore, as if she'd been screaming. She didn't remember screaming at all, but perhaps she had. Everything seemed strange nowadays.

"Sam, it's okay if you can't." He touched her hand gingerly, kneeling in front of her, the police officers flanking him on each side. The hounds were closer now.

The patio door opened again. The farmer hurried inside, dripping from the rain.

"The hounds have circled back, I think they lost the scent."

The farmer's voice was strained.

Her daddy stood. Sam would have been sure he had forgotten her but her daddy didn't let go of her hand, just gently adjusted it.

"The rain?" His voice sounded strangled. "They'll never find him if we don't tonight."

Hope. Sam swallowed.

Maybe they wouldn't find Beau or Thomas. She had to think.

The farmer answered, "Maybe not; I think they're done for tonight. The rain should pass by morning. It would help if we knew who we were looking for, Sam."

She looked up at the men in the room, meeting the eyes of each one, trying desperately to think of an answer. The *right* answer. Her daddy turned and looked down at her. "Sam?"

Suddenly, her momma was slamming her fists on the dining room table.

"Leave *my* child alone! Get out of *my house*. Leave *my child alone*! Get out there and earn your goddamn worth for a change!"

Sam watched as the anger in her momma's eyes gave way to grief, her mother collapsing into the arms of the farmer's wife.

The men all cleared their throats at different times, slowly emptying the room.

All but her daddy who refused to let go of her hand.

When he looked at her again, tears were welling in his eyes. "I am so sorry, Sam."

He wiped his eyes on his wet sleeve, stood, let go of her hand and joined the men outside.

Sam leaned against the wall behind her, breathing it all in. Everything. She stared out of the patio door, hearing nothing but the rain, the rhythmic sounds of it hitting the patio door. Exhaustion overtook her, and she slid down the wall onto the floor.

She closed her eyes, her heart aching for Beau's fur to wrap around her.

***

It was the farmer's wife who woke Sam in the end.

Sam was lying on the floor, still resting against the wall, a knitted cream blanket covering her.

"Sit up, Sam. Easy, girl." Sam was always struck by the kindness in this woman's voice.

She looked at the farmer's wife, puzzled.

Two of the older men from town lifted the dining room table and took it outside.

Sam gasped and pushed against the wall.

Just outside the sliding glass door, she could hear the two men talking as they handed over the table to the next group loading the truck.

"You see her eye?"

"Oh yeah, they think she fell coming outta the woods."

"Ain't for positive."

"Oldest was ruined anyway. Bickel boy and her. Word is she was flirting with him all year."

"Bet if we find the dog …"

Sam pushed forward to hear more, but the men had moved off the patio.

She felt a hand on top of hers.

"Sam, it's gonna be okay. You're all right now." The farmer's wife handed her a glass of cold milk. Sam took it, so thirsty she drank every drop.

Then, the farmer's wife handed her a biscuit filled with orange marmalade.

"You're almost all packed up. Be easy on your momma; she's exhausted."

Sam nodded. "Where are we going?"

"Somewhere your momma says is safe."

"Beau? Where's Beau?"

She patted Sam's shoulder, sadness in her words. "No one's seen the dog."

The farmer's wife stood and left.

Sam ate bites of biscuit in between quiet tears, abject grief filling her heart.

Sam told herself to stop crying. It took a few minutes, but by the time her biscuit was finished, she was strong again. Strong enough to face this, all of it.

Her momma took her hand. "I need you to dress your sister. Don't push her to talk. And don't push yourself. The babies are almost ready to be loaded."

Momma led Sam into the back bedroom but there was nothing in it, nothing. From there, they walked into the back bathroom where Sarah sat on the side of the tub, her thumb firmly in her mouth. Momma handed Sam two sets of clothing, clean clothes she'd never seen before.

And a white cotton washcloth.

"Sam, it's all gonna be okay. I promise." Momma pulled the door closed behind her.

Sam looked at her sister and knew that was one promise her momma couldn't keep. Everything was broken, so broken it wouldn't ever be fixed. Like the pieces of her mother's china, her world would never be the same again. Sam hoped someone had saved her a few pieces to take to this new safe place. Pieces of her childhood, pieces of Beau, pieces of her woods.

Sam slowly washed her sister's face. "Sarah, are you hurt?"

Nothing. Scratches covered her sister's torso and legs, her elbows rubbed raw too. Sarah's ankle was wrapped in a bandage and Sam was careful not to get it wet.

Sam gently put her sister's clothes on her. Sarah complied, sliding her arms into her new shirt, lifting her legs, and sliding on her shorts. Sam was careful with her sister's ankle, easing her shoe on slowly, looking for any sign of pain in Sarah's face.

Sarah just stared ahead and slowly sucked her thumb.

Sam turned to herself. She washed her face and wished for a toothbrush. When she looked in the mirror, she was immediately glad she didn't have to look long enough to brush her teeth.

Her left eye was swollen completely shut, purple bruising extending all the way down into her neck.

She touched her eye, had to. It was so swollen she couldn't believe it was part of her face.

Scratches and bruises covered her. She was sore everywhere.

She knew Sarah must have been too.

"Sarah, can you walk?" Sarah quickened her thumb sucking in response.

"Sarah, I think Beau's gone." Sarah stared straight ahead. No response.

Sam sighed, then pulled on her brand-new pair of bell-bottom jeans. A beautiful flowered, embroidered white shirt lay across the back of the toilet, ready to wear.

Normally, Sam would have been thrilled but this morning, everything dripped of sadness.

Finally, dressed, she took her sister's hand.

Sarah dropped her thumb. "Beau's scary; they're all quiet now."

Sam looked at her sister, unsure how to respond. Sarah had spoken. But what she'd said was ... *something weird.* Yet she didn't really grasp it, couldn't comprehend it.

She dropped to one knee. "Sarah, what happened? Why was he scary?"

When her sister's eyes clouded, Sam shook her.

"Sarah, please, please tell me."

Sam, realizing what she'd just done, dropped both her arms to let go of Sarah.

Sam slid down into a sitting position on the floor in front of her sister.

"I won't ever make this right, Sarah, never. This is my fault."

The bathroom door opened. Momma stepped inside.

"Don't you two girls look beautiful! Time to go!" Her voice was way too cheery for the day. Sam had seen her face and knew she wasn't beautiful, not at all.

They both followed Momma outside to the station wagon.

Sam looked around the house, seeing it empty. Everything she'd known and loved was gone.

The youngest babies were all lying on the back floorboards, the next older ones sitting on the back seat. The wayback was open.

Sam helped Sarah inside, then climbed up.

Momma smiled at them, closing the hatch, announcing way too brightly, "Away we go!"

Sam watched as her daddy pulled out in front, driving a large, rented U-Haul.

Momma started the station wagon and they pulled out, down the driveway.

As they passed across the front for the last time, Sam stared at the house, seeing the porch, then her bedroom window. They were there, then they were gone. Sam watched the trees passing behind her, then the dirt road became pavement as they headed into town for the final time.

Chapter 25

Daddy parked the U-Haul and joined Momma on the sidewalk in front of Woolworth's.

Ms. Manny waved at Momma when they pulled up.

Momma opened the hatch. "Sam, you can get out and walk around a little but don't leave the block. Your daddy and I are gonna get snacks for the drive. You remember Ms. Manny? She's gonna stay here with you and the station wagon while we go in."

Sam jumped out, seeing Momma go inside the Woolworth store, Daddy dutifully holding the door and then joining her inside.

She stood next to Ms. Manny for a second, neither of them speaking.

Theresa was posting something on the telephone pole, so Sam waved.

Theresa didn't wave back, just nodding, her hands busy. Sam quickened her step, happy to see her friend again. Theresa gasped at Sam as she got close.

"Sam, did your daddy do that?" Theresa looked at Sam knowingly and swallowed hard.

"No." Sam said it far more firmly than she meant to.

She had forgotten all about her face, and now, she stared down at the ground.

"My mama's got us all out here, posting these flyers."

Sam looked up, then was sorry she had done so. A picture of Kevin, smiling, and the word 'MISSING' in bold black letters appeared on the flier.

Sam gasped.

"I know, right. He's too mean to really be missing." Theresa finished putting a thumbtack on the flier, then sighing and stepping back.

"We're moving to town," Sam said but didn't look up.

"Well, don't be sad about it. At least one of us will get to see the world. Bet your momma loaded up like mine, packing 'em babies up tight." She looked hard at Sam. "Dang, your face looks bad. Good thing your momma can patch up anything."

"Is Kevin really missing?"

"Yeah, but I expect him to pop up anytime now. I wouldn't be mad if he never came back though. He's probably got himself under some woman."

"Under some woman?"

"Yea. Oh, I forgot. You'll understand one day. I sometimes forget how little you still are because you say such grown-up things."

"I'm not little, and I do know things."

"That's not what I meant. But yes, you certainly do know things. How's your sister?"

"The same."

"They say something happened that must have scared the soul out'a her."

"I dunno."

A police officer walked up and tacked a poster right next to Theresa's.

It was a big poster, much bigger than Theresa's homemade flier.

Sam was just grateful for the interruption, having no idea what she'd say anymore, but whatever it would've been, she was sure it would have been wrong.

A picture of a man wearing a fedora, looking more serious than necessary appeared on the poster. Again 'MISSING' appeared in big block letters.

Sam tried not to look surprised, and suddenly, the ground became more interesting again.

Theresa stood staring at the poster, as if by just looking at it like that, Kevin might reappear. Not that she even seemed to care much, either way. Maybe that wasn't the reason for her stares.

"Now ain't that something," Theresa began. "Principal Dolus disappeared in the storm last night, hunting hogs. He ain't from around here anyway. Rumor is that he's running from his ugly spinster wife. Well, I guess she's gonna try and find him."

From next to the station wagon, Ms. Manny called out, "Sam, come back over here."

Sam glanced up one more time at the pole. "I gotta go."

"I know you do. Thanks for saying goodbye. Whatever happened to your face, I hope you gave 'em hell for it." Theresa hugged her.

Sam pulled away quickly, heading back to Ms. Manny, her head beginning to swim sideways again. She breathed deeply several times before reaching Ms. Manny, fumbling in her pocket, stroking her matchbox. Hoping desperately for her strength to return, she leaned against the station wagon.

Ms. Manny looked down at her.

"You're stronger than you have any idea you are. This won't break you. You keep squaring those shoulders of yours. Not sure what happened in those woods, but I got a feeling you did this town a favor."

The Woolworth door swung open, Momma heading out first, a bag in each hand.

Daddy came out behind her, smiling.

Daddy walked up to Sam. "Is my girl ready for her new adventure?"

Sam couldn't help grinning back. He hadn't smiled in so long.

Momma turned to Ms. Manny. "Thank you so much for meeting us out here. Everyone else was so busy. After everything, I just couldn't leave them alone on the street. Even for a minute."

Ms. Manny nodded. "I got a chance to see one of my best students. My bet is she'll wind up being the one I always remember. Hang on, I got you something."

Ms. Manny walked over to her car, tugging out a big package wrapped in parchment.

When she returned, She handed it to Sam's momma.

Momma pulled back the parchment, a large quilt peeking out from underneath.

Momma gasped, wide-eyed, her hands jittering.

Ms. Manny offered, "I know you're leaving, but the quilting ladies have been working all year to give you this."

Momma's eyes teared up. "Are they sure they want me to have it? I don't think we'll ever be back here."

Ms. Manny just held her hand and shook her head yes.

"Come on Sam, hop in." Daddy had the hatch open, and Sam jumped into the wayback.

She moved close to Sarah, whispering, "I know who you meant. There's missing posters."

Sarah's eyes grew wide, making Sam immediately regret saying anything.

Momma hugged Ms. Manny a second time, harder, closer.

She climbed into the front seat of the station wagon, laying the quilt on the front floorboards, then gazing back in the rearview window. "Sam, I want you to know that the farmer will be on the lookout for Beau. If he shows up, we'll come back for him. I promise."

Sam didn't answer. Some promises just couldn't be kept and she knew that for sure now.

Watching out the back of the station wagon, she saw her little town get smaller and smaller.

Sarah quickly went to sleep, and Sam adjusted herself into a more comfortable position.

Despite everything, this was the only home she'd ever known, so she felt herself losing something the farther away it got. They turned onto another dirt road.

"Sam, you still awake back there?"

"Yes, Momma."

"Get a good last look. No more red clay dirt roads after this one. It's freeway after this."

There was happiness in her momma's voice, and hope.

Her momma turned on the radio. The happy music permeated the station wagon.

Sam watched as her last dirt road stretched out behind them.

A man stepped out from the woods, a man with a very big dog.

Sam put both her hands on the hatch window.

The man waved slowly, Sam lifting her right hand and waving back, tears hanging off her eyelid. She only wished she could cry with both eyes.

In the background, the radio continued its song.

'It's important to me, that you know you're free, 'cause I never want to make you change for me. Think of me … You know that I'd be with you if I could …'

Sam drew in a hard breath as the station wagon turned off the dirt road, the pavement appearing behind them.

Epilogue

Pulling into a parking spot, Sam shifted her car into park next to a red jeep. The sun shone so brightly that it made looking through the windshield difficult. She took a deep breath in, letting it out slowly. Stepping from her black BMW, she clicked the alarm to lock it, then clicked it again to unlock it. "No fear today. You get to stay unlocked."

The brick building, simple and adorned only by long white windows, seemed a bit lonely. She was late, as usual. Sam started walking toward the doorway. It opened, and a beautiful twenty-something woman peeked out, her long red hair flowing across her shoulders, blowing slightly in the wind. When she saw Sam, she stepped all the way outside.

"Sam, you're here."

"I am. Is your aunt Theresa here?"

"Of course she is."

"It's been a minute."

"Yeah, well that's on you." The girl stepped forward and hugged her.

"Leave it to my daughter to call me out." Sam smiled and hugged her back.

"This is a tough one."

"No tougher than most of my cases." Sam briefly eyed the ground. "She's always upset. Your aunt Theresa wasn't really made for this stuff. She's too forgiving."

"And you're too tough. We all have our faults. Anyway, I'm glad you're here."

"Elizabeth, I'm not glad at all. It's not the way things should have ended."

"No, it's not. No one will argue with you on that."

Her daughter took her hand and led her inside. As the door closed, a hearse pulled quietly by.

Entering the building, Sam noticed the room was full. She let go of her daughter's hand and began moving around the room, stunned to see how many people were there.

Has my family really gotten this large? I have to stop working so much.

A tall broad-shouldered man, looking not so happy to see her, appeared out of the crowd. "Well, look what the cat dragged home."

"Enough."

"Why enough? Your lawyer cases *not enough* drama for you?"

"Growing up without your twin *not enough* pain for you?"

He burst out laughing, then added, "Same old Sam, hard as nails."

Sam smiled at her brother. "Glad to see you're just as sarcastic as ever. Where's your wife?"

"She's doing what all the women *should* be doing, comforting everyone."

"That's never been my best act. How's everyone doing?"

"Mom's devastated, Dad's trying to act tough. Theresa is caretaking. You know, all the normal stuff."

"There's nothing normal about today."

"Mom will be glad you're here, and Aunt Theresa's been asking for you."

"She's the only normal one in the bunch."

"That's why Mom went back to that ol' hick town to get her; she needed a 'normal' child."

He reached out and drew Sam into a huge hug. "Glad you're here; it's been too long."

Sam saw her mother across the room. She drew in a breath, reached into her pocket, and rubbed the matchbox. She wasn't ready yet.

A tall glass pitcher of water with cups settled nicely beside it caught her attention.

Sam walked to it and poured a glass. She held the cold water, getting her bearings. "Why am I so upset? Jesus, Sam. Pull yourself together."

"Because your sister just died a death we all saw coming for years but couldn't stop no matter how hard we tried, that's why."

Sam stared at Theresa. Her friend's southern drawl of an accent was almost gone. Sam's momma had made sure a great education had fixed that, and even older, Theresa still glowed with kindness. Sam hugged her.

"Why do things have to end so badly?"

"You know there's stuff in between, don't you? You miss all that when you dive into work. Work that you do for free now because you've decided you don't need more money."

When Theresa had first moved in, she had been beaten almost beyond recognition. Sam remembered the day Theresa had arrived, fourteen years old, and terrified of just being touched. The world had stripped her of everything. Sam's first law case had been her mother's formal adoption of Theresa. They didn't need to because, by then, Theresa was an adult. Momma had insisted.

There was no one who opposed it; she had completed it in two weeks during the first year of law school, that and settling Matthew's accounts. Somehow, the boy had saved enough in two years to leave Theresa sufficient money for a downpayment on a house.

Sam looked at Theresa in wonder, kindness still seeping from her very core.

She never blamed anyone for anything. Sam took a swallow of cool water before responding.

"Yeah, well there are still people who need defending. People who don't have money to pay someone."

"Sam." Theresa sat in the chair by the wall, taking Sam's hand and pulling her down into the chair next to her. "We need you too."

"Look around. This family is huge. No one will miss one." Sam laughed.

Theresa did not.

"We miss you. Mom misses you. Heck, Sarah's missed you."

"How do you know? She didn't ever speak, just wasting her life by sitting around. She never did anything. No kids. No marriage. No job. Same thing every day. She just read her books and stayed in the same room for years and years, doing nothing of any value."

"She loved you."

"Not really, well maybe in her own way. She stopped even looking at me when I visited. So, I stopped coming by."

"The world isn't a place everyone can live," Theresa argued.

"If they had just let her stay somewhere, they could have helped her."

"Sam, stop that. We *all* tried. She's been in and out of psychiatric hospitals her whole life."

"You're right. I should have tried harder, been around more and maybe this wouldn't have happened."

"Stop that too; this isn't your fault. It isn't your fault she was afraid of everything. You didn't make anything happen. You're not the beginning and ending of everything. Remember, you blamed yourself for Matt's death." Theresa shook her head. "You were several hundred miles away. That wasn't your fault and this isn't either."

Sam swallowed hard.

Theresa stared into the crowd. "You need to talk to your mom. She was hoping you'd come, you know. The last fight you had really took its toll, so be kind. Ten years have passed, but the hurt is still there. And Dad didn't take too kindly to your attitude."

Sam let out a hard breath. "His attitude needed adjusting."

"Sam, not everything is a fight. You could leave his ego intact just once; it wouldn't hurt anything." Theresa patted her hand, getting up to help one of the ladies with a wreath.

Sam sat up straight, taking a deep swallow of water from her glass.

What was left to say? Why had she come? Sam couldn't answer either question sufficiently in her mind, only knowing she needed to be here. She was surprised that she had been so welcomed, having expected the silent treatment.

Her mother was standing right next to the coffin.

Sam could tell from the movements of the tissue that she was crying softly. Her mother was the strongest woman she'd ever met, but this was a crushing blow. Sam remembered the hole in the ground. She was the only child who did. As an adult, Sam understood how hard it was to actually climb out of a hole, that it would take all the strength you had and then some.

Sam walked up beside her mom; she had everything to say but said nothing.

"You gonna tell me what happened that day? What happened that was so bad it chased one of my children away and struck the other silent?" There was no venom in what her mother said.

It was a matter-of-fact tone that seemed foreign to Sam.

"I thought we settled this years ago. I don't know what happened for sure." Sam would never tell them about Thomas, about his family, or about Beau.

"Whatever it was, it killed your sister slowly, one day at a time."

"Theresa says not everyone is meant for this world."

"Well, Theresa also spent all that money you gave her buying her old homestead from her brothers, then setting the whole place on fire."

"Dang, did she?" Sam chuckled. "Well played Theresa, well played." When she looked back at her mother, Sam lost her smile. Momma looked deadly serious. Sam cleared her throat.

"I had no idea."

"You have no idea about a lot of things. You just sit in your world, playing the heroine while the rest of us struggle through."

"Mom, I'm sorry."

Her mother turned around. "I know. I know you don't belong to us. You belong to the world. Of all my children, you are the one who doesn't need us to survive. You are a force of your own. As for Sarah, well, I don't know."

"Yes, you do, Mom. Sarah was full of all the sweetness in this world. Sweetness is not what it takes to survive."

"Survive? Is that what you're doing? I called you and sent you a letter."

"And you have my address."

"Yes, and you have mine."

One of the children walked up to the coffin, grabbing her hand.

Sam looked down to see the wide eyes of a five-or-six-year-old looking up at her. "Are you Aunt Sam?"

Her mother huffed and walked into the kitchen.

Sam smiled at the little girl. "I am! And what's *your* name?"

"Samantha. My daddy says I'm named after the bravest girl in the world."

Sam hugged her and set her back down on the ground, observing her run across the room and jump into the arms of her brother.

He smiled, Sam smiled back. She thought to herself, "Boy, I really have missed a lot."

Everyone settled into chairs. Sam sat with the family; frankly, there wasn't anywhere else to sit since the place was so full. They started the service, Sam trying not to yawn.

These were always the same, with people trying to make sense of death, of the finality of never seeing someone again.

Theresa took the podium. "I have always been grateful for my place in this family. Sarah was always such a joy. She made stockings, and sweaters. She poured herself into making others' lives better. She put together care packages and sealed letters for soldiers, and she gave all she had to everyone around her. She spoke to all of us through her actions."

Sam was shocked. She stopped listening because her mind was racing.

No one had told her Sarah had ever done anything so meaningful.

When she'd visited, she'd never seen her do anything but cry.

Sam settled herself, listening as person after person came up to the podium with stories of Sarah visiting the sick, holding hands with the homeless, bringing comfort everywhere she went.

By the time Theresa came back to the microphone, tears were pushing their way out of Sam's eyes against her will. She quietly wept.

"The best thing about being in this family is that we accept each other where we are, like we are, for who we are. Sarah loved, lived, and we will miss her."

Theresa handed the microphone to the preacher.

As the preacher droned on, Sam couldn't stop weeping, everything just spilling out.

Someone tapped her right shoulder, making her glance up.

Her youngest sister was holding an infant, standing right next to her.

Her sister whispered into her ear, "So, the ice queen does have feelings."

Sam immediately squared her shoulders, weeping suddenly. She whispered back, "And you're still having babies as if it's going out of style. My God, girl, how old are you?"

Sam knew her comment had the desired effect as her sister immediately turned from her, bouncing the infant as if comforting it.

Her youngest sister habitually blamed her for everything bad that had ever happened to anyone. This had to end soon.

She was grateful for her sister's comment; at least some things hadn't changed.

The preacher continued, "To bear the burdens of the sick is a great calling for us all. Sarah's life stands as a testimony to those of us who struggle, while her silence and her pain made her reach out to those of us who hurt. She understood our pain, lessening it with her presence.

Many of you in this room are here to pay your respects to someone who's struggled along with you. She brought you food when you were hungry, cleaned your house when you couldn't, and she freely sat with the dying and the sick, for hours, in silence, absorbing sadness and grief.

She quietly worked to lessen your burdens, never accepting payment for anything. In short, she gladly gave her life to us all. We will all miss her. The church founded a mission that many of you have funded, and her wonderful work—blessed by God—will continue. Let us pray."

Sam was astounded.

How much had she really missed? As the gathering started to disperse for the funeral procession that would take Sarah to her final resting place, Sam just stared at the pulpit.

Her sister grabbed her arm.

"I don't know if you pay attention enough to even know my name, so I'll introduce myself again. I'm Anna, your youngest sister." She shifted the baby on her hip to show Sam. "This is Abby. My others are with their dad in the back. Their names are Emma, Charlotte, Isabelle, Grace and my eldest, Thomas. He's beautiful and turned sixteen this year. He was Sarah's favorite. You should come over, you know! We'd love to spend some time with you."

Sam swallowed. Honestly, it was true. She'd never paid attention to Anna; there were years between them. She just looked at her sister, and for once, was speechless.

Her sister tapped her shoulder. "Think about it, Sam, we only live five miles from you. Thomas likes Latin and you're fluent in it, so you two might like each other. Sarah named him." Anna rolled her eyes. "You look surprised. Sarah could write; you did know that, didn't you?"

Thankfully, Anna didn't wait for an answer.

Sam knew Anna was the youngest but had never bothered to learn anything about her. All she really knew was that all her sister had ever wanted was a family, a big one.

And it seemed that she had fulfilled her wish.

Sam took a deep breath and stroked the match-box in her pocket.

She'd never wanted to be a mom herself, but she'd had Elizabeth with her third and last husband. Sam had never thought she was any good at nurturing. She still believed the same.

She quietly smiled to herself, thinking, "Elizabeth would definitely agree."

Sam pulled out her keys, glad to finally be leaving. She moved out from the pew, weaving through all the people. She just had to get to her car, and her obligation was over.

Pushing open the door, cool air filled her lungs. Finally, she was outside.

She took a deep breath.

"Sam." Her father followed her outside.

Sam kept walking toward her car. If she could just make it there, she might be able to make some sense of all this.

Her father was determined. "Sam, stop running." He quickened his steps.

Sam stopped and turned, saying, "I never run. I don't have to."

"You can believe that if you want to but it's not the truth."

"Did you come out here to shame me?"

"No. Sam, stop it. You're my daughter."

"Really? I would never have known."

He was breathing heavily, years of smoking having taken their toll. Sam let herself look entirely irritated at the intrusion, but she waited for him to catch his breath.

"Please don't leave. Sarah would have wanted you here."

"Well, I came."

"Can you not let your guard down for one minute? That's why no one returned your calls; we were sure anything we said would give you a reason *not* to come."

"Oh, so you're all ganging up on me again. Really, I was beginning to believe I was *really* welcome." Sam stood as tall as she could, noticing her father did not. He looked at her with pity, and it filled her with rage. Just as she was going to speak, he held up his hand.

"Peace. Enough. I don't want more war between us. I yield. I recognize you're a force of your own, so please don't go, not now, not like this. I miss you and want you in my life, no strings. You can be sarcastic and ridiculous, headstrong and opinionated. Just please don't leave again."

She tried to hold her anger, but it slid away as she looked at her father.

She questioned if she had ever really truly looked at him before. Tears welled at the corners of his eyes as he waited for her answer. His hair was gray, and his eyes were filled with warmth.

There was a sweetness there that she'd never seen before.

"Daddy." She put her hand on his shoulder, gazing into his eyes. "I'm just going to my car."

Her father's voice cracked. "I love you."

She hadn't hugged her father since law school graduation.

He'd asked her immediately afterwards when she was going to have a child and settle down. She reached for the anger she was certain was there, but couldn't find it.

She looked at him, wanting to judge him, wanting to hate him.

She couldn't do that either. What stood before her was an old man who loved his daughter dearly. And somehow, she loved him too. She reached out. Grabbed his hand.

And said, "I love you too."

He hugged her, then pulled away, looking down and wiping his eyes. He cleared his throat and squared his shoulders. "I have to get your mother."

Sam nodded, watching as he walked back inside. She had made no promises, but somehow, things had changed. Sam turned and continued walking slowly to her car.

She put her hand on the door. She hadn't locked it.

Elizabeth appeared on the other side, popping her head over the top of the car.

"Sam!"

She hadn't seen her daughter approach.

Sam jumped. "Girl, you know how to make an entrance!"

Her daughter giggled, saying with a wry smile, "I learned from the best. Your place in the procession is right behind Grandma and Grandpa. They'll pause for you to join in a minute."

Good God, did she have a choice about anything today? Sam answered, "Got it."

Elizabeth said, "I gotta go, my ride's waiting." She winked at Sam. Sam's daughter bounced across the parking lot, where a very handsome man was holding the door for her. Sam let herself wonder if this one was a keeper. She shook her head, smiling, and got into her car.

She started the engine. Pulled into her place. Slower than she liked, they moved along. Each car parked along the graveside, and Sam didn't get out until there was a huge crowd, and even then she just stood at the back. She could not really hear what was said, simply watching as individual flowers were laid on her sister's grave. She stood there quietly, seeing the coffin get covered with flowers, one at a time, placed by the multitude of people paying their respects.

Her mother stood tall. Sam couldn't help but be impressed by the strength dwelling there, radiating from Mother even at a distance.

The crowd dispersed, people passed her nodding, expressing how sorry they were for her loss. Her mother didn't move. The cars left, only her parents remaining standing at the graveside.

Workers started removing chairs, and her brothers returned, lowering her sister's coffin into the grave. They hugged her parents and joined their own families, leaving.

Sam finally stepped forward.

Shovels of dirt had begun being placed into the hole by the time Sam joined her parents.

Her mother spoke first. "Could you give us a minute?" Sam nodded and turned to leave. "No, Sam, I was talking to your father."

Sam stopped. Her father quietly patted her shoulder as he moved toward the car.

After a few minutes, Sam broke the silence. "What is there left to say?"

"There is lots to say. But I won't say any of that today. Today is for you. Your sister wanted you to have this." She handed Sam an envelope that said, 'To be Opened Only by Sam.'

The handwriting looked like that of a third grader.

Sam never knew her sister wrote letters. "She wrote it right after you left her a box, a box filled with papers, the last time you visited her. I have no idea what was in it. She actually got up at 3 a.m. and shredded it. Right after, she started writing us notes. Notes about what kind of coffee she liked, notes that said she wanted to go to the church and volunteer, then she started writing schedules for her time. Your father drove her around. Anyway, you have a huge family that loves you. Sarah said you needed to do what you were doing so we left you to it but we never stopped missing you, loving you, wishing to see you."

There was a pause, the women's eyes locked on one another in silent affection.

Her mother said, "Thank you for whatever was in that box. You gave me back my daughter, but it cost me another."

Sam swallowed hard. "I didn't know."

"You would have if you hadn't written us off. No matter how angry we make each other, no matter what we do to each other, Sam, family is always family. You can't choose us, and you can never choose to be rid of us. We will always be a part of each other. I will never be perfect."

"I never wanted you to be perfect." Sam couldn't help interrupting.

"Yes. You did. And you expect everyone to always do the right things. None of us can, it is an impossible standard. We just try to get better each day. We will continue to make mistakes, especially your father. You and he have a special relationship. You are his equal or better and he knows it. Don't let that go to your head. You have a lot to learn too, a lot about forgiveness, a lot about loving people for who they are instead of who you want them to be. Sarah taught us all about that. You would have loved seeing her with the sick, with the prisoner, people we would never have let into our lives. Sarah used them to open our family, to heal us all."

"I don't need healing. I'm just fine as I am."

"Then why does your daughter call you Sam?"

Silence permeated Sam's mind. She had no idea why she'd never thought that was odd. It was a good point. "It's because you're larger than life, so protected you think everything is a choice."

"It is. We make choices that form who we are."

"No. Sam. Each of my children are who they are when they are born. Each day afterwards, we shame them into hiding that from everyone else." Her mother started to say more but stopped and Sam let the silence permeate the space between them.

Her mother stopped the workers.

"I can't bear this anymore. I won't watch them cover my child. Sarah wanted the shovels, and couldn't stand the idea of a machine just pushing the dirt over her grave without a thought. And a coffin, takes my breath that one of my daughter's chose to be buried in a pine box. We could easily afford better."

Her mother cleared her throat, stood tall. "Sam, do what you will. But I would welcome you home. We can cover the ground between us but it will take time. You are my eldest and your place will always be right next to me if you want it."

Sam stayed silent and nodded at her mother.

She watched as her parents drove away, leaving her alone with the workers.

They quietly waited for her signal that they could continue.

Her mind was swimming, nothing making sense anymore. Sam remembered that last day at her parents' home. All Sarah did was start crying when Sam explained it to her.

They never found the bodies of Kevin or Principal Dolus, both still considered missing persons at the courthouse.

Sam had found the newspaper clippings from all the missing girls, visited all their graves and taken pictures and stone rubbings of each one. She had researched Thomas, too, finding the graves of his wife and daughter, beautiful marble gravestones sitting side by side.

He had disappeared completely, and his family was still looking for anyone with information about his whereabouts or what happened to him.

Sam had explained to Sarah that she'd written lots of letters but couldn't figure out how to ease his family without telling their secrets.

She'd told Sarah they'd never be able to know for sure what had happened to him.

Sam had put all the articles and police reports about two little girls who were attacked in the woods at the bottom of the box with a note that said, 'We have a higher responsibility to live to our fullest, to use all our gifts to make the world better.'

When Sam had finally handed her sister the box, Sarah had wept and couldn't even look up at her.

As Sam had tried to leave, her father had yelled at her for upsetting Sarah.

And her mother … Her mother had confronted her about not being emotionally available. Sam had erupted, blind anger consuming her. Sam never remembered what she had said.

When she came to her senses, she'd left her father furious and her mother sobbing.

Someone tapped her shoulder. She turned to see one of the workers standing there.

Sam was down on one knee, weeping.

"Hey, it's getting late. If you need more time, we can come back in the morning. When you leave, check with the guard at the gate. He'll cover the grave."

"Sure thing." Sam held out three hundred-dollar bills. "For the trouble. I know I have put you all behind schedule."

"Ma'am, we can't take that. No trouble. We all loved her. We'll come back at first light."

Sam shook her head as they left.

Standing now, she still just couldn't leave, letting herself remember everything. Anger seeped into her being, but this time, she wasn't sure who she was angry with.

Sam reached into her pocket, rubbing the smooth surface. She pulled the matchbook out and stepped up to the grave. She tossed it in.

She watched it fall into the deep hole and hit the dirt below.

She still had her sister's letter in her other hand.

Looking at it, she thought about throwing it down... reconsidered...glanced around....shovels... the workers left their shovels on the pile of dirt. Folding and stuffing the letter into her pocket, Sam picked up a shovel.

She lifted the first shovelful of dirt, tossing it into her sister's grave. She cursed herself.

How could I have left my sister alone?

What was I thinking?

Sam stopped and wiped her brow on her sleeve. She could almost feel the hay as she and Sarah climbed on top of the world. She smiled, gazing upward. The vulture perched on the hay bale.

And she shoveled. Shoveled as though her life depended on it.

Those hay bales weren't so tall when you were a grown-up, she thought, grazing through time and events in her mind. She smiled, then wept, then screamed and yelled.

She just knew the guard would come over the hill any minute, but he somehow didn't.

Sam was left to her own. She shoveled, the rhythm soothing her sorrow, her anger, her joy until all the bitterness wept away and only sweetness remained.

When the light of dawn spilled over the grass, Sam was sitting beside Sarah's grave. She was exhausted, and the hole was filled.

Sam pulled out the letter, took a deep breath and opened it.

"Some things are always true.

Wild is always wild, even if you tame it. Cruelty is always cruel, even if you say it's kindness. Violence is always violent, even if it's justified. Pain is always pain, even if they tell you it shouldn't hurt. The truth doesn't always set you free; sometimes, it ties you down.

Sometimes.
It is not the things we do, but the things we leave undone that haunt us."